Dor Slinkard is an unstoppable storyteller. Be it through writing or voice, her stories will enthral. Inspired by life, especially as a jillaroo in outback Australia and later as a race horse trainer, her imagination thrives. In her lasting marriage to Wade, a jackaroo now horse trainer, they have produced two children and they, in turn, five grandchildren.

DEDICATION

To all people who in their heart feel the same way
as my two characters, Henry and Pierre.

May Henry and Pierre look down from heaven,
or wherever they are, and realize their dream came true.

Bless you all.

Doreen Slinkard 2020

ACKNOWLEDGEMENTS

My never-ending gratitude goes to all my proof-readers.
Wade, my dear husband. Sandy Batchelor, Sandy Gray,
Betty Holman, Julie Sparks, Helen Sanderson and Michael Cybulski.
If I have left anyone out please forgive me and
accept that I am most grateful.

To my patient, and dear editors, Denise Dorisarmy and
Margaret Mooney. You are my life blood of writing.

To Deb Jones, Computus Australis, thank you for
being the Angel of mercy in my technical life.

Thank you all so very much.

By the same author

For the Love of Trilogy
Book 1 – For the Love of Patrick
Book 2 – For the Love of Freedom
Book 3 – For the Love of Justice

Dor Slinkard

HENRI-ETTA

ISBN **9780648539155** (Paperback)
ISBN **9780648539162** (E-Book)

First Published 2020
Reprinted 2026

A factual point of interest.

Miss Ellen Tremayne travelled from Ireland on the *Ocean Monarch* as an assisted migrant in 1859. When landed in Victoria, Australia, Ellen dressed as a male and continued to live her life as Edward De Lacy Evans. He/she married three times. When her third wife gave birth to a baby in 1879, Edward became depressed and was committed to the Kew Mental Asylum. It was there that staff discovered Edward was a female.

CHAPTER 1
HENRY, SPEAKS

England

Sitting on my personally designed three-legged stool, painting scenes of nature's finest flora and fauna, I marvel not only at their uniqueness but at mine. What, I wonder, has made me who I am? It cannot be the blood that binds me to my parents; I bear no clear physical likeness to either, nor do I share my father's pleasure in destruction.

I am Henry, son of the Duke of Harrowfield. The Duke lives only to hunt and kill animals and sea creatures, which is most unfortunate. I treasure these living forms and try to capture and preserve their unique beauty on canvas for posterity's sake. By the turn of the century, my overweight, gout-prone, imbecile of a father and his cronies will have pushed most creatures to the verge of extinction. You may say I'm a little prone to exaggeration, and it is how I'm described by most people: a flamboyant young man who gilds the lily with his emotional and overzealous nature.

And as for my mother, Cecilia, her primary interest is in finding a way to improve the shortcomings of her appearance. The greater part of her day is spent gazing into her mirror, turning her head this way and the other to find the most flattering angle from which to view her plump, unattractive features. Then she adds lashings of powder to camouflage her true ugliness, if I may put it that way. Her secondary interest is her daughter – my sister – Gertrude, who has, unfortunately, inherited her mother's looks. I, on the other hand, have been endowed with regular features, soft topaz eyes shot with amber flecks and set well apart. I possess a straight nose, a full sensuous mouth, my ears are set neat and close to my head, and I have a becoming cleft in the middle of my rounded chin. Luckily, my parents' marriage, unlike many other aristocratic matches, shared no close blood ties, so I escaped that curse. I am sane, a talented artist and reasonably good looking, if in a slightly effeminate way. And if it were not for my love of the same sex and my easily displayed emotions, I would class myself as a normal young Englishman.

I don't *think* I display any discernible indication of my sexual longings. I try not to. However, whatever word you choose to use, the simple fact is I love men. I have always done so – except, of course, for my cruel, practical joker of a father. I suppose I must stop demeaning him, for where it will leave me, I don't know. Penniless, I assume. So, I must endure my circumstances and put up with the familial stupidity around me. Sometimes I wish I had the courage to leave, to venture out into the world, but Harrowfeild is all I have ever known. However, if I do find the strength to leave, I could not possibly do so without my dear, lifelong friend and *mon amour*, Pierre Boyar, who just happens to see me in the same way I see him. Just the mention of his name arouses such luscious thoughts! If only those thoughts could become manifest at this moment. This dashing young man, so tall and sleek with muscles bulging, the oh-so-handsome one, is my true love. Such a liaison should be illegal! As a matter of fact, it is...

There is rustling in the grass behind me. I turn – my heart flutters.

"Oh, Pierre! How lovely to see you. What a grand day it is to paint, yes?" For a moment, I study his face and my smile fades. "There is sadness in your eyes, Pierre. Is there something wrong? Are you not well?" I move to rise and embrace him but something in his serious expression makes me refrain.

He coughs to clear what Mama Duchess calls "a frog" in the throat. "*Oui*, there is something wrong, Henry, *très injuste*! Your father is forcing me to leave you. I'm to be shipped to Australia! *Sacre bleu*!" His voice is husky with barely suppressed emotion. "But, before *we* leave – yes, *we* – Sarah and I are to be married tomorrow." He stills for a moment, obviously waiting for me to digest this horrid news after my show of disbelief. "I'm telling you the truth, Henry. The Reverend Timms and Mrs Timms are to join us on the voyage. Apparently, your father has forwarded enough funds to set us up comfortably in Australia." He sighs deeply, his blue eyes glistening with tears, moved perhaps by the vision of my hands flung to my heart, accompanied by my expression of horror.

I leap to my feet, paints and canvas forgotten, and clasp his hands in mine. "Whatever for, Pierre? What has made my father take this action? I cannot imagine the reason!"

"If I may remind you, Henry, the night before last, our meeting in the stables? Do I have to say more? We were spied upon, informed upon and I am accepting all the blame – the brunt of it." He lowers his beautiful head like a serf before his king. With a tremble in his voice, he says, "It has been all worth it, dearest Henry."

"Pierre, who was the scoundrel that spied upon us?" I ask, loud and indignant.

"I don't know but it seems we are the scoundrels, Henry – you and me. Anyway, it doesn't matter. I must go. We cannot be seen together. The Duke has forbidden it. I've risked a great deal seeing you again, but I could not leave without telling you how much I love you and always will."

Pierre stands before me, head raised to meet my lips in a kiss so warm and passionate, my heart soars with the depth of his love. We hold each other in a tight embrace and with my face nestled against his, I breathe the words, "You cannot leave me, Pierre. What will I do without you?" My tears well, and without control, I weep like a child. I feel Pierre's body shudder with pain as he carefully extricates himself from my arms. He murmurs, "*Je t'aime,*" and a moment later, through misted eyes, I watch Pierre's swift departure, his long limbs striding across the clover field, a young buck escaping the hunter.

Suddenly, a vision of beauty jolts me from my despair. A godlike creature, with antlers tall and sculpted, stands only twenty feet away. He seems surreal through my tears. His coat is a glimmering golden mantle and his huge black eyes focus upon me. I am immobile, breathless, caught between his splendour and my agony.

I could never have expected in this sublime interlude. Suddenly, the crack of my father's rifle breaks the taut silence. The awful realisation that the stag's life has been taken by one bullet, one perfect shot through his head, steels my resolve. This is the final time my idiotic father will take yet another piece of my heart and stamp on it as one would an insect.

CHAPTER 2
SARAH

I am adopted daughter of Reverend Timms, and wife, Charlotte. I am mute and deaf, and it is with much concentration when reading novels, especially written by Jane Austin and teaching from my father, that I can write somewhat fluently. Although sometimes, I am so anxious to write down my feelings I stumble into stilted hand. I apologise beforehand for mistakes and ungainly writing.

We live in stone cottage on grounds belonging to Duke of Harrowfeild. Many years ago, our timber church and manse burned to ashes. My adopted father, by Duke's good grace, was given consent to preach in Duke's opulent stone church.

I remember my early days well. One year before fire, my life merged with Reverend Timms. It began on bleak winter night, fourteen years past, when he trudged his habitual soul-saving route through brothels of West End London. My mother had been young girl of sixteen, homeless and penniless. She had no choice when she was lured into the only profession that offered her existence. She became pregnant with me. Father is unknown.

Three years after my birth I saw mother giving herself to strangers in exchange for coin. It scared me. In our end of London, Reverend Timms was evangelist to the needy. On this snowy night, my mother was suffering with influenza. Kind-hearted Timms sat by her side. He held her hand and prayed Lord forgive her sins. He begged God to spare her or lift her soul to Heaven. With these last words I think my mother smiled.

"A sign, my child," Timms had said, "our prayers have been answered, Sarah. Your mother has gone to Heaven. You, child, will be christened tomorrow and my wife Charlotte and I will raise you, as we cannot have children of our own. God has blessed you, Sarah, freeing you from the dross of this life. With your affliction, being deaf and mute, you will need our love and assistance. We will nurture you into woman, one others will admire, not pity." At least, these were words I think he relayed to me some years later, when explaining that tragic night. It was moment my life changed forever.

Many years passed, and I have blossomed into the young woman I am today. Pondering my future, my father declared the following to me, as if he were giving a sermon.

"Your beauty is beyond compare, Sarah. (These are his words, not mine. I do not think myself to be attractive but perhaps my best feature is my green eyes. I have been told they are colour of the ocean.) Your sweet nature is to be commended and your intelligence to be marvelled. (Although modesty says I shouldn't, I admit this accurate.) We will make it, so you will not want for anything – you will become a good wife." This news took me by surprise, but I knew my father had only my best interests at heart. I accepted it with composure.

All of this was hand-signed to me, and exaggerated shaping of words from his generous mouth. This method of communication was first hard to learn, but as time passed, became easy. When I was young, sheets of paper were attached to square piece of wood that was tied with ribbon around large button on my pinafore. My father was proud that I'd learnt to read and write well by age five. Even today, notebook and pencil sit tucked away in hip pocket that is sewn onto my clothes.

I was four when I saw our timber church and adjoining living quarters burn to ground. My father was very upset and begged officials of Church of England to give him funds to build another church. He hoped one of stone! His demands fell on deaf ears. It was decided if my father could not come up with enough donations from the local community to rebuild his church, we were to be sent away to another parish, even to the colonies in hope of saving convict souls. My father seemed two minds about this. However, to my father's delight, Duke of Harrowfeild offered him reprieve. He would allow us to live on his property, rent free, and preach in his stone church, on one proviso – the Duke would be assured place in Heaven. My father accepted offer in exchange for Duke's promised journey, realising Duke would be in no position to complain if his destination was not one he had in mind. I must smile at that.

My previous precarious situation, along with my "rebirth", my father calls it, has been used to edify parishioners on many occasions. And these times, my hand is squeezed by Pierre, who is the estate's stableboy and son of Duke's gamekeeper. When I first arrived and met Pierre, friendship developed between us. I looked up to him as young sister would to caring, older brother. Pierre introduced me to his dearest friend Henry, Duke's only son, and I came to value Henry as close companion. Henry sits most days at his easel, painting in fields while Pierre and I watch. We often make statues of ourselves, so Henry may sketch or paint us; we three rarely part company. Henry makes me laugh. He is funny the way he conducts charades for me, so I feel included. But I adore Pierre; he produces magic with horses. He controls and coaxes them only through gentleness. For me when I stroke horse's head, it's like happy ending of fairy tale. When I'm permitted to ride with Pierre on these graceful animals, my spirit transcends to another realm; we ride as one, as if we belong together.

When Father made his announcement that I was to marry tomorrow, I expected he had some upstanding member of his parish in mind – perhaps a young widower or even much older bachelor. Therefore, the revelation I am to marry Pierre was sudden and unexpected but not unwelcome news. Father then told me, Pierre and I, along with my parents, are to be sent to Australia. Duke has prepared our voyage along with funds to build church and home for each couple. This, Duke announced, or I should say, bellowed at us this morning. This was after my father had discussed with Duke what he called "urgent business". What, I wonder, had caused the Duke to puff up like bullfrog? His face became bright red, so his blood looked ready to ooze from his skin. And then, for Duke to suddenly announce such an unexpected turn to our future – why? The plan, when I take time to think about it, I do not find disagreeable, as I have dreamt of such union with Pierre. However, our dear, charming and funny Henry, where does he fit in? Our hearts will surely shatter to leave him so suddenly and all alone with family he does not treasure as he ought.

CHAPTER 3
PIERRE

I am from French nobility. It was during the French Revolution, 1789, that most of my ancestors perished. Luckily for me, two young Boyar brothers, Charles and Guillaume, from noble birth, managed to escape France across the English Channel. They were eventually taken in by a sympathetic English family and worked for many years on a large estate until it was safe for them to leave and make their own way in the world. My mother, Mary, is thoroughly English, previously a schoolteacher from a country village. *Mon pere*, Charles, is the great-grandson of Guillaume. I see myself as humble, like my mother, albeit with a strong determination to succeed, a trait I inherited from my father and the other members of the Boyar family who still reside in France. Together they have built a successful winemaking business there and our many visits to their French vineyard has given me a deep connection to my past. I tend to speak the odd words of *francais* at times. It has become a habit I seem unable to break ever since being reunited with my family in France.

My father is *le garde-chasse* (the gamekeeper) for the Duke of Harrowfeild and is well regarded by the Duke. He ensures the estate's pheasant and deer are safe from poachers, and subject only to the Duke's deadly aim. *Ma chere maman* spends much of her time painting and writing books about flowers. And of course, educating me to a higher level in all spheres. Her work is highly prized and has been published, along with articles printed in the newspaper. This fact has endeared her to Henry, the Duke's son, who loves all things to do with nature, in stark contrast to the Duke who cares only for drinking whisky, hunting, shooting and chasing down any attractive female he can catch.

I have only two real passions in life. Foremost are horses and my dream to one day breed thoroughbreds to win races at the best tracks in England. My second passion is, of course, my dearest Henry. However, if Henry were to know I placed horses above him, it would surely break his heart, as he demands my complete love and attention. We have been close since we were boys and this closeness bloomed into a deeper passion as we grew older.

Our voiceless friend, Sarah, outside of each other, is our favourite. She is a delightful innocent, full of life and a loyal friend. Although not conventionally pretty – a fact her father has yet to admit, rather he exclaims the opposite – I see her as somewhat attractive. She has the most beautiful green eyes and auburn hair, both of which amply compensate for the plainness of the rest of her features. She usually smells like a sprig of lavender, except when she helps me muck out the horse stables. The three of us have been quite inseparable during our years growing up together and we never thought too much about what the future may hold. Somehow, we just assumed that we would all continue living happily on the estate when Henry inherited the title, and when old Ted the head groom retired, I would have been advanced to his position. *Mon dieu*, that will never happen now, for the Duke has decreed that I am to marry Sarah and, with her parents, travel to Australia. There we will live for the rest of our days and I will be bereft of Henry's love. How I will bear this I do not know.

The only brightness to assuage my grief at leaving my family and dear Henry behind is the Duke's gift of a thoroughbred stallion and a mare to begin my breeding campaign in Australia. This will keep my mind and energy involved in my new dream, breeding the fastest horse in the colony. My grief and sorrow extend to poor Sarah, for as much as I care for and admire her, she will be lumbered with a man who does not desire her physically as a woman needs to be desired. However, I vow I will care for her and treat her tenderly. I can only hope this will suffice.

CHAPTER 4
HENRY

This unjust and unexpected separation from my darling Pierre fosters in me the utmost self-composure, which is due to my father's constant trickery. Therefore, I speak calmly about Pierre's departure during our usual formal dinner the same evening. I know the servants standing to the left and right of me already know as much, if not more, than I do.

"Father, why is it you suddenly decided to send my dear friends away? And to where, may I ask, have you sent them?' I inquire solicitously.

With a gruff, spluttering cough, the Duke lifts his head from his bowl of venison soup and proclaims, "Henry, it is with regret I must tell you this sudden departure of your friends was brought upon by the condition of Sarah Timms. Yes, you may as well *all* know," he gives a fleeting look around at the servants before continuing, "Sarah Timms is with child. Boyar's the culprit. And I will say no more, and hear no more, on the subject. They have left us, and I have been more than generous in my donations to Reverend Timms. He is to set up his own ministry and lodgings in another land. Yes, another land, Henry. This is all I will say. Now eat your dinner, there's a good lad." He resumes his slurping.

"Yes, Father," I meekly reply, *which is not like me, I can assure you.* I continue my dinner. For a moment, I almost believe him, about Pierre and Sarah, I mean. But then how many times has my father tricked and deceived not only me, but others who have shared his company, being mocked and humiliated when the truth was revealed. His fabrications and pranks are notorious. Many of his victims had simply laughed at his trickery, but some had fainted when opening the bed covers to find an enormous spider, dead of course, lying upon their sheets. Others had braced their gun for the perfect shot when hunting, only to find the gun was unloaded. "I was sure I loaded my gun," they would say with one eye screwed half-closed and the other glaring down the gun barrel as my father looked on, smirking. One terrible night, I remember hordes of lavishly dressed guests arriving for a formal ball, only to be sent away in dismay as my father laughed uproariously at their discomfiture as his personal butler and accomplice Formidable George, as I call him, announced, "You have the date wrong. It is to be held next month."

Even though the Duke's extravagant hospitality on the next occasion outshone the shabby memory of being shunned on the former, I remain unable to fathom the humour in the episode, but my father laughed himself silly for a week, merely proving to me yet again what an imbecile he truly is.

Now I will spend my time working on a plan that will allow me to at least see my darling Pierre again, if not live with him forever. I must be tactful and refrain from emotional displays. I must outwit my father – yes, beguile him into believing I am happy and carefree although my friends have departed for foreign shores. I must never let on how heartbroken I truly am. I know, I shall simply relay to him my ardent desire to travel the Continent to pursue my interest in art. Yes, I intend to paint the world! I will start with France, for Paris is where the seriously dedicated artists begin their journey into enlightenment.

I am quite convinced the Duke has pressured the Reverend Timms to support this "marriage" with his promise of funds to settle in Australia. Certainly, I am the one to know. After all, I have witnessed my father's treacherous bullying my entire life. He would not see it as such, of course, no more than he would see playing yet another devastating practical joke as humiliating and hurtful. As for my inclination to kill my father, *well, not really, I don't have the heart for killing.* I shall for the moment exercise restraint. Instead, I will endeavour to find Sarah and Pierre in Australia and never again will I have to endure the Duke's company. Nor will I miss my sister and my mother - at all – I shall be rid of the lot of them! Yes, the aspersions my father has cast on the characters of my beloved Pierre and dear Sarah will prove the catalyst for me to find the courage to leave the security of my home and venture into the wide world.

I shall paint in my studio from now on, until I leave these premises for good. I will always in the Duke's company pretend to be happy and carefree; I will hide my broken heart. He will be baffled by my composure and be unaware I'm planning revenge. With cunning, I shall extract money from him, or more the point, obtain my inheritance. I am positive he will never suspect *me* of the same duplicity he exercises to manipulate people. My delight lies in using one's wit and intellect to spar with a clever opponent, not in the use of ridicule to demean others. Oh, my vengeance will be delicious; I am about to indulge in treating him with the contempt he so richly deserves.

CHAPTER 5
SARAH

One week after Pierre and I were married by my father, we left England to begin our sea voyage to Australia. Colony built by convict labour and free settlers. We should arrive, all going well, within three months.

Pierre and I are yet to join as husband and wife. I long, as I have done for some time, for Pierre to become my husband in deed as well as word. From my memories as child seeing my mother with many men, some rough and some not so. I have vague understanding of what goes on between man and woman. I know in my heart Pierre will be gentle when time comes. However, what troubles me is he shows no desire to satisfy his manly urges with me. I may be deaf and mute, but I am not blind. I have seen more love and passion in Pierre's eyes for Henry than ever for myself. I would say Pierre's feelings for me are more of kindness and perhaps sympathy. Love in way, yes, but not burning desire one shows when adoration for another is beyond control. It fuels suspicions I have about why we four have been banished to colonies. Perhaps my father witnessed what I suspect, that Pierre's love for Henry is physical. I can only assume this to be correct. I cannot understand, but perhaps time, in addition to me being alone with Pierre, will dull his longing for Henry. I cannot bear to think that if Pierre is so inclined, he may fall in love with another man and keep me to camouflage his true desires. It is with great sorrow I acknowledge such feelings but there is no use dwelling on these. I shall now brighten my disposition and concentrate on adventures that lay before me. Being morose will not bring Pierre closer to me.

Firstly, I shall explore this fine ship and learn something about sailing. Let other passengers see me as confident and charming. I will have them believe my affliction is nothing for which I need to be either pitied or ashamed. My father has instilled me confidence with aim of showing people I am quite normal, other than fact I am unable to speak or hear. My communication skills I believe are better than the speaking fraternity, and with it I have a sense of humour. I have ways of brushing aside anything that will harm my nature, which is pleasant and obliging. I choose to be that way. I have found laughing at myself prevents others from laughing at me.

Day two on board ship after breakfast, I helped Pierre to feed and groom his two horses. They were gifted to him by Duke in appreciation for his dedication to his craft. The black stallion, Satan, stands 16.2 hands high with eyes like doe, and neck so strong I'm sure he could haul ten men from quicksand. Satan has enormous apple-shaped rump and gaskins of prize fighter. The dappled grey mare, Cheval D'Azure, is 15.3 hands and displays prettiness of her Arabian ancestors. She is fine of frame, intelligent, and swift of foot. Pierre stroked her head while she munched hay. He turned to me, so I could read his lips. "Both these horses I would have chosen, Sarah. It was very kind of Duke to gift them to me, under the circumstances." Pierre's eyes clouded, I assumed with his last memory of Henry, and he suddenly lowered his head. This gave me an opening.

"What, pray tell, Pierre, *are* circumstances which led us to be married and shipped off to Australia in such urgent fashion?" I asked this in sign language, head tilted to one side, my eyes wide.

"You really have no idea, Sarah?" Pierre replied.

"I do have some idea, Pierre," I confessed. "However, I need my observations confirmed. Remember, I am not blind. I see and feel things better than most."

Pierre dropped his pretty head once again. Raising it slowly, he studied my face with look I was familiar with part pity, part affection. My fingers moved quickly, and my lips tightened.

"Please do not give me that look, Pierre. I am not to be pitied. Even Henry treats me without pity. I imagine you love Henry in way God intended you to love women." His shamed expression tells me I was correct. I took deep breath and continued, my fingers flying. "In that case, if we are to remain married, I request you reward me by siring my children. In return, I will love and care for you as good wife should, and I will make you happy in any way you wish. I truly feel for you, Pierre. I do not envy you being inflicted with such strong desires that are not natural. Therefore, it is I who pity you."

Pierre's tears welled, clouding his brilliant blue eyes. He pulled me close to his chest and his embrace felt benevolent – grateful, even – especially with brief softness of his lips upon my cheek. He stepped back to smile at me shyly.

"*Pardonnez-moi.* I will try, Sarah, I promise I will try." But then he was gone, out the door with scamper of small boy not wanting to face his punishment. Yes, punishment. I would be punishing him by forcing him to make love to me. But who knows? When Pierre performs his husbandly duty as promised, he may enjoy the soft plumpness of my breasts and thighs.

I have read pamphlets that Mother, speechless with embarrassment, gave me after Father told me I was to marry Pierre. Also, as I mentioned, I had observed through crack in door, my mother earning money that way when I was young. It was not always offensive. I remember old man visiting and giving Mother cake of sweet-smelling soap. He asked her to wash before he introduced her to well-dressed young man who was coming to visit. Later, the young gentleman edged his way nervously into my mother's bed chamber.

That night was first time I'd witnessed my mother caress and kiss man, showing him affection. After their act, they gently stroked each other as they lay entwined. I wished he would stay forever. In fact, he did return many times and never without gifts for us. Unfortunately, it was around then my mother became deathly ill. She refused to eat and therefore the fever claimed her in the end. My poor mother; I am determined to live my life well for her.

Day three. The ship hit turbulent seas throughout night. Our attempt at consummation was prevented by tumultuous waves, so violent at times I near fell out of bed! At least when this happened I was held close by Pierre, secure in his embrace – that feeling I will cherish. His warmth and caring perhaps is all I need. But I want to produce strong healthy children, and with God's help and Pierre's promise, it will be done.

Day four. Pierre became violently ill after eating his dinner. All night he heaved over side, as he held on to railing of ship. Our consummation was postponed yet another day.

Day five. Because Pierre was still squeamish, I cared for horses. Feeding, grooming then walking them in fresh air up and down the ramps for so long as I could keep them calm. These chores filled in my day. That night my interest for anything other than sleep was beyond stirring.

Day six. I have decided not to go on with my sea journal. The long journey will no doubt mean that each day will blur into one another with monotony. I do not expect there will be an appropriate moment to consummate our marriage. The seas are far too rough. This voyage is taking its toll on all our senses and our time is consumed with caring for the horses. Instead, I will spend my time with the people my father has summoned to listen to his sermons. Some of these people are also interested in learning our skill of communicating by hand movements. They may never need this skill, but it certainly helps allay boredom and fear of drowning during this seemingly endless sea voyage. The poor people enduring this voyage in the hull also need our help. They have health problems, and children learn sums and letters. Theirs is wretched trip. I take pity on them huddled like livestock sleeping in stinking hole below.

However, if any interesting things happen I shall write about it, as my passion for writing is equalled only by my passion for reading. I have learned much about the world through reading, and I hope one day to write novels of my own. Foolish idea perhaps but it would give me known voice amongst my readers – I trust. I enjoy recording my thoughts and feelings on paper; its helps assuage my longing to speak. I must now add that I have a new friend, Amy Watson. Amy is three years older than me; she is twenty. Amy is heading to the Blue Mountains to become schoolteacher. We have begun changing lessons. I teach her sign language and she helps me with my writing. This is exciting me!

CHAPTER 6
HENRY

Almost one year has passed since the departure of my dearest Pierre and Sarah. I have since polished my acting skills and managed to convince my father I am being sensible and sincere in my wish to travel, although I see him searching my eyes whenever Pierre's name is mentioned. I wonder if he, too, has desired the odd fling with a male counterpart. No need to consider that; it would be the stuff of nightmares. I am more concerned with my own feelings than to worry about my father's dalliances.

Since Pierre left, my father has persistently and annoyingly produced, it seems from nowhere, many pretty and some quite unattractive young females who flutter their eyelashes at me constantly. Perhaps this is the new fashion. I swear I will never be seduced by this new mode of courtship. I have only one love binding my heart – Pierre. And I will find him if it takes eternity and every penny I am entitled to, as well as some of my father's money, should my clever attempt to swindle him be successful.

I am near to twenty-one. For my travels, I will not need the Duke's consent, but more importantly, I will be entitled to my money. Though his wish for me is to stay home and marry, I promise myself it will never eventuate. But in view of the Duke's intransigence, I wonder if I should use another tack? Pretend to fall in love with a pretty girl, marry her, and take her on a long honeymoon overseas? Surely, I will find Pierre, then I can send the unfortunate girl home. The marriage would be annulled as it would not have been consummated and she could soon find herself another suitor. However, on second thoughts, this brutal type of behaviour is something my father would do, and I have vowed never to do anything hurtful to another, if I can help it. No, I will delete the thought from my mind. I shall set my sights only on the target – my darling Pierre. I will keep to a simple plan.

Not one day has passed since Pierre's departure that I have not discussed with my father my need to travel. I am determined to persist.

Even my sister Gertrude seems excited about my travels and therefore inquires of our father if she may join me. Thank God, the Duke protests loudly, for I'm sure I would have, had he not.

"Schooling, especially in deportment, will come first, young lady! No travelling abroad until you are at least twenty-one!" Gertrude is crestfallen but accedes to her father's wishes as a dutiful daughter should.

He then turns to me. "Well, Henry, you've worn me down, and I give you permission to go abroad. Not that I needed it; I simply play along. You can thank the Lord I am allowing you to travel before your twenty-first birthday. When exactly is that?"

"Not until next year, Father. But I do appreciate your trusting me to travel alone." I can hardly contain my excitement and I smile endearingly at my father and manage to maintain my insincerity sufficiently to bestow the same smile upon my mother and my sister.

"No such thing, Henry. I do *not* trust you! What kind of fool d' you take me for?" My father eyes me sternly. "I am sending Georgie with you as your chaperone. He has served me faithfully for thirty years without so much as a day trip to the beach. He is still young enough to keep a close eye on you, my boy. And without his usual duties, he will no doubt have the energy to keep up with you." Father nods towards Georgie, who gives a smug, yellow-toothed grin in my direction. *Mmm, I'm sure he's never had a day trip to the dentist either.*

It takes considerable self-control not to howl in frustration at this turn of events, but I will deal with it somehow. I smile back at Formidable George, revealing my own perfect white teeth. "I agree wholeheartedly, Father. Well done, George," I say happily. "I may be able to teach you how to paint on our journey." I stand and bow. "Now if you will excuse me, Father, I shall bid you goodnight before this thrilling news preoccupies my senses and makes me unable to sleep."

I walk backwards, delighting in their shocked expressions. The Duke, I'm sure, is hankering for a fight, or at least a heated protest. I must say, I am proud of my efforts to stay calm under such adversity. The Duke scratches his newly clipped beared, and his look of disbelief fixes upon me. I bow once again, execute a dainty pirouette and leave. Yes! I am so proud of myself. Perhaps I should take up acting professionally. However, my departure from this castle should be made swiftly before any further attempts to outfox me.

Despite the news of George joining me on my travels, I sleep well, and as usual my dreams are of Pierre. I can feel his light touch upon my skin, tantalising my senses, his sensuous fingers slowly finding their way between my thighs. Softly at first, then with an exquisite rhythm he is awakening me to his seduction. My eyes open to view his beautiful face… "Oh, my God!" I shriek. "It's a WOMAN!"

Fully awake now I find one of the wenches previously sent by the Duke to distract me from my "unnatural" proclivities. She is fondling me – nicely, I must admit. Don't get distracted, I tell myself, think quickly! Remember, Henry, this is a game between you and my father. He has paid her handsomely to seduce me, I know. I compose my features and smile winningly at her. She is duped and so tilts her pretty head.

"Oh, Henry! I love you so. I want to please you," she claims. There goes the flutter of the eyelashes again.

"Of course, my lovely." I close my eyes, lay back and imagine it is Pierre's ministrations I enjoy, and before long I am satisfied. I continue to act out the role the Duke has prepared for me. I hold her to my chest and moan with delight. She seems pleased. I know she will report to the Duke what a great lover I am, especially when I have recovered enough strength to enter her as I must if this charade is to be believed. He must think I am totally stupid. This bogus act has made me even more determined to outmanoeuvre him and that I shall do.

Politely, I ask the wench to leave my bed soon after I have performed the distasteful deed. I must say, it took quite a bit of my imagination to become erect and do my duty. Fortunately, I have a very active imagination.

"I am unable to sleep a single wink with another person in my bed," I tell her sadly. "I hope you understand, my sweet?"

She accepts my excuse with a smile, blows me a kiss and tiptoes out of my room. I feel disgusted and sleep comes slowly after I shed tears of longing into my pillow. Oh, Pierre – the amount of deceit and shame I must endure to be in your embrace once again. It's so demeaning.

In the morning when I enter the dining room, I am shocked to find the wench – I must stop calling her that, what is her name? Winona? Yes, Winona – sitting straight-backed and confident at our breakfast table. The Duke coughs, his usual introduction to a speech, especially one which is peppered with untruths. I sit silently at the table, preparing myself to do battle.

"Henry, I have been in serious discussion with Miss Winona Burke." He nods towards the fair temptress, her eyes shining with victory and her posture upright and confident. "Apparently, Henry, last night you invited Miss Burke to your room, plied her with brandy and took advantage of her innocence, taking her to your bed and forcing yourself upon her! Therefore, I have no other option than to insist you marry this young woman! We will not tolerate this family's reputation being dragged through the mud! It may well be that Miss Burke is now with child. She has told me, Henry, you spent yourself with her. Is this not true?"

My God! Does his temerity know no bounds? Though this hurdle is high, I will also leap it.

"Father. Sir, you forget your notorious reputation for trickery, which is discussed with horror from one side of this country to the other. I cannot possibly see how my experiencing a little dalliance with a young lady who was placed in my bed, by *you*, specifically to seduce me, would drag *our* name through the mud as you imply. The opposite, in fact, would be the case. It is *her* reputation that is at stake, Sir."

Winona, looking less victorious by the second, casts my father a frightened glance. I continue. "Ah, they would say. Henry has at last shown some good old Harrowfeild form – just like his Papa! Well done, Henry, you are a man at last!" I pause to sip my tea. "Honestly, Father, you must stop this silly charade and give me leave to do as God intended," I pause again to take delight in his horrified expression. "And that is to immortalise the world in my paintings so not all is lost to the destruction of time. I believe I have a gift, a spectacular talent that must be allowed free rein. If I am to leave this house penniless, so be it. I am prepared to starve my body to feed my soul. Do you understand, Father?" I ask sweetly.

Father's face becomes enflamed; he seems unable to speak. Perhaps he will have an apoplectic fit. What fun!

I turn toward Winona. I can't help but notice the disappointed pout of my pretty seductress's pink lips. I stand and step closer to her, placing my hand gently on her shoulder. I bow and say, "A sterling effort, my dear Miss Burke." Her chin trembles quite becomingly and her eyes glisten with unshed tears. I turn and leave my father coughing and spluttering into his kippers.

What next, I wonder, will the Duke throw in my path. I detour to the kitchen; my stomach complains as I have forgotten to eat my breakfast. Nothing like a victory over the old man to whet the appetite. As I enter the kitchen, my darling Rosie, our cook, who has been more of a mother to me than the Duchess, holds me to her luxurious bosom and cries.

"Oh, Master Henry, I will miss you so!" My face is pressed within the cleft of those massive, wobbling jellies. I love it! I have never received such pleasurable affection from my own mother, the empty vessel that she is. I am released and then kissed by lips that deliver the last dregs of honey they held.

"I will miss you even more, Rosie," I tell her sincerely. "Wherever will I find a pair of bosoms so delightfully large and soft to rest my weary and miserable head upon?" She laughs, and her entire body shakes.

We sit and chat while I devour bacon and eggs that Rosie ordered the kitchen maid to cook. I'm able to make Rosie laugh easily and I'm aware my humour is perhaps what she will miss the most. She, like me, enjoys a clever wit, and not the type that belittles or plays tricks on another person's feelings. Rosie is my confidante, my treasure chest of secrets, truth and fond memories. I hold her as dear as any man would his own mother. Because I am her fondest love, Rosie announces that she has saved sufficient funds to help pay for a sea passage for me to escape. Yes, escape from the continuous torture of living with my family, with whom I honestly believe I do not belong. If my father refuses to pay for my passage and give me my rightful endowment, Rosie will at least be able to help send me on my way, and with my own more than meagre allowance I will have enough to keep me fed and modestly lodged for several months. Precious Rosie, how blessed I am to have her as my loyal friend. I decide that if absolutely necessary, I shall accept her offer. Better still, why don't I take her with me? Yes, I will! I should not leave Rosie to bear the brunt of my father's rage.

"Rosie, would you like to come with me?" She gasps and clasps me to her breasts once more. "Please! One day you will go too far and suffocate me!" I say with stifled breath and a mouthful of bacon.

"I just can't help it, Henry. Oh, thank you for offering to take me. I'll be beside meself when you go!" She lowers her gaze as she dabs miserably at her wet cheeks with the corner of her apron. "But I must stay and try to cover your tracks."

"I must admit, Rosie, I will find it hard to survive without your cooking and motherly affection." I return her hug, and all is understood between us.

I amble off to my studio a little more confident about the outcome of my argument with Father. This morning I shall paint and let my disgruntled feelings be calmed. I lock the studio door against physical intrusion, but my large uncurtained window allows me to be viewed like a goldfish in a bowl by nearly all who live and work on the Harrowfeild estate. As they pass by my studio on their duties, their expressions range from sympathy, mainly from the gardeners whom I respect greatly, to disgust, mainly from those servants who are in my father's direct employ. And now my sister loiters, with a condescending look on her plain face, or is it a look of jealousy she has just thrown at me? Now she strolls on, arm in arm with Mother, who makes a point of looking in the opposite direction. Yes, *the traitor son*! I know what she is thinking. I am a disgrace to the family.

Well, I think her to be a disgrace after the way she has treated me, ignoring me most of my life. And whenever she does pay attention to me, it is to chide and chasten me. "Your shoelace is undone, Henry," or "Your hair needs combing, Henry." Not one pleasant word has been uttered from her thin and bloodless lips. My father, for all that he is a bully, has been kinder in a way than my mother. At least through disinterest he has allowed me to do mostly as I wish. He has not spent too much time persuading me to learn the running of the family estate. I would detest being boxed up in a dark office for most of my life, working with figures and sharing long meetings with archaic advisors and stuffy bank managers. No, I am an artist and I must be left to follow my instincts, not be immobilised like a human machine, generating money for the benefit of the Harrowfeild seed that may follow. My life should be spent capturing whatever does not need embellishment – all of God's glorious creation.

CHAPTER 7
SARAH

We are within one hundred nautical miles of the continent of Australia. And finally, our intrepid journey is blessed with calm seas. I am now able to admire the sheer beauty of the ocean flowing like diamond-studded silk. Though in my heart it still feels like the devil in disguise.

I am so delighted with the company of my newfound friends, Miss Amy Watson and her brother William. Amy, as I wrote, is to be the schoolteacher in a new town called Blackheath, which is set amongst the Blue Mountains of New South Wales. I have spoken to Father about also settling there and he has agreed, mainly because Amy's father, Ted, and her brother William, are carpenters. Father has commissioned them to build our homes and his church. I am so excited I can hardly write for my hand is shaking so. It seems to me our meeting with the Watsons was planned from above.

I have written Amy a note about my interest in becoming an assistant teacher, and she has accepted my offer with pleasure. She has also helped me with my writing. I feel so confident now, adding conjunctions, pronouns and adjectives, which I tend to leave out with my haste to communicate with hand signs, and therefore, it carried onto my writing. Amy thinks having my affliction is a fine way to teach children compassion towards the less fortunate in our community. I may have influenced her decision to take me on because when I hold my class to teach sign language each day, the number of interested children has increased threefold.

I am now impatient to see what they call the Blue Mountains. We hear good pastures abound there for us to raise our horses. Pierre is looking forward to it so much. We had to convince Father of the benefits of living in the mountains. Fresh air, much cooler in the summer, and a reminder of England in the winter, as it snows frequently during what would be summer months at home. It will be strange to think of December through to February as being summer, and not winter.

We have disembarked at Sydney Cove; I must say a little worse for the voyage but perhaps not as bad as the two hundred or so passengers who were cramped below deck. They've been living communally, sleeping and eating together in very sorry circumstances. I feel for their terrible experience and pray they will find a better life here in Australia.

I stand for a moment; shaky, still feeling the rolling of the deck although we are on dry land. I walk carefully, feeling the firm ground beneath my feet but at the same time I'm enthralled by the stunning scenery. Such an intense blue sky meets the sea. It creates an illusion, a mirage, a glimmering sheet of silver – jewels dancing on the skin of the ocean. The sun is embracing us in a warm welcome. Somehow, I think it wise not to stand under it for too long. I feel it burning through my clothes already, and I make a note to retrieve my parasol from my trunk. Huge rocks of earthy colours surround us, the relentless waves slowly sculpturing them into what appears to be living forms. The horseshoe-shaped harbour gives shelter to the ships at their moorings. Tall, white-trunked trees with dusty green leaves stand as sentinels around the higher perimeter. They provide us with a scent that clears the head and delights my senses. I feel a sudden rush of affection for this strange, new land. I am pleased we are here and to know this is where I shall raise my family.

We reach Sydney Town. It is alive with all types of people, some in shabby clothes and some dressed like royalty. Urgency is in the air we breathe, and a certain rhythm gives this new colony the energy to forge ahead. For the majority, it will provide a better life than the one they have left behind in England. I am caught up in the buzz and hum of it. I notice all stores and hotels are doing a brisk trade with hordes going in and out. My father notices the vast number of people surrounding us. I know he is counting each one as if they were to join his congregation. He looks at Mother and me, and says earnestly, "I can see a great opportunity to preach to hundreds here and not just the few who may actually reside in the mountains. Do you think we should change our plans and stay here in Sydney?"

I shake my head most decidedly. I have dreams of living in the Blue Mountains, away from the crowds of single-minded people who wish only to make a fortune or climb to social heights, things I'm sure they would never have the chance to do in England. I need the gentler side of life, as I know Pierre does and Henry would too. If he were here. Perhaps we can settle not too high into the mountains. I hear that a racecourse has been built near the Hawkesbury River. Settling there means we'd be close enough for Pierre to race his horses, when they are ready, of course. I can see it now. By the time Cheval D'Azure's first foal is old enough to race, at three or maybe younger, I will be a mother of two children and maybe have another on the way.

The business of planning our continued journey to the Blue Mountains has taken us one week. We have purchased cart horses, wagons and supplies to see us through. By way of distance, we were told the Blue Mountains area is not too far away and probably the quickest way would be to sail up the Hawkesbury River and then unload at Windsor. But Father says he does not care to see another large expanse of water, other than one which is necessary for us to survive. I must agree. After our stay in a noisy, rather tawdry hotel in Queens Street, Sydney Town, we prepare to head off in a convoy with our new friends, the Watsons. Father has set up an account with the Bank of New South Wales, investing most of the money given to him by the Duke. He has on his person only the amount he needs to pay the Watsons to build our homes and buy stores; a wise and cautious man, my father. My mother is sweet natured and forever obedient to my father, although he only ever asks her nicely, rather than ordering her to do things for him. I feel truly blessed to have had them adopt me and treat me as their daughter. I am happier than I could have imagined, even though my longing for Pierre's physical love gnaws at me. I do forgive him though, as our sea journey placed many barriers to us joining together. I trust once we settle in the mountains, Pierre will fulfil his promise and we shall begin a family.

CHAPTER 8
HENRY

I am delighted to say the Duke, after a frustrating twelve months, seems to have tired of the game we have been playing and I'm sure he will be pleased to see me leave. Although I know he does not entirely believe the casual disregard with which I have treated my friend Pierre's departure, he has agreed to give me the funds to support my journey around Europe. Unfortunately, it is still to be taken with Formidable George. Oh well, the game will continue, until I think of a way to be rid of him. My bags are packed and I'm ready. But first my magnificent residence calls me to bid it farewell. After all, it has been my home from the time I was born.

Its charm and elegance are to be admired, not be taken for granted, or seen as a mere symbol of wealth and power. She is a grand, artfully sculpted old lady who has witnessed many memorable events. People from all walks of life have taken refuge under her many roofs. She denounces none, only the people who own her do. I feel a sadness creeping within me, now I am leaving such a treasure behind. Her three stories are of stone and marble, with a sweeping mahogany staircase and delicately carved balustrade.

Fifty rooms are adorned with the most expensive furniture, and ornaments of the finest porcelain, glass and ivory acquired by past generations sit on most surfaces. Many of the rooms have secret hiding places, and as a child, I thrilled in their use when playing hide-and-seek with Pierre and Sarah. Priceless paintings hang on every wall. The ones I favour most are the Chinese works by William Alexander. I also revere his self-portrait. It portrays strength of character, and if I am to be honest, William's features are comparative to mine, although I do have sight in *both* eyes. I have never discovered the truth about William being blind in one eye, as the black patch would suggest. He may have simply wished to add another layer of intrigue to his character.

Our grounds of our estate are abundant and lush; their beauty will remain in my memory forever. Who knows, one day I may return. The future is so unpredictable. I hear that Australia radiates light and is filled with rugged beauty. I'm sure it will be of great inspiration, especially painting the scenery and animals, so dissimilar to those in England.

My heart begins to ache upon seeing our faithful, kind staff of twenty lined up outside, some with tears welling. I shake their hands and accept their sincere good wishes for a safe and prosperous journey, although I cannot believe Rosie is nowhere to be seen.

"Father, where is Rosie?"

"Rosie has asked that you forgive her for not being here to farewell you. It seems she cannot bear to see you go, Henry. She told me to wish you Godspeed."

"Is that all?" I am forlorn by her absence.

"I'm afraid so, Henry," my father says gravely and for once he seems sincere.

I sigh deeply, thinking of the heart-wrenching scene Rosie no doubt would have created at my departure. I know she loves me like her own child. It must be unbearable for her. But I cannot allow myself to weaken and stay for that reason alone. Rosie, I'm sure, will recover and maybe when I'm settled in Australia, I will send for her. Yes, this thought gives me the strength to be on my way.

Kisses on both cheeks for my mother, the Duchess, whose eyes, like my own, are dry. I turn to see a satisfied smirk on Gertrude's ferret face, which I choose to ignore. Once again, my acting skills come to the fore.

"My darling sister, how I will miss you! Please do not fret for me. I promise I shall return. *Maybe*." She stiffens with a look of disbelief as I smile sweetly and plant a kiss on each of her papery cheeks.

Turning to my father, I shake his hand. Oh dear, one last joke before I go. A false hand falls limp in my palm. I play it up for the staff. Horrified, I throw the hand to the ground. The staffs' tears of sadness have now turned to tears of laughter.

"My, my, Father, you are such a scoundrel! You got me this time. I shall miss *some* of your jokes." I shake his real hand and he returns the grip firmly.

He laughs heartily, but do I detect a tear in his eye? I wait for more. Oh, no, it seems one lonely teardrop is all the Duke can muster. Never mind.

"Come, George," I command like a general. "Let our adventure begin!"

Our first night on board ship is rather entertaining, especially being seated beside the Captain, a humorous fellow with tall tales to tell about his countless voyages. Thankfully, I feel no sea sickness at all, and I enjoy my meal. But alas, poor George becomes quite ill and must leave the dinner table. On my way back to the cabin, I come across George still heaving over the side. He manages to look at me for a moment then says in a hideous croak, "I – I thought we – were going straight to France, Henry, Sir?"

"I have chosen a roundabout way to France, George," I inform him airily. "Before I eventually settle in Paris, where I intend to polish my artistic technique and learn from the masters, we shall travel the sea road to Italy, then perhaps Spain. I am an open book, waiting to fill my pages with beauty and travel experiences. I do hope you feel better soon, old chap."

I smack George on the back, which makes him heave again. I must say though, I do feel some sympathy for him, suffering such dreadful nausea.

Happy to be alone behind the locked door of my cabin, I proceed to unwrap a special parcel I had secreted amongst my possessions. Luckily, I am the same height and much the same weight as my sister Gertrude, and when I recently took a trip to London, I obtained two lady's outfits from her dressmaker, explaining they were for my sister. This is how I plan to cleverly deceive Formidable George and everyone else. On our first shore excursion in Italy, I will disembark disguised as a woman and, no doubt, leave George busily searching the ship for my good self.

I had previously booked in the name of Miss Henri-Etta Brown for my immediate passage to Australia from Spain. This was organised by Rosie, who on the pretext of visiting an ailing relative, travelled to London two weeks prior to George's and my departure. My masterly plan could not have been achieved without my dearest Rosie, and my heart now aches that she was not there to see me off. I console myself with the fact that she was spared the heartbreak of our last goodbye.

I surprise myself at not feeling nervous about my plan. I am excited to be free, finally, and dressed the way I have secretly desired to be all my life – as a female. I would love to hang my beautiful dresses in the wardrobe, but if they were discovered, my future would be ruined, and all would be exposed. I again wrap them carefully, with hope in my heart.

CHAPTER 9
SARAH

Our way to the Blue Mountains was mapped out by a Sydney surveyor. It was easy to follow and after two days, we reached the basin of the mountains. Time, it seemed, has moved quickly, perhaps because of my delight in seeing such strange native wildlife. Kangaroos have, from time to time, bounced along beside the carriage. They are inquisitive by nature, it seems, until suddenly, a strange noise causes them to flee. Whenever we stop to "boil the billy" – a large tin can – for a cup of tea, other strange creatures are often observed. We have also seen Aborigines, some dressed in European clothes, and some carrying spears in their native state of undress. They have not been menacing toward us; they simply looked our way as they went about hunting food – not us, thank Heaven! I have fallen in love with this country, even the pesky flies, which would have perhaps driven us mad if they had not been thwarted by Mother's ingenuity. She has fashioned nets that completely cover our hats and faces. Even the men are now wearing them. Mother said she may be able to start a business selling her homemade "fly nets". They are comparable to the netting the women in England wear attached to their fashionable hats. This made us laugh, but I thought it was not such a silly idea, especially as she was designing fly masks for our thoroughbred horses to wear, as otherwise they would also be tormented by the flies. Pierre has been bathing their eyes morning and night, trying to rid them of the fly mite that has become lodged in their eyes, causing pus to accumulate. Mother just may be on to something worthwhile, I think. I must say, at this point, how proud I am of my writing. Amy says I have improved incredibly. I have none other to thank but her. Thank you, Amy.

On our sixth day of weary travel down dusty roads, we set up camp on the Sydney side of the Hawkesbury River, an expansive, powerful watercourse. We discussed if perhaps we should settle here in this town of Windsor. Its name conjures up memories of Windsor in England, as I'm sure it did for Governor Macquarie when he named it in 1810. We took a walk to view the Governor's home. It was well kept, built from timber and sat high on the Sydney-side bank of the river. I would have liked to venture in. Maybe I should have knocked on the door, but then it is most difficult for me to communicate with strangers, and besides, my father thought we should not intrude. Never mind, I just stood out the front admiring the cottage garden. It gave show to dahlias, pansies, roses, creeping jasmine and many other flower varieties.

I sighed and remembered that settling here would be out of the question, especially for Amy Watson, as she had been contracted to teach at the Blackheath School and I have promised to be her assistant. Father agreed that we should venture on and see what fate had in store for us there. If it turns out we are not happy in the mountains, then we would return to Windsor, as he had a good feeling about this place, as did I.

We took another walk around the town and on the outskirts. Father stopped to admire the grand Anglican church, Saint Mathews, and at the same time, he seemed amused at the Catholic church that bore the same name. It sat across the road to the left. Both churches were impressive. Alongside the churches were the fine, solid brick homes of the clergy. It appeared the growing population in Windsor was certainly Christian minded. Father sighed, considering this, and I could tell he wished his church to be built here.

"I feel the Lord has sent us here, Sarah," he said, after turning to face me. "This is where I should like to build our Church of England – well, not exactly here. Perhaps further down the river, or closer to the town centre." I stroked his back and smiled, then tugged his arm so he'd walk me back to camp.

We stayed another two days in this quaint, welcoming town, where some buildings were of timber and some of brick, but all had generous verandas at the front, built for much needed shade. The Macquarie Arms Hotel was a rather grand two-storied, cement-rendered building. After enjoying our lunch there, Father inquired of the manager if we could possibly be given a tour of the premises. To our delight, he complied. The interiors were lushly decorated and the rooms most spacious. However, I was soon horrified when walking down the many narrow steps into the cellar where I saw iron chains embedded in the walls.

"This is where the prisoners were chained during the night, and by day they laboured to build the town," the manager informed us. I shuddered to think it was only ten years earlier when men were treated worse than mongrel dogs.

All around, and on both sides of the river, lay market gardens. The produce was loaded and carried on barges down the Hawkesbury River all the way to Sydney Town, where I was told the growers received good prices. They seemed to be doing well, as did the graziers of sheep and cattle. Those properties were mostly beyond the river flats, running into the foothills of the mountains. It appeared fruit and vegetables were in ample supply now. We were told this by a local man, Joseph Toonage, that it had been a good season with plenty of rainfall, but he followed this with a warning. "You'd better keep stores and save y' money for the drought years, m' friends, because they can be devastatin'."

With his cautionary words still fresh in our minds, the next morning we waved goodbye to our new friend and continued our journey. Not too far from Windsor we came across a racecourse. We stopped and inspected the track. Already there were professional trainers setting up stables around the perimeter. Pierre looked at me with longing in his eyes. I knew what he was thinking; he would like to stay right here. But once again I reminded him of our commitment to first reach the Blue Mountains before making any other decision. This reminder consoled Pierre and we headed off with the thought of perhaps returning to this area.

After another three days and nights travelling in the rain, up and down the mountains, we arrived wet and bedraggled at Faulconbridge. It was only a matter of another twenty-five miles to Blackheath, but Mother had caught a severe cold. She was not well so we had to find dry, warm lodgings. The Watsons decided to leave us at Faulconbridge, as they needed to be settled in Blackheath before school began. Mr Watson has already purchased a large barn for shelter while he and his son build their grand home next to it. He would then use the barn for his business dealings and storing timber.

Father secured our lodgings in a local boarding house where, from the veranda, we bade farewell to the Watsons. When we returned inside, Father handed money to Miss Fielding, the proprietor of the house.

"We may have to stay many days," he explained to Miss Fielding. "I suspect it will take quite a while before we can determine if Mrs Timms is well enough to continue our journey. She will need constant warmth and rest to recover before our hard work begins in Blackheath."

Miss Fielding smiled and told us, "You are welcome to stay for as long as necessary."

A few days turned into a week and still Mother's health had not improved. The doctor who visited her this morning was grave as he delivered his diagnosis – Mother had pneumonia. We needed to take her to the nearest hospital, which was located back in Windsor. Luckily, the weather was kinder now and we could make Mother comfortable in a bed within the wagon. It would be another long journey back down the mountain for the three of us, as Pierre has decided to continue to Blackheath in search of acreage for his horses and the land on which to build our homes.

I could only pray Mother will recover.

CHAPTER 10
HENRY

I have hardly slept a wink on my final evening on board ship. Thinking about being reunited with Pierre after so long concerns me: has he found another love, or perhaps fallen in love with Sarah? I try hard to lighten my thoughts by concentrating on the morning sunbeams filtering through the porthole. It illuminates my cabin and allows good light by which I can shave my whiskers, sparse and though they are. A gown of pale yellow, which I think highlights the gold flecks in my eyes, is laid out upon my bed. Feeling a tingle of delight, I carefully unpack the cosmetics I bought in London, applying some powder and adding a touch of rouge to my cheeks and lips. I darken my naturally long lashes with a small brush and some of Monsieur Rimmel's mascara. Voila! I look stunningly gorgeous, and the wig sets me off – I am the most glamorous woman I have seen on board! Naughty me, I mustn't fall in love with myself.

I shall skip breakfast and be the first passenger to disembark. Of course, I shall leave my belongings on board, all except for my personal papers, one suit of my own clothes, my feminine attire, cosmetics and the like. No one will ever know what has happened to Henry of Harrowfeild. It will be the gossip of the ship for many years to come, I'm sure. However, I shall not burn all my bridges. Who knows what trouble could befall me, and I may need a safety net. Though turning twenty-one years I did receive a large payout from my inheritance; that I'm feeling more than pleased about. I also feel exuberant, because at last I am myself. I am totally free to pursue my love, Pierre, and maybe my future as a woman. Also, I have overcome my trepidation of venturing out into the world on my own. Yes, I am now brave.

"Good morning, sailor," I say sweetly, with a flutter of my darkened eyelashes. There you go! It works on him. He blushes as he comes to my assistance, undoubtedly taken with my beauty, I'm sure.

"Good morning, Miss. You're up bright and early. No time for breakfast?" he asks.

"No, I must hurry. I am to meet a friend." As I move towards the gangway, he raises his hand to stop me.

"Excuse me, Miss, but I'm not supposed to let you go without y' givin' me y' name, Miss." He regards me apologetically.

"Oh, but you are a cheeky devil! Next you will be asking me out for the evening and then …" I giggle, hurrying past so closely I almost push him into the sea.

I'm surprised at how confident I am walking in my high-heeled boots. I stride out even more quickly down the gangway when I hear the Captain ask the sailor, "Who was the young woman who just left our ship?"

"I don't know, Sir. She said she was in a hurry, had to meet someone. It's strange, Sir, because another older lady left before her and said the same."

I dare to look back. I watch the Captain place his arms behind his back, turn and walk to the companionway, presumably to partake of breakfast before the official roll call. If all goes to plan, I will be well out to sea by then.

The ship sailing to Australia will leave in approximately an hour. Despite my hunger, I plan to go straight on board and lock myself in my cabin. My journey to the ship, however, is interrupted by several handsome young men, all offering to help carry my trunk. I also receive a tap on the bottom and a wink to go with it. I must say I find it flattering, and not offensive at all. Yes, I've heard about these swarthy Italian men. Oh dear, what would become of me if I were a real woman? Easy game, I would think.

The charming words and admiring looks follow me, as ticket in hand, I make my way up the gangway and then to my cabin. I explain to the young steward, "I'm not feeling well, and I do not want to be disturbed. But, perhaps refreshments could be brought to my cabin in approximately one hour?" I throw him a suggestive smile for good measure.

"Will your mother be wanting refreshments also, Miss Brown?"

"My mother?" I ask, so completely shocked I almost faint.

"Yes, Miss. Your mother is waiting for you in your cabin."

With difficulty, I regain my composure. "I shall ask her, thank you, young man." How could my mother possibly be here? How could she know my plan? How could I have avoided her on board the ship from

44

England? My heart is racing! Oh well, this will at least be interesting, if not disastrous. Before entering, I take a deep breath, and open the cabin door. I'm ready for battle but instead my heart melts with joy, "My goodness me! Rosie, my darling!" I cry and throw my arms around her.

"Yes, it's me, Henry." She steps back from my embrace and looks me up and down – with pride, I think – and says, "Well, I'll be damned! It's a fine lookin' woman y' are!"

"I love it, I simply love that you are here with me, Rosie. I made excuses for you not being there to wish me farewell. Now I see the reason why. What an utter joy it will be to have you travelling with me as my mother."

"Well, if the truth be known, Henry, I'm old enough to be y' grandma," she says, holding my gloved hands in her own.

"I don't think so, Rosie. You haven't a wrinkle on your face!"

Rosie laughs raucously. "I think it might be the fat that has pushed the wrinkles out, Henry."

With that outburst, I suddenly realise our conversation may have been overheard by the steward. I open the door and pop my head out to peek along the corridor, but he has gone, no doubt to see other passengers to their cabins. I sigh, relieved, shut the door and settle on the bed next to Rosie, where she begins to acquaint me with the latest details.

"Now Master Henry, I mean Miss Henri-Etta Brown," Rosie giggles. "I've received word from Reverend Timms and Sarah. They've reached Sydney Town and have begun their travels to the Blue Mountains. It all sounds very exciting and romantic. Sarah met a Miss Watson on board ship, and she offered Sarah a job as her assistant teacher in the Blue Mountains. Of course, Sarah seems most pleased about it. It's all I know at this stage. But at least we know where they be."

Rosie's eyes well up and she hugs me for dear life. Once again, I am enveloped within her bosoms. My wig slips sideways, a victim of her enthusiastic embrace. We hold each other apart and laugh.

"Oh dear, I must remember my wig when we're in company," I tell her as I straighten it. I frown at her. "And pray tell, how on earth did I not see you on board the ship from England, Rosie?"

"In a minute, Henry, I mean Henri-Etta. Just let me have a good look at you." She scrutinises my face and I strike a pose, making her laugh. "You've done a fine job transformin' y'self – and what have you done to y' eyes? They look amazin'!"

"Later, Rosie, I'll show you how I do it," I promise her. "But now, tell me about your masterful plan." We sit side by side on the bed and settle our skirts.

"Well, dear Henry – Etta, I booked m'self under Roslyn Brown. The same surname I booked you under for this trip. I just stayed in me cabin all the time. Said I wasn't feeling well. I had all me meals brought to me. They musta had a gay old time talking about the woman in cabin ten, who said she wasn't well but ate like a bloody horse!" She slaps my arm playfully.

I giggle, but notice something in Rosie's expression, a trace of hesitancy, maybe? Rosie meets my gaze, and her eyes linger on my face for a long serious moment before she confesses. "Henry, I've held a secret for a very long time. But now we are free from your family, I must tell you. I know all things will become clearer when I do." Rosie coughs twice, clasps her hands in her lap and sits up straight. "Now, Henry, your grandfather, the old Duke, whom you never met, was…" she takes a deep breath "your father!"

The reflex of flinging my hands to my heart when surprised takes over. Rosie clasps my hands and holds them to her bosom.

"It's not all bad, Henry, please hear me out. You see I lost my daughter Emily when she gave birth to you at sixteen." Rosie shakes her head, looking sorrowful. "Only sixteen she was. Y' see, y' family, especially y' grandad. Sorry, y' father, was very good to me, bein' an unmarried mother and all. He took me in and said if I was a good cook he'd keep me on – and he did. He gave me a roof over my head, and he loved young Emily, he did. She be thirteen when I got the job, I was only a young twenty-nine meself. She was always a bit too forward, was young Emily. And bein' a widower, the old Duke was always lookin' for a bit, if y'know what I mean. I was real cross at first when I heard what was goin' on. But by the time he had his way with her she was sixteen. He said this be the age of consent by the new law. He said he would marry Emily. I couldn't have been happier." Rosie's smile turned downwards. "Well, that's not quite true. I thought if he be twenty, or even thirty, it would be grand. But a sixty-year-old? Well, that was a different matter. Nevertheless, the old Duke said he would marry Emily and he told everyone he did. But then the saddest thing happened. On the day Emily told the Duke she was carrying his child, he died of a heart attack. All the family knew about her situation and his promise to marry her, including your half-brother, the Duke and his young wife. So now you understand, Henry. You are really Gertrude's uncle. Cecilia, the Duchess, is your sister-in-law and, of course, the Duke is your half-brother, and I – I am your grandmother!"

The silence lay heavily between us as Rosie waited for my horrified reaction. But there is none, for I know instinctively this story to be true. It does not surprise me at all, as I've never felt a common bond with my supposed mother, or my sister. My father, who I now understand to be my brother, yes, there was always a remote feeling of being kindred spirits, if I may describe it so.

"Anyway, Henry," Rosie continues briskly, clearly relieved by my acceptance of her news. "Poor Emily died giving birth to you, and against Cecilia's wishes, your brother adopted you and raised you as their own son. This means, Henry, it doesn't matter which way things go in your life, you will, after your half-brother dies, inherit the Harrowfeild estate."

Rosie's touch upon my cheek is so gentle and loving. I know I truly belong with her.

"Oh Rosie, I mean Grandma, I always knew deep in my soul I did not belong to my mother. And to have had your unconditional love all my life has been such a blessing. You will stay with me forever, no matter what? You will, won't you, Rosie? Even if I become poor and bedraggled and nobody else loves me?"

I cried unabashedly, and my eyes became a black sticky mess. My painted lips smudge beyond repair and my rouge smears all over Rosie's blouse. I clasp her to me as she strokes me gently on the back.

"There, there my sweet. I will never leave you, Henry, I promise. I'll always love you, no matter what."

If my spirits are not already lifted enough with the excitement of dressing like a lady, they soar with this news. We sit apart and study each other's features for a moment until Rosie smiles and says, "Don't worry, Henry, Emily was a pretty little thing. Not like me. She had perfect features, just like you, my darling. I've kept the only photo I had of her. Thankfully, it shows Emily with your father, the old Duke, standing arm-in-arm in the Harrowfeild garden." Rosie removes the photograph from her purse and hands it to me. My tears well without warning. I finally see a family resemblance to someone. My mother was so pretty.

"May I keep this photo, Rosie?" I ask quietly, my throat tight with emotion.

"Of course you may, Henry. Though better still, I thought you may like to paint it. And now I'll show you something else. I kept a few sketches, drawn by your mother."

Rosie hands me the stunning charcoals, which are mostly of the castle and grounds. But there is one of a deer, looking so much like the stag my brother shot on the day of Pierre's departure. At that moment, I somehow felt the presence of my mother, Emily, very close and reassuring.

Our continued time on board ship, as grandmother and granddaughter, works well. Rosie shaves my whiskers each morning. Not difficult, as I have so few, then she helps me dress. Her laughter is contagious. She, too, thinks it such fun, like a stage play we are acting out.

However, there are personal problems. I am admired to the point of receiving two marriage proposals from two beautiful young men within the first two weeks on board. These proposals did not, of course, sway me from Pierre. Rather, they stand as mere tests to my never-ending love for him. Despite these unsettling attentions, I am determined to continue the pantomime all the way to Pierre and then I will let him decide if I should keep up the pretence of being female. Yes, it may be our only way to stay together forever.

I must admit though, one romantic star-filled night as the full moon bewitched me, I allowed myself to be kissed by one of my suitors, a Mr Edward March. I wanted to see how a man kissed a woman. I must say I was surprised by the immense passion and urgency in his kiss. I became considerably aroused before I regained my senses.

"My dear Mr March!" I gasped breathlessly. "We must not do this again, for my feelings have been stirred by your kiss and I am promised to another man. I am on this voyage to meet him in Sydney Town and we are to be married the following week." Poor Teddy, I call him, looked crestfallen but ever the gentleman, he kissed the tips of my fingers and bade me goodnight.

I lied, of course, but it sounded so good to say I was marrying Pierre. Wouldn't it be the ultimate? I must stop dreaming of things that cannot possibly be, especially since he is already married to dear Sarah. I wonder, have they consummated their marriage yet? Has Pierre turned his affection from me and fallen in love with Sarah? It pains me to think of such things, so I stop.

Mr March and other admirers continue to speak of their love for me. It is a difficult journey in this respect. I have never imagined such favourable attention from so many young men. And while it flatters my ego, it also saddens me to think I am not who I should be, meaning I should have been born a woman. This is a double-edged sword that may be the end of me if I don't keep my wits. Thank heavens I have Rosie to stand guard on most occasions, especially when my emotions begin to heat up.

I'm sure I can speak for Rosie, when I say I am delighted to finally dock in Sydney Harbour and be rid of my captive admirers.

CHAPTER 11
SARAH

Our journey back to Windsor Hospital was not in vain. It had taken all of six weeks for Mother to fully recover from pneumonia. She was still a little weak, but determined to go forth and settle in the mountains before winter set in. In the days Father and I spent in the Hawkesbury Basin waiting for Mother to be well again, I have had time to reconsider our initial plan of putting down permanent roots in the mountains.

Father has spent most of his time in Windsor praying for Mother. When not praying, he has introduced himself to the local Anglican minister and the Catholic priest. He told me they have shown the greatest kindness to the poor unfortunate souls in the area. And they agreed that yes, a Church of England would be a beneficial addition to the general congregation. I felt as Father did; we might return here if things did not go smoothly in the mountains. I wrote my feelings on paper and sent a letter almost every day to Pierre Boyar, care of the Blackheath Post Office. His single reply held good news; Pierre had found suitable land for the horses and a picturesque site on which to build our home.

We arrived in Blackheath eight weeks after Pierre's letter and found him fencing paddocks for the horses. He had already purchased the undulating block, two miles out from the village. I'd almost forgotten how handsome he was. His skin had tanned from working outdoors and he looked lean and muscled. We embraced warmly, and he clasped Father's shoulder and shook his hand. He swept his arm expansively and said, smiling, "One hundred acres will be plenty to run our horses." He turned to me; his eyes bright with excitement. "Sarah, this is a perfect training ground. The limestone will provide calcium, which young horses need to grow strong bones. Working them up the hills will produce good muscle, and the clear water, running down from the mountains, feeding into our own private stream, will provide good health."

His face was radiant. A vision of his future was set here on this splendid piece of earth. Our home site overlooked the horse paddocks and afforded spectacular views to the higher mountains, according to Pierre and Mr Watson. I stood on the very spot and took in the panoramic view. The blue hue of the endless sky meeting the mountain peaks felt timeless. It was like nothing here would ever change; its majesty would live forever. Pierre squeezed my hand and turned to face me.

"I have put a deposit on a smaller block of land for your parents, but it's big enough to build a home and a church next to it, with room for a sizable garden and a vegetable patch. I'm sure with your mother's ill health and her now being rather frail, she will be happier living in a cottage nearer the township, rather than a grand home. The cottage will be warm and cosy in the winter. It faces north so in the summer the westerly sun will not interfere with the coolness offered by the wide verandas we have designed. *Mais certainement*, your parents will have the final say."

I stroked Pierre's arm and kissed him on the cheek. What a lovely man, I thought. How I longed for the moment when we would unite in love – then my happiness would be complete.

Upon returning from his and Mother's inspection of the parcel of land Pierre has selected for him, Father stepped down from the buggy and congratulated him. "Pierre, you have done well, my son. I'm sure the Good Lord has guided you in our absence." He coughed then lowered his head, but I was still able to read his lips. "I'm certain you have been praying for the Lord's assistance, in more ways than one. And I'm sure, you know what I mean. Mother and I will be overjoyed to have grandchildren. And the sooner the better." He slapped Pierre's back heartily and I imagined his laughter echoing in the clean, crisp air.

Pierre hung his head, embarrassed. I felt for him, but I knew Father's wish would come true. I am determined.

The stables were constructed within four weeks after the felling of many trees. Timber was in ample supply and we began to build our home. The frame was built from timber, but the outer structure would be built from sandstone, quarried from a nearby mine. Verandas were a must, we had been told on arrival in Sydney. They would be a cooling place to sit and enjoy the afternoon breezes.

Months passed, and I continued to help Pierre in every possible way. I created a vegetable garden and helped him care for the horses. We were overjoyed to see Satan had done his duty by serving Cheval D'azur; the mare is now in foal. Pierre has worked out the birth date. He told me that by the time we move into our home, in nine months, the foal should be born. We have laid bets on this happening, and even though Father does not believe in gambling, he thought this wager to be fun.

School has begun, and Amy begged me to begin working with her, but I was unable to do so if our home was to be completed in good time. Amy understood and on occasion pitched in to help us whenever she could, so our teaching together would begin sooner, rather than later.

Thankfully, Pierre and William have already built a solid, high-roofed barn, containing four stables. Two were for the horses and the other two made do as our living quarters for the time being. Father and Mother took refuge with the Watsons, closer to the village. It saddened me to be apart from them. Perhaps I would not have been so sad if Pierre had done his duty to me as Satan had done for Cheval D'Azure. I know this was putting it crudely. However, it was the way I felt. Pierre forever made excuses: "I am too tired, Sarah. I have a bad back, Sarah." His excuses were beginning to vex me. I was frustrated physically and mentally. It was tormenting to lie beside him at night with his back turned to me. I also had to keep making my own excuses to Mother as to why I had not yet conceived her first grandchild.

I took to walking in the bush, which seemed to calm my senses and distract me from my longings. There were so many different varieties of wildflowers, many of which I picked, pressed and sent back home to Mary, Pierre's mother. My favourite was a tiny star-shaped flower, mauve in colour, which always lifted my sombre mood. In her letters, Mary told me how she had become enchanted by the Australian flora and promised to come here soon and stay for a while. I could not be happier with this news. Perhaps she would speak with Pierre? She could remind him why this had all come about and how he must fulfil his duty to me. I cannot explain how frustrated I have become, perhaps even like a bitch on heat. I know I shouldn't write such things, but I am bursting with love.

One fine morning, after doing all I could to help Pierre, I decided to take a long walk – on my own. I packed lunch, leaving Pierre's lunch in our newly built meat safe. The safe is one piece of furniture I know we could not do without. It has a large hook attached to the roof and sections cut out where wire netting is put in place to keep the flies and insects out. A tray of water sits on the base of the safe, cooling the air as it flows through the netting. Simple but ingenious.

On this day, I felt the need more than ever that I must be alone to think about what would become of me if I could not share Pierre's physical love. My juices were flowing, and my urge to have children was beginning to drive me mad. I could now understand why those men came to visit my mother and paid her money to relieve their pent-up desires. But I was a woman and I did not think it would be the same for us; I know now that it is. I was driven by a burning desire for Pierre to make love to me to feel him as close as possible. This feeling was much stronger than the simple desire to reproduce, even though having children was my dearest wish.

The path I took through the bush was my usual one. I had marked trees and tied pieces of ribbon to their branches, so I was sure to find my way home. I had been warned by the locals that it was easy to go missing in the mountains. Some walkers, I was told, had even lost their lives, becoming enthralled by the scenery and forgetting which way they had come. I heeded the warning and took no risks. I had packed ample food and water for my walk and took good note of many landmarks along the way. My only regret was not being able to hear the sweet songs of the birds flittering around me. I saw the breeze ruffling the leaves on the trees and wondered at the sound they might make. The deep dark depths of the rock ledges had water gliding down and over their smooth surfaces. What sound did it make? Did it all meld together like a symphony, creating a harmonious and haunting tune? My walks took me far away into a secret realm. There I felt my mind and body at peace.

I had ventured further than ever before. My weariness after two hours forced me to rest and eat my lunch. I sat on a fallen log and dreamily took a bite of my sandwich. To my complete shock, it was suddenly grabbed out of my hand from behind. I could not scream, so I threw my arms about, trying to be rid of my attacker, who came around to stand in front of me. He smiled at my outrage, which only provoked me further and I clenched my fists. He sat on a rock and devoured the sandwich. I stared at him, angry though afraid to move, but at the same time, my curiosity had been piqued. It seemed he did not wish to hurt me. Maybe he was simply lost and hungry?

My note pad was at hand and my pencil was sharp. I wrote:
I am unable to hear or speak. Are you lost, Sir? You
must be very hungry to have forgotten your manners
and grabbed my sandwich so savagely. If you are lost,
I know the way out of here and you must come with me.

53

I shall give you more food and then see you on your
way to the closest town.

I thrust the note towards him. As he read, I studied his finely chiselled features. His full lips curved in a smile as if my note amused him. His teeth shone white against his suntanned skin. A taut, fit body was clad in well-cut, tailored clothes. A fine silk shirt floated about a pair of well-fitting breeches. His long dark hair gleamed and was tied loosely with a cord at the nape of his neck. His long boots were of fine leather. He fascinated me.

He stood slowly and gently extended his hand for my pencil. I watched him write fluently. He was well educated, I was sure. He returned my pad and I read.

Dear Miss,
Please do not tell anyone you have seen me. I apologise
for my poor manners in snatching your sandwich. I was
indeed very hungry. I assure you I am not a murderer.
I merely helped a friend who was in grave need. My
actions have placed me on the wrong side of the law.

I looked up to see him studying me with piercing blue eyes. I found it hard to leave his gaze, but I forced myself to lower my head and read on.

However, I am not lost. I have taken refuge in a cave
further along the ridge. You appear to have an angelic
quality, Miss. I have been watching you for many days
on your excursions. I would appreciate your friendship.

I sighed, and wondered: do I make a sound when I sigh? My shoulders relaxed, and I tilted my head to study his face. I felt I was a good judge of character and I was sure this young man was telling the truth. I suddenly saw an amusing side to our encounter, and I smiled involuntarily. It could be fun, if not exciting, to help this dashing miscreant. I smiled more broadly and handed him the rest of my food. He thanked me with a deep bow and ate with a little more grace.

I wrote on my pad.

I shall return tomorrow, Sir. It is getting late. I will bring
you more food. But then you must tell me your name and
your whole story. I will not feed a common scoundrel.

He nodded, and I rose and turned to leave but before I had walked two steps away, he reached for my hand and pressed my fingers to his lips. I blushed and dropped a small curtsy.

This unexpected meeting made my heart race. It enticed my imagination. Maybe this was something that could distract me from my longing for Pierre?

CHAPTER 12
THE DUKE

"How long has it been now?" the Duke bellows at the police sergeant handling the case of the still-missing Henry.

"My lord, please have a little more patience. It has been only four months. We truly feel master Henry is alive somewhere. I believe it to be three years before we can legally call him deceased. We are doing all we can to track him down. Bulletins have been sent out all over the world, showing the picture you gave us. Surely, someone will recognise him soon. We suspect he may have had some accident, perhaps he hit his head, and this may have affected his memory – amnesia, you know," the police officer explained.

"I know that, you fool! I warn you, Sergeant, my patience is wearing very thin. Now, get out of here and don't come back until you find Henry – dead or alive!"

"Dead, I hope," the Duchess whispers as she smirks across at her daughter. Gertrude, who suppresses a giggle.

Yes, my lord. Of course." The sergeant makes a rapid exit.

The Duke, emitting a sigh with enough force to blow out ten candles, collapses heavily into his armchair. He frowns at his wife, who shows no sympathy for his distress.

"I know you don't care an atom about Henry, Cecilia, but do you have to make it so bloody obvious? And you, Miss," he shakes his finger at Gertrude, "you have been poisoned by your mother's dislike for Henry, even though Henry has been most kind to you all your life. I'm assuming your mother has told you, against my wishes, that Henry is in fact your uncle – not your brother? Well, whichever way you are related to Henry, he deserves your respect. You might like to remember that this estate will be left to Henry after me, and whether you are permitted to continue living here will be up to him. It would pay for you both," the Duke's stern gaze rests on the faces of his wife and daughter, "to be a little more circumspect in your treatment of the next Duke of Harrowfeild."

Gertrude tries hard to muster an expression of remorse, but Cecilia fumes upon hearing the stated truth. Most of the money needed to keep Harrowfeild in fine order over the past twenty years was, in fact, part of her dowry. Cecilia's extremely wealthy father had found it almost impossible to marry off his ugly daughter – there is no other word for her misfortune – to a Lord. Harrowfeild Hall was in grave need of repairs and the servants had to be paid. A huge amount of money was offered to the old Duke to make Cecilia his daughter-in-law. On top of that, Cecilia's father had offered a generous allowance for the next fifty years. The old Duke quickly accepted. He demanded his son, Albert, marry Cecilia. If they wished to save the Harrowfeild estate from bankruptcy, there was no alternative. Cecilia knew that there was not a hope she would be able to undo the trust account set up by some of the best lawyers in England. Albert now held all the power, especially as he was shrewd in his business dealings. He had accumulated even more wealth than the old Duke could have ever imagined. If only Cecilia could have borne him a son and heir. Unfortunately, complications arose with the birth of Gertrude, and Cecilia was made barren.

Cecilia looks hatefully toward Duke as he slumps further into his armchair and wearily rubs his face.

"I must admit I do miss Henry, and I am determined to find him! So, please show a little compassion towards my feelings, or take yourself on a sea voyage – somewhere far away!" he sighs again, resting his chin on his beefy hand, his eyes downcast.

With that, the rustle of taffeta sweeping across the tiled floor announces the departure of the two women.

After some time reflecting on Henry's disappearance, the Duke is drawn once again to look at Rosie's letter. With great effort, he heaves himself from his chair, shuffles across to his mahogany desk, opens the top drawer, and withdraws the letters.

To the Duke of Harrowfeild.
My Lord,
It is with the deepest sorrow I must bid you farewell. I cannot possibly stay a moment longer without my beloved Henry. I have saved enough money for my needs and I will be moving to the home of my elderly sister in Devon. She is in poor health and needs someone to care

for her. Please, if you will, Sir, could you send me a note,
just to let me know how Henry is faring?
Thank you for all you have done for me over the years.
Our secret will always be held in confidence.
Yours sincerely,
Rosie Pierce.
Willow Cottage, Potts Lane, Devon.

"Hmm, written on the night before Henry's departure. I shall seek out this elderly sister in Devon. Perhaps Rosie can shed some more light on Henry's vanishing act," the Duke says aloud while pacing the floor.

Dutifully, Rosie has covered her tracks. Rosie's sister in Devon is in fact Bethany Pierce, a close childhood friend with whom she's kept in contact all these years. Rosie had taken the surname Pierce when hiding from her violent father. Bethany is wise in assuming the Duke will sooner or later send a messenger trying to track Rosie down. So, when George, who had returned with his bad news of "losing" Henry, is sent to Devon to inquire about Rosie, Bethany explains the situation to him.

"Well, seeing ya's asked, Sir, Rosie fancied a trip to London Town, she did." She smiles feebly at George and wraps her shawl more snugly around her bony frame. "I 'aven't 'eard from 'er for over a week now and she said she was 'avin' a grand old time, she was." A husky chortle escapes before she continues. "I think she may 'ave even found 'erself a fella. But she did say in 'er letter she'd be 'ome 'ere before the month ends. Me 'ealth fluctuates badly, y' know, Sir." Bethany gives a few shallow coughs for good measure. "Do y' want me to let 'er knows you was lookin' for 'er, Sir?"

"Yes, Missus, tell Rosie the Duke needs to see her urgently!" George takes one of her gnarled hands and presses a few coppers into her palm.

"I certainly will, Sir, as soon as she comes 'ome, I will." Bethany nods obsequiously as George turns and strides down the path. She goes back inside her cottage, closes the door and leans against it, wondering how long it will be before George returns with more questions. *I'll keep 'em guessing, I will. Rosie's promise to keep me well looked after 'as been kept so far. This mornin' me second payment came by messenger. I shan't let me best friend down. No, I won't.* She clinks the pennies in her hand and regards them disdainfully. *Mean as cat shit, that tosser!*

CHAPTER 13
HENRY

"I must say, Rosie," I observe as I gaze out of our hotel window, "this town is alive with all sorts. It seems England's class distinction is nowhere to be seen here in Sydney, except for some 'two bob toffs' as my fath… I mean, my brother would say, strutting around as if they own the place. I find it refreshing to be in a new colony and on the brink of our exciting adventure, Rosie. Do you think it safe to remove my feminine attire now? I feel overwhelmed by admirers. It tires me, saddens me, and at the same time excites me." I turn to Rosie, longing to remove my wig and give my scalp a good scratch.

"I know, Henri-Etta," Rosie says, smiling down at yet another young gentleman who's looked up and tipped his hat in my direction. "Just a little longer and we'll be on our way to Blackheath and then it will be a good time for you to be a man again. I hear it's not safe for a woman to go traipsin' off into the wilderness on her own, at least not without a man. We'll buy a rifle, I'll drive the buggy and you can ride shotgun," Rosie says with a determined nod of her head.

"But, Rosie, we have only one trunk each. Don't you think it would be simpler to go by train?" I confess the mention of firearms disconcert me a little.

"I suppose so, Henry, it's just I thought it be better to have our own transport. But come to think of it, we should be able to buy a horse and buggy in the mountains. After all, it's supposed to be quite civilised now." Rosie busies herself unpacking our clothes.

"And I ask you, dear grandmama, what exactly are we going to say about you and me turning up on Sarah and Pierre's doorstep? That's if they have their home built by now. Though knowing how industrious Pierre is, he should have a mansion built within the near two years since we have seen him."

I move from the window to sit of the edge of the bed, carefully arranging my skirts.

"Mmm, I haven't made me mind up yet," Rosie says with a serious look upon her face. "I thought I could say you were my young cousin. And since I'd retired from Harrowfeild, I thought I'd take you on an adventure to see some of Australia. This means, Henry, you'd have to stay in costume."

I throw my head back, laughing so hard my sides began to hurt, and Rosie joins me. It seems we have the same picture in mind.

"Dear Rosie, how delicious!" I lie across the bed with my chin propped in my hand. The thought of flirting with Pierre whilst in my female guise is quite titillating, but my thoughts then turn grim. "But will I fool them? What if they see straight through my charade?" The thought of being ridiculed for posing as a woman is too hard to even contemplate.

Rosie pauses in her folding of a voluminous pair of bloomers to give me a direct look. "I'm being honest with you, Henry, when I say if I hadn't known what you were up to, I would never have recognised you. I do think though, if we stayed long enough in the company of the Reverend Timms, he may see a resemblance between Henry and Henri-Etta. But we won't be payin' him a visit. We'll go straight to Pierre and Sarah's home, we will." Rosie nods her head adamantly, her usual fashion when stating something that brooked no disagreement.

I sit up, my fears allayed. "Yes, you're right, Rosie, and I think I should stay dressed as a woman until either I reveal myself or they realise who I am. I do love this game. I wonder how long it will take them to recognise me. Maybe I should have a new name. What about just Etta? I've always liked the name Etta. It's simple and sweet."

"Alright, to them you'll be Etta. But I think Henri-Etta suits you better." Rosie smiles at me indulgently.

"I've just had a good idea," I tell Rosie. "Let us stay in Sydney Town. You write Sarah a letter telling her of our arrival. We will wait here for her reply. I know it will hold a welcome for you and your cousin Etta. This way, I will quench my thirst for sightseeing and meet some of the locals in Sydney Town, albeit in men's attire. It seems my female appearance brings a little too much attention. What do you think, Rosie?" I ask while removing the last traces of paint and powder from my face.

"That *is* a good idea. If the truth be known I wouldn't mind a coupla days to take things easy. I'm not as young as I used to be, my dear," Rosie reminds me.

"Wonderful, Rosie! And now I'm going to enjoy a long luxurious bath while you write your letter."

We then decide that a nap until high teatime is in order. We fall asleep like contented babies. Several hours later I wake, turning my head to Rosie who is blinking wearily, and I yawn my words.

"I'm going to dress in my men's suit, Rosie. I won't shave. A little show of whiskers will help my manly image."

"As you say, Henry," Rosie yawns loudly. "Just be careful no one sees you leave this room dressed like a man."

"I'll be cautious," I assure her. "I shall take a walk and post your letter to Sarah."

The golden hues of twilight spread enchantment over Sydney and its people. The setting sun shows crimson before it disappears over the western horizon. Yes, whoever said Australia radiates magical light was correct. Such a feeling of peace and freedom I have as I walk to the Post Office, which by now is closed, so I deliver the letter through a slit in a large red iron box standing on the street outside the building. I sigh, knowing it could be over a week before we receive Sarah's reply although I'm confident her letter will hold words of excitement and longing to see Rosie. I can picture the scene when we arrive. But will my overwhelming joy lead me to immediately give away my true identity? I may not be able to hold my feelings together long enough to act out the charade. My need to embrace and kiss Pierre has now reached boiling point. No, I must never relent. The true situation between Sarah and Pierre must be shown to me before I display my emotions. In the meantime, the suspense may just kill me.

Head lowered, I watch my step as I pick my way carefully down a steep and slippery hill. When I look up, I not only notice the glimmering harbour, but I a group of young men talking and laughing outside a public house or "pub", I think the colonials call them. On closer inspection, one tall well-muscled dark-haired fellow gives my heart a jolt. From a distance, he looks like Pierre! I take a few more steps towards the group. My heart soars. This is when I need to brace myself, and I do.

"Pierre, is it you?" I ask calmly.

Pierre's gaze meets mine and the current between us flows. "Mon dieu!" he cries, and hurries to enfold me in his arms, and through my tears I see bewilderment on the faces of the other men. Quickly I recover and make excuses for our exuberant embrace.

"I do apologise, gentlemen. This is quite a shock for us both!

After not hearing from each other for quite some time, I assumed my close friend, Pierre, was dead! Apparently, he thought the same fate had befallen me. Is this not so, Pierre?" I grab his shoulder roughly and give him a shake.

"Oui – yes, that's right. I'd had word that you had been killed in a terrible accident!" Pierre says, quickly regaining his composure. "My friends, c'est merveilleux!"

The young men shrug and smile, any suspicions hopefully put to rest by this explanation. Pierre introduces me as one of his oldest friends and they offer their hands to me in welcome.

It transpires that these young men are horseracing enthusiasts, and Pierre is doing business with them. They are interested in breeding thoroughbreds to race and had heard of Pierre's well-bred stallion. As Pierre needed supplies found only in Sydney Town, he had agreed to meet the gentlemen there to discuss the service fee for Satan. I am desperate to be alone with Pierre, but he must, of course, finish his business. There is more talk about a live-foal guarantee (whatever that is) and the price for sending two or more mares to the stallion. I try hard to show interest, and I certainly do not want to drag Pierre away from his future livelihood, but my heart is almost exploding with love, and I fear I will do something quite silly if I do not leave soon. I am sure my desire is beginning to show, so I bid the group farewell after writing down my address in Sydney and handing it to Pierre.

"It was so good to see you again, Henry. I shall pay you a visit." To ward off any suspicion, Pierre adds, "Has your wife journeyed with you on this trip, Henry?"

Luckily, I was quick on the uptake. "Of course, Pierre, I would never leave my dear *Rosie* behind!" I tell him emphatically.

He tilts his head with a look of puzzlement before the penny drops. "Certainly not, Henry! I know how much you adore *Rosie*. Silly question really. Au revoir."

Once out of their sight, I run with gay abandon back to the hotel, bumping shoulders with the rough element of Sydney by night. I care nothing for their shallow threats of violence; my wild happiness makes me feel invulnerable. Totally breathless, I arrive at the Paten Slip Inn. Rosie, looking concerned, sits waiting in the foyer.

"There you are, Hen…" she begins but quickly continues in a much louder voice, "I must say you look rather flustered, Master Smith.

Are you alright? I've been waiting for quite some time, you know!"

"Yes, Mrs Brown, I'm quite alright, thank you. I'm sorry I'm late. Shall we go for our supper and I will inform you of my good news." I take a deep breath, regain my composure and calmly proffer my arm to Rosie. We walk briskly into the hotel's dining room, selecting a table for two in a quiet corner. I rush my words with excitement, throwing my arms about, and adding to the drama of my meeting with Pierre. All Rosie can do is laugh in her wobbly way, which makes me adore her more.

"I'm so happy for you, Henry," she whispers. "And you know this meeting with Pierre will make it easier to fool Sarah. Well, until she needs to know."

"I know. Pierre is coming to our hotel room later, so can we make it a quick supper? I don't want to miss him."

With supper over and indigestion creeping up, we go back to the hotel foyer. Luckily, the desk staff are nowhere to be seen and we make it to our room without being noticed. In my note to Pierre I had instructed him to ask for the room of Mrs Rosie Brown. And so we wait, me with a stomach full of butterflies dancing the highland fling, and Rosie belching out a congenial tune named "Oh, them onions." Finally, a knock. Rosie struggles from her seat and opens the door to an emotional Pierre. Once again, his passionate embrace is all I need to know he still loves me.

"Do you two want me to leave?" Rosie asks with a sweet and knowing smile.

"No, thank you, Rosie, our love can wait a little longer. We three must discuss a plan of action," I say, although I am still clutching Pierre's work-hardened hand.

One hour turns into two, before we relate our individual stories and reach an agreement on what to do next. However, I am surprised when Pierre divulges the fact his parents knew from the beginning about my relationship to Rosie. Also, Pierre shyly explains, that although he does love Sarah – in a brotherly way – he has been unable to make love to her and give her the children she so ardently desires. He feels he has wronged her and is full of self-remorse.

"I can't explain it, Henry, only to say my heart is so full of love for you that I was willing to go through my life without having another lover. I truly feel sorry for Sarah. I wish I could at least give her children. But I look at her and nothing happens. I can't do it!" Pierre shrugs, and

Rosie tilts her head to one side, her finely plucked brows furrowed in thought.

"I find it intriguing, Master Pierre. What do you think it is? Do you think you were just born this way, or do you think it might be something from a past life? Like Henry may have been your wife in a past life?"

I'm sure it is the seriousness with which Rosie has asked her fanciful question that caused us to laugh so loudly that the person in the next room bangs on the wall.

"Quiet down, you lot, or I'll report you!" comes a gruff voice.

Still trying to stifle our laughter, we say our goodbyes. Pierre and I leave Rosie to enjoy a good night's sleep, while we lovers hurry to Pierre's hotel, where our rising passion is to be released for a night of unsurpassed bliss.

The following morning after a tender farewell, Pierre, holding our secret close, is on his way back to the Blue Mountains and Sarah. Rosie and I wait another four days before Sarah's letter arrives. It is, as I imagined, full of excitement and welcome. Sarah writes:

> *My Dear Rosie,*
> *I will be delighted to see you and to meet your young cousin, Etta. What a wonderful time we shall have. I hope you have time to stay for quite a while, as I am rather lonely up here, high in the mountains. I eagerly await your arrival.*
> *With love,*
> *Sarah.*

I must say my heart goes out to Sarah, poor little darling. How are we ever going to sort out this entanglement? And I must say her writing has become so fluent it impresses us both. *Maybe Sarah will write her novel after all.*

As I had suggested, Rosie and I travel to the Blue Mountains in a rather charming steam train. It chugs its way through inspirational scenery, and every so often we catch glimpses of the strangest creature I had ever seen – a kangaroo! And what most delights me is the little joey popping its head out from the mother's pouch.

"I just have to have one as a pet," I say excitedly to Rosie, tapping her on the arm with my fan.

"Now, Etta, they are wild creatures, my love. I don't think it would be wise to just lasso one and take it home."

A man's voice interrupts our conversation. "Ladies, excuse me for eavesdropping, but I can tell you a thing or two about kangaroos, if you wish."

Well, if it didn't take this man at least one hour to tell us all we needed to know (and a lot we didn't need to know!) about kangaroos. In fact, it took two! I turned my pretty head toward him and peeped coquettishly over the top of my fan.

"Thank you *so* much for your information, Sir. Perhaps you should write a book about Australian wildlife? I'm sure it would be a bestseller!" I can't help but be a little facetious.

"I am doing just that, Miss. And I'm wondering if you might like to join me on an occasional nature walk?" His eyes seem to twinkle with delight at my appearance. At that, Rosie joins the conversation.

"I'm sorry, Sir, but my young cousin here, Etta, is to be married soon. There'll be no nature walking with strange men. No! Indeed not!" Rosie draws her skirts around her in an affronted way.

"I do apologise, madam. I assumed, of course, you would accompany us." He has the good grace to look at least a little caught, and I hide my smile behind my fan.

"No, thank you, Sir. I'd rather view the wildlife from here, sitting comfortably in a train." Rosie's tone indicates the conversation has come to an end. He withdraws to his seat and says not another word for the remainder of the journey.

Blackheath village sits perched on the highest point in the Blue Mountains. The fragrance of eucalyptus flows about. I inhale deeply as I take in the sights. I am surprised at how established this township is. It tickles me to see fresh produce sitting in wheelbarrows outside and under the protection of the shop verandas. Some of the shops are tearooms, having tables and chairs taking pride of place out front, where fashionably dressed ladies sit sipping tea and nibbling cake. How delightful!

"Oh Rosie, how charming this town is, and the air is so fresh! Do you not love it as I do?" I demand happily.

"Yes, Etta, I do, of course I do," she says distractedly as she looks around for Pierre who is to meet us outside the post office where we wait.

"There he be Etta." Rosie points her fat little finger towards Pierre, who has just tied his horses to a hitching rail alongside a drinking trough.

"Hello, ladies!" Pierre calls as he hurries across the road and kisses our cheeks before ushering us to his buggy, carrying a trunk in each hand.

The sight of his enormous biceps straining to carry such weight makes me melt. "Be still my heart," I mutter.

As we jog along in the buggy, we speak continuously of our admiration for the mountain scenery, which consists mostly of dense ferns, gumtrees and the occasional pine tree. It seems not too long before we reach the entrance to a partly cleared acreage. Pierre eases the horses to a walk and then halts them as we survey the property. A large stone house is built on the highest point of a hill. I can see a rose garden has been planted in front of the generous veranda. Many different trees, including young native conifers, surround each paddock, which is what I was told the settlers call the fields here. It takes my breath away for a moment.

"Oh Pierre, this is wonderful! What an ideal setting your home is built upon, and what a grand home it appears to be!" Pierre's eyes are shining with pride at my sincere compliments. "And what a fitting name for your beautiful property – 'Mountain View'," I add, reading the words carved into the rail either side of the entrance.

"Yes, we were lucky, Etta. It only took half the time we allowed ourselves to build, due to the many parishioners who helped us. It also has four bed chambers, especially for guests, as we live so far away from Sydney. Plus, I built a small cottage at the end of the barn for staff, and though I should, I haven't as yet hired anyone. Reverend Timms can be quite persuasive when he needs to be. His parishioners are some of the hardest working people I have met and very willing to help." Pierre smiles and eases the horses to a walk, as we enter the long driveway up to the house.

Sarah stands on the veranda with her hands upon her heart, seemingly overwhelmed to see us. She smiles broadly, her eyes shining when shaking my hand and betraying no hint of recognition. Sarah turns to envelop Rosie and nestle her head into Rosie's bosom. I can understand; it is also my favourite place to seek comfort. It takes many moments before Sarah's eyes are free enough of tears to write, *Welcome to you both.* This simple note makes *my* eyes water; I am unprepared for such emotion. Never did I think my meeting with Sarah again would be so – so heart-wrenching. She is like my little sister; we grew up together. Pierre and I had protected Sarah and now I am about to deceive her. How can I? Oh, control yourself, Henry. Your future with Pierre is at stake. I take Sarah's hand in mine and curtsy, lowering my head, so she cannot witness my raw emotions.

Meanwhile, Pierre stands rigid, waiting I'm sure for the moment when Sarah recognises me. He relaxes only when he realises Sarah has simply assumed I am the young lady who was introduced to her, Rosie's young cousin, Etta.

At this point, I begin thinking of all the times Pierre and I could now take long walks to be alone in each other's arms. We know our dear Rosie will give aid to our undercover romance. What a gem she is, and what fun we will have.

As Pierre ushers us inside, he announces that the Reverend and Mrs Timms are to dine with us this evening. I am not in the right frame of mind to meet them, so I decide to have a raging headache. I excuse myself almost immediately and go to my room for the evening. I spend a restless night either dreaming of Pierre or berating myself for deceiving Sarah. In the morning, I am presented with a bunch of wildflowers Mrs Timms left, along with a note to say how sorry she was not to have met me. I let out a sigh of relief, and my wretchedness is soon forgotten upon catching Pierre's burning gaze across the breakfast table. I am besotted!

CHAPTER 14
SARAH

I am overjoyed to see Henry after such a long absence. As soon as he stepped down from the buggy I recognised him – I almost laughed out loud! Not that it is possible. How funny! It took all my strength and cunning not to let Henry see that I recognised him almost straightaway. His eyes gave him away. People's eyes do not change, no matter how much paint and powder they apply. And poor Pierre – standing there so frightened. I can't imagine what they thought I might do – it was most amusing. But I was genuine in my pleasure in seeing dear Rosie again. What a charade they are all involved in. Poor Henry! I truly feel for him with his hidden desire to be a female, and I am aware of how difficult it must have been for him to escape the grip of his father, though it has taken almost two years. I must say, to see Henry dressed as a woman has truly impressed me. What a fine female he makes! If I were a man, I would most certainly take a fancy to him myself.

Yes, this reunion could not have come at a better time. James, the charming sandwich thief, has proven to be more like a knight in shining armour. We have been meeting frequently when I take my walks and, like a delicate blossom yielding one petal at a time, our affection and admiration for each other begins to bloom. Soon our secret longing will reveal a glorious declaration of love – and, eventually, a child of my own, I hope.

The first time we touched physically was when James stroked the bare skin on my arm, pretending to brush away some imagined dust. I could not help but lean forward wantonly to kiss him. He held me from him and gazed into my eyes before his lips softly met mine. I needed him so badly that I strained against his hands on my shoulders, grabbing the lapels of his jacket to draw him closer. But he stopped me, kissed my forehead and told me to go. Many times after that he would take my hand when we met, often raising my fingers to his lips. He would sometimes kiss me goodbye, touching his lips briefly to mine. I could see the strength of my growing desire reflected in his eyes. I longed for the time when we might throw propriety aside and embrace each other with unrestrained passion.

Several days later it was unbearably hot, and we swam in our undergarments in a rock pool. When our clothes were wet, we were as good as naked. I could not take my eyes off him and felt no shame as he gazed appreciatively at the curves of my breasts. Although I know we were both sorely tempted, we took things no further. We lay side by side on the bank of the pool, letting the sun dry us while our fingers intertwined. We dressed slowly and then he was gone, after teasing me with a sensuous smile. My need to make love to James preoccupies my every waking moment, and my sleep is full of such dreams! I blush when I think on them.

I decided to take things into my own hands on our next meeting. I was determined that I would break down his reserve – I would join his game. It was very hot and humid, and as we sat by the rock pool, I raised my skirts over my knees and slowly unrolled my stockings. I felt his gaze but pretended to be unaware as I dabbled my toes in the water. I slowly undid the buttons of my blouse, leaning forward to show the curve of my breasts as I cupped the cool water and let it trickle over my neck. I raised my skirts to my thighs and stroked them with my wet hands, all the while pretending not to notice that James was watching me intently. I lay back against the ferny bank, my arms stretched languorously back over my head. Only then did I openly meet his gaze, my invitation clear and unequivocal. The food I had brought remained untouched as James leaned over to place his lips in the hollow of my throat. I closed my eyes and felt his hands undo the remaining buttons on my blouse. As his lips traced the swell of my breasts, I felt his hand slide under my skirt, and I opened my thighs. His hand stopped in surprise when he did not encounter any undergarments. At this point I opened my eyes and smiled at him, drawing him down to kiss him with ardent desire. We both knew there was no turning back and with deliberate slowness he undressed me, then removed his own clothing. He lay down beside me and we stroked and touched each other until we could bear it no longer. We were finally joined together in our longing and love. I felt no shame or guilt; I know the Lord has sent James to me as recompense for the hurt I have endured with Pierre. Although my heart has not wavered from loving Pierre, I simply acknowledge he holds a deep and different love for Henry. I am quite certain God sent James to love me as a woman needs to be loved and, God willing, our union will eventually be blessed with a child.

CHAPTER 15
PIERRE

I am in such torment! I cannot bear having Henry so close to me and yet remain unable to hold him. When he arrived, I was petrified that Sarah would see through Henry's disguise, but fortunately she showed no sign of recognition. She is clearly happy to have visitors and I confess to feeling relief that Sarah now has something to divert her. It is lonely for her here although she seems to take great solace in her frequent excursions into the bush. In fact, she has seemed much happier these last few weeks. I have offered to accompany her on her walks, though she insists that she is perfectly safe, and has come to know the surroundings well and will not get lost. In truth, I have enough to occupy me with the horses and my plans for the future, and I am content to let Sarah pursue her own interests. But how will I endure being apart from Henry? It is only the first night.

**

Sarah writes:

Good morning, Etta. I trust you slept well and are rid of your headache? Rosie answers for Henry, in sign language.

"Etta says thank you for the flowers, Sarah, and yes, she slept well. She's going to take a walk to the horse yards. Etta loves horses and wishes to ride. Pierre told her he has two good hacks that are quite suitable and said he will ride with Etta and show her over the property after breakfast."

"I think that is a wonderful idea, Etta, as I will not be here." I sign to Rosie, "You see, I walk in the bush every day collecting wildflowers. I then send them back home to Pierre's mother. She is writing a book about Australian wildflowers, including illustrations. I would take you with me, Rosie, but sometimes I must climb high cliffs and walk many miles. Perhaps tomorrow, I will take a shorter walk and you can join me?"

Rosie duly translates to Henry (or should I say Henri-Etta), then signs to me, "Yes, tomorrow would be better, Sarah. Today, I thought I'd put me culinary skills to work and cook a fine dinner. It will give you a break and I'll enjoy doing it."

I cannot be happier with this arrangement and with Rosie's help, I merrily prepare a hearty breakfast. I cook extra lamb chops and bacon, hoping Rosie does not notice me wrapping some and placing the parcel aside for James. Soon we all go our separate ways. I place the food I have prepared in my flower-collecting basket, then wave goodbye to my guests and Pierre before slipping away down the track to my love. James sits waiting in our usual spot. He stands and holds me close before smothering me with kisses. I cannot wait a moment longer, my hands moving quickly to undress him, and he reaches for me with equal urgency. Before too long we become one and our mutual desire is satisfied in a shuddering climax. I hold him tightly and pray his precious fluid will produce my first child. Please, dear Lord, please let it be.

CHAPTER 16
HENRY

It is six months to the day since Rosie and I have been living in the company of Pierre and Sarah. I find it hard to believe Sarah has still not recognised me nor grown tired of our presence in her home. It is beginning to tease my intelligence. Does she also playact? And why does she take long walks almost every day alone through the bush? Some days I notice it is almost nightfall before she returns, and occasionally her basket is empty. I should not complain, or even inquire, as it gives Pierre and me precious time together. I shall leave well enough alone and let sleeping dogs lie, as they say. However, there is one thing I'm positive will divulge my identity to Sarah: I have begun to paint. Surely, she will see the likeness to Henry's style, though yet, I have not shown her my work.

Pierre, when not alone with me, spends his time with his horses. His meeting with the racing enthusiasts in Sydney has turned out to be most profitable. The property is now almost overflowing with mares all waiting to be served by Satan who seems more than anxious to begin the Australian breeding season. Spring, in this new land, begins on the first of September. Meanwhile, Cheval D'Azure is heavy in foal again, and is now ready to give birth to her second foal. Her first foal is a yearling colt and looks the goods, as far as a racehorse goes. I have taken enthusiastically to painting horses, and the magnificent black Satan is my first attempt. So far Pierre has given his approval. My equine work, he says, shows excellence, especially in portraying the true nature of the beast. He flatters me, though I confess I must agree with him.

Tonight will be another test of my acting skills. So far, I have avoided meeting the Reverend and Mrs Timms. I mean, how many headaches can one have? It has become obvious I am eluding them so I shall be brave. But I will hide behind my fan and, of course, I know Rosie will back me up. "Etta is very shy," she will say. I pray to God we manage to keep our charade up a little longer. It would crush me totally to leave Pierre again.

Early evening brings a gentle, albeit hot, nor-westerly breeze, so we gather on the veranda. While sitting in feather-cushioned cane chairs, we wait for our guests to arrive. It is an ideal place to relax, sip sherry and watch the fiery orb sink below the horizon. Such a vivid sunset is surely a sign of a long, hot summer to come. The sky darkens, enough for a few stars to be visible. There is such splendour in these mountains that it almost takes my mind off being back at home in England. Well, most of the time, for there are moments when I feel the need to travel home to my half-brother the Duke to tell him what I now know. *It has all been a bit of fun, dear brother, but now I must tell you the truth about my real reasons for wanting to travel abroad.* I wonder how he would react. Overwhelmed with joy? Disappointed? Perhaps, but hardly. Angry as a charging bull? Probably. Three years, they say, it must be before I can be declared "deceased". And then my fortune will go to my niece and her mother – my pseudo-mother – who is devoid of feeling for me. Will I let this happen? I don't know at this stage.

Ah, there they are! The Reverend and Mrs Timms, driving cautiously up the path, smile and wave abundantly, but who do they have with them in the buggy? Mmm, quite a handsome young man I see now as they come closer. There is something quite familiar about him, I think, as he helps Mrs Timms down from the buggy. After straightening her skirts, she gives him a brief curtsy then hurries to reach us on the veranda. She embraces Sarah, but only for a moment before holding her at arm's length with what appears to be a very firm grip. She narrows her eyes, tilts her head and gasps excitedly, "Oh Sarah, can it be true? Are you with child?"

Sarah blushes, and I near faint at this unexpected question. I need to take hold of a chair to steady myself. Pierre's mouth drops open. Rosie's chuckle builds into a bubble of mirth as she watches us. Clearly, she has known of Sarah's condition and has let no word slip to either Pierre or me. Sarah blushes again and sighs. She signs the words to her mother. "Mother, you have spoilt my surprise. I was going to announce it after dinner." She throws Pierre a "please forgive me" look, her eyes pleading with him. I know Pierre as well as I know myself, and he seems shocked to the bone.

There is a momentary and uncomfortable silence before Reverend Timms comes to the rescue. "Well, ladies, I must say, this is welcome news and very exciting, though we are forgetting our manners." He moves around Mrs Timms to the side of the gentleman. "Pierre, I believe you are acquainted with Mr March. He is one of your horse clients. It took us totally by surprise when Mr March knocked on our door this morning after being told by the postmaster to seek our help in finding your property."

Pierre shakes himself back to reality, coughs, stands up and extends his hand.

"Now I remember, Mr March. We did meet briefly in Windsor. I am delighted to meet you again, Sir, and I now share good news in person. Only yesterday I posted you a letter. Your mare was the first to be served by Satan, and I believe her to be in foal." Pierre continues to explain, his shock at Sarah's condition momentarily forgotten as he expounds on his favourite topic. "You may not be aware, Mr March, but it is a sure sign of pregnancy when the mare goes straight off-season once served. Nevertheless, the vet checked her and will again, in 20 more days. Everything going well, she will then be ready to travel home to your property. Where exactly is Goulburn, Sir?"

Looking very pleased, Mr March replies, "My property is a long way south. Goulburn is on the way to Melbourne."

The men exchange a nod of understanding and the introductions continue. Rosie, thank heavens, hands me my fan while helping me to remain upright. My knees are still shaking, and my heart feels like it will stop beating with the knowledge that this is, in fact, the same Mr March who had been my suitor on board ship. I proffer one hand and with the other, I fan more quickly. Bowing slightly, he says, "I am very pleased to see you once more, Miss Brown. Forgive my impertinence but I thought perhaps you would be married by now. I had given up all hope of ever meeting you again." A smile (or was it a smirk?) appears on his handsome face before he lowers his head and kisses my hand.

"You have met Miss Brown before, Sir?" Reverend Timms inquires, somewhat surprised.

"Yes Sir, Miss Etta Brown and I had the pleasure of sharing each other's company on board ship. I am overwhelmed and most delighted to meet with Etta once more. If I may be a little presumptuous," March turns to look me in the eye as I raise my fan up higher to cover my horrified expression, "may I divulge the fact, Etta?" Without waiting for my response, he continues, "Whilst on board I fell in love with Etta and asked for her hand in marriage, to which she replied, 'I am already taken. I am promised to a gentleman who has recently set up business in Sydney'."

I am struck speechless by his indiscretion and I dare not look at Pierre for fear of what I might read in his expression. It takes all my resolve not to punch Mr March on his aquiline nose when he reaches for my hand, which he begins to kiss passionately, if it's possible to attribute such an expression to hand kissing. Oh, dear me, but it does send shivers to where it should not. Rosie hurries away before her introduction, making the excuse, "I have to check on dinner."

Thank you very much, Rosie!

I am then properly introduced to Mr and Mrs Timms, who seems not to recognise me at all. Perhaps it is Mr March's revelation that distracts them from studying my face. As night cloaks us in total darkness, we make our way inside. Candlelight flickers entertaining shadows around the living room as we take our seats but Reverend Timms remains standing. Under the soft glow of candlelight, he looks younger than his years.

He clears his throat loudly to gain our attention. "I would like us all to drink a toast to Sarah and Pierre's success in finally producing an heir. But before we drink, I should like to confirm this welcome news is in fact true." He turns to face his wife Charlotte. "Hopefully, my dear wife has not jumped to conclusions due to the weight Sarah seems to have accumulated around her middle," Timms says light-heartedly.

Sarah sits next to Pierre and squeezes his hand, looking deep into his eyes. "I apologise for not telling you, Pierre," she signs. "I was afraid something might go wrong. I was going to tell you tomorrow, please believe me, I was." She hangs her head, fighting back tears, I think, from what I can see.

Pierre's response is intelligent and calm. I expect nothing else from my love.

"This is wonderful news, Sarah. I am so happy for you – I mean us." He manages a wry smile then kisses her forehead. "This should be a celebration, Sarah, so please don't worry about not having told me." Pierre is making sure Sarah can see his mouth clearly forming these words to her. She is so good at lip reading now that they rarely resort to pen and paper.

Though Pierre can't help but look a trifle nonplussed, Reverend

Timms prevents another awkward moment by raising his glass. "Alright then, it seems we are to be grandparents at long last! Let us drink a toast to the new arrival. When is the baby due, dear Sarah?" he asks her, waiting for her calculations.

"I'm sure it is due around the end of December, Father," she writes boldly on her writing pad. "But now you all know about it, I shall go to the doctor just to make sure all is well. I would be surprised if it was not," she writes, quickly adding, "I feel wonderful."

With that done, we raise our glasses and drank to the baby's safe arrival and good health.

Mr Edward March, or Teddy as he insists we call him, sits as close as possible to me at the dinner table. I feel his leg rub against mine occasionally, and each time I nearly fall off my chair as I move away, such is the effort it takes me to assure I am not complicit in his impropriety. It seems he is not going to give up easily. His wayward hand keeps fumbling under the table. I am almost titillated by his groping but if he is successful, what he discovers will certainly shock him out of this house, if not the country. I can do nothing but excuse myself, once again relying on one of my debilitating headaches as the cause. Reverend Timms is most caring and offers to escort me to my room, but once again Rosie liberates me from his ministrations.

"I shall take Etta, Mr Timms, thank you all the same," Rosie says firmly, taking my elbow in a proprietary way. "I know just what she needs when these dreadful bouts come upon her so suddenly."

Luckily, I have a bottle of "medicinal" brandy placed on my bedside table. I drink an ample dose to calm my nerves, then another measure and then several more which knocks me out. Come morning, my complaint is genuine. A raging headache truly does prevent me from facing our overnight guests at the breakfast table. However, Mr March refuses to go with the Timms and remains to wait patiently for my recovery. Pierre will now have to take valuable time from his work to drive him back to Blackheath. I feel it unfair of him not to consider this.

But I'm also worried by something Rosie has just noticed – Pierre shooting the odd admiring glance towards Teddy, and Teddy reciprocating. *Mmm.* I have never been jealous of Pierre before, but somehow this intrusion by a man whom I can only describe as being outstanding in every way, is becoming more than a tad daunting. If I weren't so in love with Pierre, I may take the risk of shedding my feminine attire and see if there were a glimmer of hope for myself, with what I may describe as, a both way, Mr March. Oh, dear, this is becoming messy. What is his pleasure, I ask myself?

To distract me from my doubts, I think about Sarah being pregnant. Who, I wonder, could possibly be the father? I must speak with Pierre and confess my suspicions, especially about Sarah's long solo walks through the surrounding bushland each day. Maybe she has a hidden lover – the only explanation. I am now amused with the picture it paints. She must be a darn good lover to keep a man waiting for her to return each day.

Rosie knocks on my door and pops her head in to inquire after me, distracting me from further speculation. "My dearest Etta, how are you feeling? I've brought you some toast and tea, my dear, and I'm obliged to ask if you are up to seeing Mr March. He is most concerned about you." Rosie speaks loudly, presumably to maintain my charade in case of eavesdroppers, but it rumbles my headache to the point of explosion.

"Shush, Rosie," I whisper. "I truly do have a headache this morning." She spies the empty bottle of brandy and gives a knowing grin.

"I must say, Henry – Etta. My sympathy is a little less forthcoming now I've seen you've given *that* a good nudge!" She tilts her head in the direction of the empty bottle and places the breakfast tray gently on my lap. "I shall inform Teddy you are still not feeling well, so he is best to go home now. I'll bring you a headache draft directly, my love." Rosie plumps the pillows behind me, kisses my forehead, and leaves to do her duty.

My imagination runs amok. I visualise Pierre and Teddy in the buggy, peering around for any passers-by, before allowing their passion for each other to totally consume them. No! My headache is the least of my worries now. I must join them on the journey back to Blackheath or, better still, take Teddy there myself.

Thank heavens, Rosie returns quickly with the draft. She helps me shave my faint whiskers, then dress. I soon appear before Teddy like a yellow bee floating around, ready to suck pollen from him. It seems to tantalise his senses, as I notice an alert stiffness in him. *Oops, lift your eyes, Henry.*

"My, but don't you look lovely this morning, Etta? I must say, yellow seems to be your colour and you look a lot better. Are you feeling well now?" Teddy inquires solicitously, strategically placing his hat over the front of his trousers. I can see the colour in his cheeks is not the only thing rising. I giggle in my best girlish manner, which has certainly taken ages of practice to perfect, and bat my eyelashes.

"Yes, thank you, Teddy, I feel wonderful." *A lie.* "You don't mind if I call you Teddy, do you?"

"No, not at all. I have taken the liberty of calling you Etta. I must apologise. I did not ask for the privilege."

Once again, I giggle, and tap him on the wrist with my fan. "You are welcome to call me Etta, Teddy." I give a little gasp and say quickly, as if I had just thought of it. "Oh! I just had the most wonderful idea. Pierre is *so* busy; would you like *me* to drive you in the buggy back to Blackheath? Or, you could take the reins if you wish. I'll be quite alright to drive back home alone. It's not too far."

"It would be very kind of you, Etta, and then we will have time to talk – in private." He looks around like a sleuth before resting his eyes on mine.

His smitten gaze gives me reason to gather my composure. I must think of something shocking – horrifying – that will send him away from me – from us – forever. My request to borrow the buggy is met with a curt nod of consent from Pierre. Do I detect a look of displeasure before he heads to the stable to harness the horse? I choose not to comment. A short while later, Teddy and I head off in the direction of Blackheath.

Along the way, we discover we share the same profound interest in nature. I am impressed with Teddy's knowledge of the botanical names of the many wildflowers and plants. Suddenly, he points to a barely noticeable bellbird. I am delighted, as ever since I arrived in the Blue Mountains, I have been wondering about their pinging bell-like sound, and I had yet to see one. I ease the horse to a stop to take a closer look. Teddy points to the little bird, which I think resembles a budgerigar in shape and size, although it is not as colourful. It sits to attention on a branch, its moss-green chest puffed proudly as it settles its variegated, pale brown-grey wings. I am amazed to think how such a singularly loud call can possibly come from such a small bird. Teddy sits silently for a while. From the corner of my eye, I can see him studying my face. Is he amused at my amazement? He interrupts my trance.

"Perhaps you would feel up to having dinner in the Scotch

Thistle Inn, Etta, before I need to catch my train – in the morning?" His naughty wink exposes his intentions.

This is the moment I must find the strength to divulge my horrid past – the one I have concocted, of course.

"I would be delighted, Teddy. But there is something I should tell you first." I clear my throat and sit upright to deliver the blow. "You see, I did tell you the truth when I said I had a suitor waiting for me in Sydney. I have not referred to the matter since you mentioned it last night at Pierre's home. The reason is that my engagement has become quite complicated and embarrassing. But now I must tell you the whole truth. The fact is, Teddy, I have been fighting all my life with an unnatural fondness for my own sex." I pause to turn and study his expression; it is one of interest, rather than revulsion – not what I was hoping for.

"Go on, Etta, I must say I'm more than a little fascinated," he says with enthusiasm.

Oh dear! But this is going to be difficult. Why can't he be repulsed by my admission, then throw himself from the cart to walk downheartedly to the train station, leaving me alone to gloat over my victory? I take a deep breath and let the words flow.

"Well, the problem began, Teddy, when I felt the need to determine if I were imagining my desires or if they were in fact real. So I allowed my fiancée to seduce me. I found the whole experience profoundly nauseating. Yes, sickening. I fled from his bed in distress. I could not return." I hang my head in shame, before delivering the final, knockout blow. "Now there you have it. I am a *lesbian*!" I say triumphantly, hoping this will turn him away from me once and for all. To my dismay, it has the opposite effect. Teddy reaches out to comfort me.

"There, there, Etta, I don't think we should give up easily," he says, with his arm around my shoulder and smiling into my eyes, searching for a glimmer of hope – I assume.

"I don't think you understand, Teddy!" I yell at him, frustrated by his unruffled response. I go for the jugular. "I'm a raving lesbian! I've had affairs with hundreds of women of all classes, including prostitutes! You don't realise how desperate I get!" My anger rises to the point where I feel like pushing him out of the buggy. But he simply laughs like a hyena. Damned fool, he is!

"You're a wild one, Etta. I've always fancied the wild ones," he says in between hoots of laughter.

"You cannot possibly be serious, Teddy. I mean, how could you love me after knowing what I am? I am the lowest of the low. A gutter wench. A trollop! I will embarrass you and I will make your life a misery!"

He laughs uncontrollably, so much so, he can barely speak. "Etta, Etta, my dear young lady – or young man. You are *such* an actress. I beg for an encore – I simply love what you are trying to do. But please, do answer me truthfully. If I were to allow you to live your life in the guise of a woman, would you marry me? We could live as husband and wife and no one would ever be the wiser." He regards me hopefully.

I gaze at him with a mixture of horror and excitement. Oh dear, what is a girl to do?

CHAPTER 17
PIERRE

Alors! Henry has just now left in my buggy with a man I do not entirely trust. While Henry has been honest with me, and we have even laughed about the marriage proposals he received from Teddy while on board ship, I can see this March is a very determined chap. And now I cannot help but wonder why Henry insisted they go alone to Blackheath.

Although, perhaps I *should* be more concerned about who has Fathered Sarah's baby. I know it is Sarah's dearest wish to have a child, and even though I promised her I would help her achieve it, our efforts to consummate our marriage come to nothing. I was in fact quite relieved when she stopped making overtures to me at night because I was fast running out of excuses. When I think about it, she has been very happy and content these last months. I simply assumed she had adjusted to our new situation, but clearly there has been another reason. Tomorrow, I think I might follow her when she takes her walk. I'm sure she must meet her lover there. I am not jealous of whoever it may be, but in truth I feel a little disappointed that Sarah could not confide in me. Tomorrow will no doubt reveal what has been going on, but today I have other more important things to concern me.

The vet is coming to pregnancy test twenty mares. Most breeders do not worry about such tests, but I find it necessary as it removes the guesswork and helps me to judge correctly if a mare has conceived on the first service. My vet, Percy Smith, has the unenviable job of pushing his hand, indeed his whole arm, into the mare's passage where, I hope, he will discover a tightly closed cervix with a sizable fluid swelling produced by the foetus at the base of one of the uterine horns. I can see his trap coming up the track now – I had best join him for what will be a laborious job that will take most of the morning.

Sitting on the veranda afterwards, Percy and I gratefully sink into the cane armchairs to enjoy the refreshments Sarah and Rosie provided earlier.

"Pardon me, Percy, but my mind has been elsewhere today," I offer my apology to the vet. "I feel embarrassed. I was distracted and not on the job, so to speak. However, finding eighteen of the mares were in foal is good news. It will make my work a lot easier and I dare say Satan's as well, not that he would ever complain."

"Don't worry, Pierre. I really don't know how you accomplish running this place on your own. You have work cut out here for at least three men. Why don't you hire someone to help you, man?" Percy asks as he refills his cup.

"I'll think about it," I say, lowering my head. My mind is already preoccupied with Sarah and the baby's father.

When Percy leaves, I walk to Satan's paddock and lean against the post and rail fence, letting the sun warm my back. Satan has never looked better; his temperament has changed to one of quiet pride and confidence. He was a fiery young colt when he first arrived here but after serving fifty or so mares, he has matured into a powerful stallion. I think about Henry's painting and how he's captured Satan's air of self-assurance, his true spirit shining through his eyes. The painting would win any prize on offer, I'm sure. I must speak with Henry about it later.

By the time the sun disappears behind the mountain tops, my day's work is finished, and I relax on the veranda for a while until I realise I have not seen Sarah all afternoon. I become worried – where is she? And for that matter, where on earth is Henry? Rosie appears, offering me a calming sherry. Her eyes are dark with anxiety. As usual, she rises above her own worries and offers me comfort, the dear sweet lady.

"Do not concern yourself, Master Pierre. I'm sure they will be home soon."

A moment later, we turn upon hearing the back-door squeak open and shut with a bang. I stand and call, "Is it you, Sarah?" I immediately curse myself for my stupidity – *she cannot hear, you fool!* Despite her bulk, Rosie beats me to the kitchen, where behind her generous form, I stand in shock. Sarah's eyes dance with delight and her hand moves so quickly over the pages I am unable to take in all the words she is trying to convey. My attention is focused on the young man standing beside her. Long dark hair, his eyes pools of mystery, the physique of an athlete. And his features – *mon dieu,* he is amazing.

I step forward and extend my hand to the gentleman while Sarah busily continues writing down her story. *"Bonjour.* I am pleased to meet you, Sir. May I have your name?" His handshake is strong, in keeping with what I think him to be – a fine character – and I know without looking at Sarah's writing that he is the father of her baby. Well, it will be good looking, at least.

"Yes, of course. My name is James Howard and I'm most pleased to meet you, Mr Boyar. I do hope you will remain pleased when I confess my sins. Perhaps alone?" He glances at Rosie with a raised eyebrow and a wry smile. I ignore his suggestion and turn to Rosie, who is staring quite openly at the handsome stranger.

"Please excuse me, Mr Howard. May I introduce Mrs Rosie Brown? Rosie is a very dear friend of the family. Anything you must say, Mr Howard, may be said in front of Rosie. We keep nothing hidden from each other." Rosie's face flushes in appreciation of the respect I have shown her.

Sarah hands me the pages she has written, although I am sure I could have written them myself, having put two and two together very quickly. However, there is one twist to the story – James is a fugitive from the law. I'm sure my stunned expression was the reason for James stepping close to Sarah and placing his arm protectively around her shoulders. They breathlessly await my response, like two naughty children clinging to each other after they being discovered doing a very bad thing. I must say I find this *très amusant.* How could I be upset by Sarah's behaviour? I still love her as my sister, but at the same time, I am ashamed at not having been able to fulfil my promise to her. It does not need too much sense or sensibility to see the two souls who stand before me are in love. I am sure the situation can be worked out to the benefit of us all. If I feel anything, it is relief.

I look up from the pages held in my hand, and smile. "Welcome to the family, James."

CHAPTER 18
HENRY

It is hard to believe Teddy's handsome face can so quickly turn so ugly. "Stop pretending, Etta," he snarls, grabbing my wrist and twisting my arm. "Don't try and tell me you didn't know that I knew what was going on? What do take me for, a complete fool?" Teddy's features are warped with anger, revealing a hitherto unknown and very dark side of his nature. Suddenly he pulls me hard against his chest, kissing my mouth urgently, his tongue forcing itself between my lips. His hand dives to my crotch and through the layers of my dress he fondles my penis which, to my horror and embarrassment, approves of his touch. This is preposterous. I must stop him! I shove, heave and push at him with such force that Teddy March tumbles from the buggy headfirst. I slide from the buggy to watch him roll uncontrollably down the steep embankment before coming to an abrupt stop, as his head hits a large rock ledge jutting from the earth. The crack of his skull is audible. I stand stunned, waiting for him to rise, but there is no movement. I scream, "HE'S DEAD! My God, what have I done?" My hands clasped to my face, I counsel myself: *Go down and see if he is breathing, Henry!*

With my skirts gathered high, I scramble down the embankment. Thankfully, the horse, well trained by Pierre, stands stock still. *Please – please, don't think of Pierre, Henry. What will he think of me now, now I have killed a man? Just shut up, Henry. Check his pulse. You don't know if he's dead yet. Feel his pulse!*

There is no pulse I'm sure and blood is pouring from his head from where it hit the rock. He's dead, I'm certain. What should I do now? *Think of a story, Henry! Think!*

I sit close to the dead body and nervously rack my brain for a simple explanation for the tragedy. I have it! I am closer to Blackheath, so I shall go to the police station and tell them that Mr March merely needed to relieve himself and tripped while stepping down from the buggy. *Brilliant! You've got it, Henry!*

"Now, I must leave you, Teddy," I say, after I have managed to climb up and down again to cover Teddy with the knee rug. I drive the horse at a brisk clip towards Blackheath and the police station.

I deeply regret having killed a man, albeit a man who was either out to ruin me or devour me with his unnatural lust. What am I saying? I have the same lust, only that mine is for one man, my darling Pierre. My thoughts of Pierre calm me while I travel the lonely road to Blackheath.

Whimpering and snivelling (for in fact I am upset by the recent turn of events), I present my miserable self at the front desk of the police station.

"Oh, dear sir, a terrible tragedy has just occurred. I beg your assistance." My voice wavers and I blow my nose into my lace handkerchief, perhaps a little too loudly for a lady.

"Now, now Miss, calm down. I'm Constable Lamb. Now tell me, Miss. Exactly what seems to be the problem?" the policeman asks. He is a middle-aged gentleman with the innocent face of a choir boy.

I tell him all that has happened to poor Mr March. He listens with what appears to be sympathy and a good dose of intellect.

"It certainly is a tragedy, Miss, but please don't distress yourself. It was an accident. There is nothing you could have done," he assures me while hurrying around from the desk and placing his large hand on my shoulder. "I will accompany you to the spot where you left him. And I'll have my assistant follow with the paddy wagon to carry his body to the undertaker."

I feel immediately relieved. My story, it seems, has gone down like hot chocolate on a cold night.

Constable Lamb and I soon become acquainted and we even share a few chuckles along the way. In an attempt to lift my spirits, he regales me with some of the humorous cases he has attended over the years. His face is glowing red and his blue eyes glisten with laughter until he returns to the reason for our journey and adopts a more appropriately sombre tone to say, "Mind you though, Miss Brown, I have never had to pick up the dead body of someone who had fallen out of a buggy and hit his head upon a large rock!" He shakes his head in dismay, but he still is quietly amused, I'm sure.

"I can imagine you haven't, Constable Lamb. Who would ever believe this could possibly happen?" Our conversation comes to an end as we approach the scene of the accident.

From time to time, I applaud myself on my ability to observe and remember details, especially when it comes to episodes of importance, and the scene of Teddy's demise is certainly one such instance. However, when we reach the location on the road where we had stopped and look down the embankment to the exact spot where I had left Teddy, he is nowhere to be found. The blood on the rock is still there, but there is *no* Mr Teddy March and *no* knee rug. Constable Lamb and I look quizzically at each other before it dawns on us. Teddy is not dead as first thought, but then – where *is* he?

Our search begins and goes on and on with the three of us calling Teddy's name loudly throughout the surrounding scrub, until our voices are hoarse. It is then we decide to drive to the nearest property further along the track. A small white-washed weatherboard home soon appears, tucked away amongst bushland a little way off the road. No planted gardens take pride of place, instead the local wildflowers had grown almost right up to the cottage. To my surprise, an elderly Englishman opens the door. He is well spoken, and I take delight in hearing the Queen's English used so fluently. He wears a rather dapper tweed jacket in colours of brown and beige, a golden cravat is folded neatly around his neck and tucked into his spotless white shirt. I am most impressed.

"How do you do? I am Theobald Tootle. Please, do come in," he says, with his right arm spread wide in welcome and what looked like an uncontrollable winking of his right eye. "May I offer you a cup of tea, or something stronger?" His smiling face surveys each of us, as he waits for our reply while his eye continues its wink, wink, wink.

"No, no thank you, Mr Tootle, we don't have time. We're looking for a gentleman who has perhaps lost his way after having an accident," Constable Lamb says, after which he makes the introductions and explains the whole scenario, much to the obvious interest and enjoyment of Mr Tootle, it appears.

"Dear me, the poor man. I have heard of such cases. He may have what they call amnesia. It comes when one has a decent bang on the head, particularly when one is knocked unconscious. This could be a tragedy if he is not found. The man won't have a clue where he is – or even who he is. I suggest, Constable, you gather a search party immediately. If Mr March goes wandering off into the bush at night, he will end up dead after all."

As Theobald Tootle is giving this sound advice to Constable Lamb, I stand viewing Mr Tootle's paintings. I assume they are his, as his paints and easel are set up beside a large sun-filled window. When he's finished talking, I take the opportunity to question him.

"Mr Tootle, I have been admiring your paintings. They are your works, no doubt?"

He looks pleased. "Yes, they are, Miss Brown. Are you interested in art?"

"I am, indeed, sir. I also dabble. I'm staying with friends, not too far from here, a Mr Pierre Boyar and his wife, Sarah. Pierre stands a thoroughbred stallion named Satan on his property." This elicits a chuckle from the men. "I know, it's such a devilish name, isn't it?" I say with a giggle. I am so proud of my manufactured girlish giggle that I give another just for good measure. "Satan is my study now; my work is almost complete. I see you have captured this horse very well, Mr Tootle," I say, nodding toward what I thought to be a masterpiece although a little jealousy prevented me from saying so. He has depicted in oil a chestnut mare leaning over her foal, and the love portrayed in their eyes almost has me weeping. A treasure to behold, I think.

"Thank you, Miss Brown. I would be honoured to view your painting, when finished, of course. Would it be possible?" Wink, wink.

"Yes, more than possible, sir. I would be honoured to show you, but I must beg you to not judge me harshly, Mr Tootle, as it is my first attempt at capturing the essence of a horse. I have in the past concentrated on deer, rabbits, birds of all varieties, as well as the farm hands going about their duties. In England, of course." I smile sweetly at my countryman.

"And where may I ask do you hail from, Miss Brown?"

"I come from a small village within the perimeter of Northumberland, very insignificant, I'm afraid." I flutter my fan along with my eyelashes and thank the Lord when Constable Lamb interrupts our conversation.

"We should move on, Miss Brown. Time is of the essence as Mr March may not survive the night. The temperature will be next to zero by morning light."

"Yes, we must, Constable." I turn with haste, and dignity of course, and proffer my gloved hand to Mr Tootle. "It was a pleasure to meet you, Mr Tootle. I would like to talk with you further about art, if

89

you agree?"

"Dear Miss Brown, it will be my pleasure." His blue eyes sparkle. Well, one does as the other is too busy winking. "Soon, I hope. Please call on me anytime you wish."

We exchange a few more pleasantries and are out the door and soon on our way back to Blackheath. About halfway there, I panic. "Oh dear!" I exclaim. "I have forgotten Pierre and Rosie! They will be so worried about me! I..." I am speaking in the lower register of Henry's voice, before I cough and miraculously Etta's voice comes back to me, high pitched and sweet.

"Well, of course your friends must be worried about you, Miss Brown," Constable Lamb says with a quizzical squint of his eyes. "I do apologise. It must have been the fact I was enjoying your company so much I continued towards Blackheath. I shall hop on aboard the paddy wagon with young Keegan there." He points his large finger towards the wagon in front that holds the skinny youth who's said nought since he'd helped call for Teddy March. "Could you hurry the pony up a little, Miss Brown? I'll call him over, there's a good lass."

Once our transfer is accomplished, we say our goodbyes.

"Don't you worry, Miss Brown. We'll gather a search party. Hopefully before nightfall we'll find your Mr March. Please don't fret. But it would help if you would ask your friends to join us in the search," Constable Lamb looks at me hopefully.

"Certainly, Constable, I'm sure they will be more than willing to help. Thank you for everything you have done." I give him one of my best smiles.

However, soon after parting company with the erstwhile officer and his sidekick, my horse becomes lame. What can I do but disembark from the buggy and walk beside the poor injured creature. I know if Pierre had been there, he would have checked the horse's feet and found that the horse had picked up a large stone, lodged in the cavity between the frog and the sole of the hoof. Instead, this is discovered only after I reach home exhausted and awfully sore-footed myself. It is after dark when I arrive. "Pierre, Pierre!" I call from outside the front door, horse in hand.

To say he rushed to greet me would be a gross underestimation of the unbridled enthusiasm with which he met me. His warm embrace is followed by a barrage of kisses on my neck. This becomes a little embarrassing when I realise we are being observed by a total stranger, albeit a *very* good looking one.

"I must say, this new colony has a way of attracting handsome young men to its shores," I say when Pierre releases me and stands alongside. I assume he has not heard what I said, due to his next remark.

"We have been so worried about you, Hen… I mean Etta. Where on earth have you been?" Pierre asks with genuine sincerity. Would I expect anything else?

"It's a very long story, but first things first, Pierre. The horse seems lame. I think it's his offside hoof?" I look down at the horse's leg as Pierre picks the hoof up and dislodges a large stone. I should have inspected the hoof myself. However, it seems since becoming female, I appear to have lost some of my physical abilities – except, of course, when they are required to push one scheming, overzealous man from my buggy. Oh dear, I do hope Teddy's not gone in the head. Or do I?

Once our sweet horse is put to bed with a poultice on his hoof, we go back to the house and I am properly introduced to the handsome James. We all sit in silence for a moment before I find the words to explain my extremely late arrival. I tell my story uninterrupted except for the "ohs" and "ars" of my audience.

"I feel dreadful," I finally say, "because it is too late now to join the search. But first thing in the morning we must."

I look beseechingly at their stunned faces. Rosie nods solemnly. Pierre, I know, is thinking: *Do we really need to find Teddy?* Sarah, sweet thing she is, shows a great deal of compassion. Our guest, James, sits next to her, holding her hand, but betraying no emotion. However, he must have some tender feelings to have won Sarah's heart and mind – and body! Suddenly, I am desperate to know their story.

"Pierre!" I demand imperiously. "You simply must tell me what's been going on with Sarah and her young man. I'm simply *dying* to know!" I turn to James. "Please forgive me, James, but would you prefer to tell all?" I ask with head tilted to one side.

"No, I will let Pierre do the telling." James goes to fetch a glass of water, then returns.

I listen to Pierre's revelations about Sarah and James, including him being on the wrong side of the law, for now, until he can prove his innocence. I nod understandingly whenever appropriate. I realise the situation has already been calmly discussed, accepted and put to rest well before I arrived home. I offer my unequivocal support to the plan of having James live at "Mountain View" as Pierre's assistant. God knows he needs one – his energy level has been worrying me lately.

"Yes, what a grand idea, James. You will no doubt be of great help to Pierre. He works far too hard and his energy is spent by evening. Which is a shame." I wonder if my insinuation has reached its listeners. Because we are exposing secrets this evening (it's fun, like playing "the truth game"), I decide to make a final confession.

I rise gracefully from my Queen Anne chair and sashay around the tastefully furnished living room before halting in front of the cavernous fireplace. Bathed in the flattering light from the kerosene lamps, I begin my story. I am not too long into it when I notice Sarah giggling, albeit silently, behind cupped hands. It is most distracting, especially as I have just divulged the truth about Etta not being Etta, but, me – Henry. I give Sarah a stern look and she tries with little success to control her amusement. It leaves me a little lost for words, but not Sarah, who offers me an explanation with her accomplished hand signs.

"Oh Henry, you didn't *really* think I was fooled by your acting? I have known you far too long, darling Henry. And I have known all along that Rosie is in fact your grandmother."

My heart plunges. This is the second time today that those I had set out to deceive had seen my feminine masquerade. I can't stop my tears from welling. This is when Sarah comes to me, gently comforting me until I can control my emotions.

"Henry, dear Henry," she tells me with her delicate hand movements. "You make such a beautiful woman. I think you should remain one." She pats my back and kisses my teary cheek, then her lips shape the words, "I tell you what, Henry, let's go shopping together. There is a lovely clothing shop in Blackheath, particularly for ladies. What do you say, Henri-Etta?" She laughs (silently) before kissing me on the cheek again. I sniffle away my tears and hug her tightly before holding her from me.

"You forget, Sarah," I say carefully so that she can read my lips, "that we are to join the search party for Mr March tomorrow. We must find him alive. I had no desire to kill the man, just push him from my life." I place a hypocritical hand on my heart.

We all agree: the search *should* come before frock shopping. I do hope we find Teddy – quickly!

CHAPTER 19
SARAH

Well, what an evening this has turned out to be! A most perfect scenario has transpired, the culmination being when Rosie revealed her secret of being Henry's maternal grandmother, though I already knew. We are initially all quite shocked by the turn of events but now we are most comfortable within our shared bed of truth. What an utter relief it was to accept and understand each other's feelings and desires. However, it must remain hidden from my parents and I feel a little guilty about this. I will pray every night for their forgiveness, which is all I can do. I trusted God would understand that our collective predicament was essentially caused by love and loyalty. After all, Father has always preached to his parishioners that "The Good Lord is our loving Father. He will forgive us all our sins – if only we ask."

However, we are left with the problem of my James-the-outlaw having a price on his head. How can we keep him hidden from the eyes of the law? Especially as there are likely to be visits from Constable Lamb since Henri-Etta and he have become new friends.

James turns to face me and speak, although I assume it is meant for all to hear. I feel the vibrations of his conviction through my arm as I hold his.

"Please do not worry, my dear Sarah. I would have been forced out from hiding sooner or later. I'm pleased to be here and still be free to support you. Whatever happens, I'm sure it will be for the best. And I have a good idea! Seeing Henry in a frock has given it to me!" He turns to Henry with a broad smile, his dimples adding to his charm. "What if I were to also dress up?"

This is met with protests and a violent shaking of heads before James shrugs, defeated. I smile, amused by his suggestion of donning feminine attire. Yes, his face is beautiful, but his physique is purely male: broad shoulders, narrow hips and a taut behind. Not exactly the right shape for a woman.

"Well, perhaps I could dye my hair and cut it short? It's not as if you have many visitors here, and if you do, I would be busy working most of the time. Maybe I could pretend to be unable to hear and speak, too? There are many ways to avoid suspicion. I've been hired by Pierre as his assistant and a capable one I will be. You see, my father has bred many talented thoroughbreds in England. He owns a fashionable stallion along with many fine mares. Some of their offspring have won The Derby – and even The King's Cup." James sighs deeply, his broad chest rising and falling. "Oh well, it will sort itself out, one way or another. Though another matter, which is in no doubt, I shall have to change my name." He wrinkles his brow in thought. "Ah, I have it, 'Jimmy MacKay'. He's a close friend back home and the luckiest man I know." We all take note and agree.

James, or Jimmy, and I leave our friends to mull over his other suggestions. It has been such an extraordinary day I feel the need to sleep and be comforted by James. "Come this way," I sign, and he smiles. Since our first meeting, James has been quick to learn my sign language; he took to it like a bee to nectar. I am amazed how fluent he is after only six months.

Pierre's expression is one of relief mingled with affection as James and I bid everyone goodnight. It almost has me in tears – tears of happiness, tears of regret and a little sympathy for us all. What a mixed lot we are. There's dear Rosie, happy to be finally known as grandmother to her only grandson, Henry. He and Pierre are finally able to sleep together as a couple. I am bearing the child I prayed so desperately for, and James seems very happy with his lot – I hope. If his words of love and devotion are genuine, and I'm sure they are, then I am the happiest woman on earth. However, I have but one regret; I have not kept my promise to Amy Watson to accept her offer as teacher's assistant. For this she said she has forgiven me. Amy understands – the pregnancy has prevented it. Perhaps when the baby is born and is old enough, Rosie will care for it for a few hours each day, so I can take up the teaching position? If so, my life will be fulfilled.

I feel fortunate beyond belief to have James finally lying beside me between clean sheets. I assume he feels the same. With his touch, soft as satin, brushing my nakedness, I tingle with his slow exploration of my body. The nipples of my tender breasts are teased erect by the wet smoothness of his tongue while his gentle fingers do their work below. Soon my body arches, begging him to take me, and he does not disappoint me. Later, we lay enfolded in each other's arms. This could only be true love, I tell myself, before I drift into a deep and contented sleep.

CHAPTER 20
HENRY

I stir just before dawn, not in the least wanting to face the day ahead. I would prefer to stay, eyes closed and wrapped in the warmth Pierre's arms. In my languid state, I think I may have only dreamed of last night, or has my dream finally come true? I tweak Pierre's nipple just to make sure. He flinches and moans – oh, how I love it when he moans. Ooh, yes, now all his senses are alert. We burrow back under the sheets.

All too soon we are forced out of bed by the morning light and a sense of urgency. What trouble lies ahead; we can only guess. Rosie has been up earlier, preparing a hearty breakfast she has laid out on the long informal kitchen table that seats at least twelve. We take our seats as the others arrive. I take a quick glance at our lovers sitting across the table to know their first night spent together had been perfect. And I'm sure when Sarah smiles back, she can see the same is true of Pierre and me.

"This should keep our hunger at bay for the day. Then after y' eat y' breakfast, Master Pierre, I suggest y' feed the horses and we'll all be on our way to help with the search for Mr March," Rosie says, her wooden spoon pointing in Pierre's direction.

A collective "Yes, Rosie" reverberates through the cavernous room which contains all our cooking needs – a giant wood-fired oven, a large scrubbed kitchen table centre stage, with pots and pans hanging above in easy reach, and there is a well-stocked pantry off to one side.

Yes, all is well, as we bask in happy chatter until a sudden loud knock on the front door startles us. We each look to the other, as if to say, *Well, who's going to get it?* Pierre takes charge and strides to the door while we creep behind like thieves about to jump an unsuspecting victim, except for our "Jimmy MacKay". He's gone to ground, hiding in the stables, I presume. Pierre opens the door, tentatively at first then gives a sigh of relief and stands aside to usher in Constable Lamb and a bedraggled Teddy March. To say I am relieved to see Teddy alive would be an irony, in a way. Then fear takes hold – has Teddy confessed the truth to Constable Lamb? Has Teddy revealed my identity? Has he claimed I had tried to kill him? *Pull yourself together, Henry,* I tell myself. I shall rise above whatever accusations he has made. After all, I have witnesses who will vouch for me.

I play the role once more of distraught female. "My dear Mr March," I whimper, stepping forward to place my hand gently on his shoulder. "Thank heavens you were found alive! One can only imagine how bewildered and terrified you must have been upon finding yourself left alone beside the road. I had to push my pony almost beyond his physical capabilities to reach help. I honestly thought you were dead after *you got down from the buggy, tripped and fell down the embankment, cracking your head horribly on that rock!*" I dramatically emphasise the chain of events and cry a few crocodile tears into my delicate handkerchief. *Boo hoo!*

Teddy March's head is bandaged heavily – Egyptian mummy style. He even looks like one with his eyes staring straight ahead, glassy and dazed. I can't help but tilt my own head from side to side, puppy dog fashion, while awaiting his reply.

Constable Lamb says quietly, "I'm afraid, Miss Brown, that Mr March here," Lamb nods towards the patient, "doesn't seem to remember anything. As Mr Tootle said, we fear he has a case of amnesia. He doesn't even know his name. We simply assumed it was him. The doctor wanted to keep him at the surgery for a while longer, but I said we'd better see if he is the one who went missing. If I don't take him for verification, then I must continue searching." His worried expression leaves his face as he continues. "You have now confirmed, Miss Brown, that this is, in fact, Mr Teddy March. And thank heavens!" He wipes his ruddy brow, only for effect, I'm sure, as it is quite a chilly morning. Rosie pushes me aside as she grabs Lamb's arm.

"Y' must be worn out and freezin', not to mention hungry into the bargain. Come into the kitchen, Constable, and I'll be dishin' y' up a decent breakfast. Come along, Mr March," Rosie commands while waving her other chubby dimpled arm toward the kitchen. God bless her; she can solve any problem with a good lashing of food. Our plates are soon piled to overflowing with lamb chops, bacon, eggs and tomatoes (home grown by yours truly).

I notice Teddy is only picking at his food with vacant despondency.

Poor chap, I think, I wonder if he will ever know again who he is. More to the point, what in the name of justice are we to do with him? Once we have finished eating and are sitting around a large pot of Rosie's special blend tea, I broach the subject that I am sure has been on all our minds.

"Constable Lamb, I suppose we should take care of Mr March until we are able to contact his family in Goulbourn." I take a ladylike sip of my aromatic tea while awaiting his answer.

"Yes, Miss Brown, thank you – a perfect solution," he replies before taking a manly slurp of his own.

Goodness me, where are his manners? Though I am sorely tempted to do the same, so delicious is Rosie's brew.

"I will be sending a message from Blackheath Police Station. It will be forwarded along the line until it reaches the Goulbourn Police. I'm sure then we will find out the full details of Mr March's position in the community and the whereabouts of his family," Lamb says in a hurry. Obviously, he likes to drink his tea hot.

Rosie, as I have explained before, is a fusspot over other people's needs, but this morning she absolutely dotes on Constable Lamb. Being most observant, I do not have to look too hard to see Rosie's intentions. I decide to ask a few personal questions of our congenial Constable Lamb. "Constable Lamb, you have done us a great favour indeed by finding Mr March and returning him to us alive," I say with a giggle. "Your wife, I'm sure, will be happy to have you keeping regular hours from now on. The good woman is probably preparing your breakfast right at this very moment." I take another sip of my second cup of tea.

"Just doing my duty, Miss Brown. As for my wife, I doubt she'll even have missed me." He smiles at me briefly before looking at Rosie in a meaningful way. *Mmm, I'm onto something here.* Just look at the interplay. He looks into his empty cup and a second later a simpering Rosie fills it once again. "Thank you, my dear," he murmurs and continues, "I must say, with six littluns the Missus is kept very busy. There isn't much time left to care for my needs, if you know what I mean." The poor constable looks a bit embarrassed after divulging this piece of information, but at least he's honest.

"I can only imagine, Constable. Her work would be never ending. Does your wife not have help with her tiresome chores?" I ask sympathetically. *Poor woman, I'd feel the same in her circumstances.*

"Oh yes, she does. I engaged a fella quite a few years back, name of Joe. His parents died of influenza when first arriving in the colony. He chops the wood, runs the errands into Blackheath and so forth. I don't know what the missus would do without him, although he is a sandwich short of a picnic, if you know what I mean."

"What a shame," I say sincerely. "But what a wonderful thing it must be for Joe to have found a good home with you and your wife, Constable."

He smiles and nods. Then, from under his heavy brows, he looks at us squarely with his clear blue eyes and adds in a conspiratorial tone, "All but the first-born bears a real likeness to Joe, if you know what I mean?"

I take his meaning quite clearly, having a decent dose of deception myself. It is obvious that Mrs Lamb has found a pleasant diversion from her daily chores. It seems Joe is a young rake. I give my silent consent to the incipient love affair blossoming between Rosie and Constable Lamb. What a hoot!

"I think we all know what you mean, Constable, and seeing that our friendship will surely continue into the future, would you allow us to call you by your Christian name? In private, of course," I add.

"Yes, I don't mind at all, Miss Brown. My name is Ernest. Ernest Lamb." He gives Rosie a dashing smile and her cheeks turn scarlet.

What a happy little lot we are, all except Teddy March, although he does seem comfortable in his own delirium. Mmm, I think I prefer this situation after experiencing the true Teddy March. I immediately banish this unpleasant thought.

"More tea, anyone?" I ask gaily.

CHAPTER 21
PIERRE

I am the first to leave the breakfast table. Shaking my head in dismay as I walk away, I try to dispel the thoughts of the tangled web we are weaving. *Sacre bleu!* I need to clear my mind and concentrate on my own dream – to breed the fastest racehorse in the country. I don't know if it is possible, but I will do my best to succeed. Some say the love of horses is like a disease, one that never leaves you. I am convinced this is true; it controls my every thought, other than my never-ending love for Henry.

As I go about the duty of feeding my team of horses, I take pleasure in the sun warming the morning stiffness from my joints. Here in spring, and even winter, can be as warm as summer in England. In Australia, the sun is so much more consistent, shining all year around. As I busy myself mixing horse feeds, thoughts of home cross my mind. I still miss it keenly, holding a fondness even for those grey English skies. I notice some wild daisies growing beside the water trough and they remind me of my mother and her promise to come and visit us. But what would she come to? A home where a continual pantomime with a twisted, perhaps even a perverted, plot is being played out?

The way things are turning out, I decide I will stay only until I've broken in the first colt by Satan out of Cheval D'azur. It will be best to do his initial training here at "Mountain View", being the familiar ground he was born on as this will help calm him into submission. I'll then spend a season training the colt at the Hawkesbury track. Its proximity to Sydney will allow me to easily take him there whenever a suitable race is held. Sarah will be well occupied with her baby and by then be living happily with her newly named "Jimmy MacKay". He will remain here to care for Sarah and the rest of my horses if he proves as able as promised. Henry, my love, will come with me but no doubt Rosie would rather remain here with Sarah and the baby when he or she arrives. By the look of things at breakfast she will also prefer to stay close to Constable Lamb. My plans will keep me focused and finally sharing my life with Henry will make me happy.

"Pierre, I'm here to help y', mon," says a voice behind me, one with a very poor Scottish accent indeed. I turn with a smile.

"Jimmy, 'tis you, me lad! I think I'll be needin' yer help verra much, och aye!"

We have a laugh as he smacks me hard on the back. Maybe it will work out.

I watch James, or Jimmy, as he opens the gate into Satan's yard. The slow gentle way he approaches the horse impresses me. James allows Satan to sniff his hand, then his hair, before he reaches up to scratch the horse's wither. It shows Jimmy has the right tactic to befriend a horse, and it obviously delights Satan who snorts and shakes his head for more attention when James stops his scratching. I smile, knowing that I have a true horseman here to help me with my never-ending workload. I feel sure all will be well, and pray I am not making a mistake.

CHAPTER 22
SARAH

Nine months has almost elapsed and I am anxious to give birth. I am the size of an elephant and beginning to feel extremely uncomfortable and more than a little grumpy. I am so thankful to have Rosie with me. She is such a darling, meeting all my wishes in between knitting and sewing clothes for the little one. My mother is overjoyed for me to have Rosie taking care of me, as mother has never completely recovered from her severe bout of illness. She is weak, to say the least, and Father refuses to leave her side for any length of time. This situation, although it saddens me, helps to hide our secrets.

Rosie returned inside after collecting the mail. What a treat it was to have our mail delivered. It showed that progress is being made and one day this colony will grow into a great and sophisticated nation. Rosie handed me the bundle, which I sifted through, and with a good deal of excitement I opened one and scanned its contents. I mouth the words, "I have received a letter from Mr March's only relative, his sister Mable March. She is a spinster. Would you like to read it, Rosie?" I asked, holding the letter towards her.

"Yes, but after you, Sarah," she rubbed my arm gently, her way of saying she was there for me, whatever news it may have brought. I kissed Rosie's pink cheek and placed the letter down on the table so we could both read it.

> *Dear Mrs Boyar,*
> *I thank you for your correspondence on behalf of my ill-fated brother Edward, or Teddy, as you call him. I can only explain my situation and hope you will understand. I am unable to care for my brother as I, too, suffer with ill health and must pay a live-in nurse who is more than busy with my needs. I am not a wealthy person as my*

*much younger and only brother, Edward, inherited all
our father's wealth and property here in England. I
have an annual allowance that should be just enough
to see me out for the rest of my days. I am afraid that
unless you could somehow, on Edward's behalf, sell his
property in Australia and send him home to England
with the funds and a nurse, I cannot be held responsible
for him. Or you may wish him to remain amongst
friends. In that case, his money is yours to be used for
his care in Australia.*

Yours most sincerely,
Miss Mable March.

The letter was disappointing to both Rosie and I because *our* Teddy
had not recovered one iota from his head injury, and we appeared to
be the only ones who were prepared to look after him. The manager of
his property refused to care for him personally, saying it was too much
responsibility, given all the other duties he had. Our Teddy rarely spoke,
and when he did, we wondered what on earth he was talking about. The
only thing that seemed to bring him joy was when Henry read to him or
took him on nature walks. Sometimes, Henry sat Teddy beside his easel
where he seemed content to watch Henry paint. In other words, he was
only happy when he was with Henry, who remained dressed in women's
clothes. Perhaps Henry reminded Teddy of his sister? Anyway, I needed
to write to Teddy's lawyer, informing him of the latest turn of events and
we would take things from there.

Pierre burst through the back door, putting a stop to my pondering.
Although I did not hear him, I saw Rosie turn when she heard him enter
and she smiled at what Pierre had to say.

"Come and watch, ladies. James, I mean Jimmy MacKay, has
the colt going really well. He's cantering him around the yard." Pierre
took me by my arm, forgetting how heavily pregnant I was as I stumbled
alongside him in his haste to arrive at the round yard. Before us was a
beautiful sight. The colt, as black as coal, cantered smoothly around the
yard, his neck was arched, and his tail held high. His gait was so proud
he was surely asking us to admire him – he was a showoff, I thought.

My hands moved quickly. "Oh Pierre, you have bred a fine

horse. He will do you proud on the racetrack. I am so happy for you and delighted James can assist. You make a great team." I took one step closer to the fence when something happened. A gush of warm fluid broke from within me and flowed down my thighs. I staggered, a little shocked, before I realised the baby was on its way. I grabbed Pierre's arm and pointed to the puddle at my feet. Pierre immediately lifted me off the ground and carried me inside to my bed where the surging pains began.

I have refrained from going into detail but suffice to say three hours later I lay between fresh clean sheets, nestling a beautiful baby girl against my breast. James sat alongside, stroking the golden down covering her tiny head. Her sweetness filled our hearts. She was so pure and so new that she brought tears to our eyes. When I said *our*, I was referring not just to James and myself but to our happy little community – Pierre, Henri-Etta, Rosie, and Teddy – who all huddled around the bed in total awe of our new miracle. I named her Sascha. It was the name of a beautiful character in a wonderful novel I read a long time ago and it had remained with me like the memory of a glorious spring day.

CHAPTER 23
THE DUKE

"I will not have it, doctor! George is not dying! He can't die! I'm about to send him to Australia where he is to trace the whereabouts of Henry. Can't you do something? George has been my servant for as long as I can remember. Do something!" The flustered Duke points his finger towards poor George who lies motionless on the bed.

"The precise problem, my Lord, is I can't do *anything*! George has been here since well before you were born. Unfortunately, we do not live forever, and I'm afraid George's heart is past its ticking time. It will stop shortly." The doctor places his hand on the Duke's shoulder in a gesture of comfort. "I must take my leave, my lord; there is nothing more I am able to do for George."

The doctor pauses for a moment, studying the redness and the sweat beading on the Duke's face. "Forgive me, my lord, but I must say you're in for the same fate as George if you don't take care of yourself. Here, I insist you take this medicine every day and try to calm yourself. I'm sure your blood pressure is about to blow your head off. And a little less weight around your middle would help." With a shake of the head the Doctor hurries to leave.

Although the Duke pays scant heed to the doctor's warning, nevertheless he swallows the proffered medicine, its bitterness showing in the Duke's grimace. Shortly after, his anguish abates, and a calmness settles upon him. Once left alone, he leans closer to the prostrate form of his lifelong friend Georgie, upon whose ashen face the green tinge of death is slowly creeping. "I'm not sure whether you can hear me, Georgie, but I must tell you, I do love you. You have been everything to me – father, mother, brother and faithful servant. All I can say is that I hope you find peace and happiness in Heaven, and I'm sure one day we will meet again. After all, the Reverend Timms has promised it."

Bereft, the Duke whimpers as he bends his enormous frame over

Georgie to place one last kiss on the forehead of the man he would miss most in the world. George's eyes flicker open, he smiles weakly, and with a sigh, takes his final breath. The Duke weeps uncontrollably as he clutches George's bony hands in his own. It is some time before the tears subside and he finds the strength to rise and seek help with preparing George's body for burial. It will be done without haste and with great ceremony; the Duke simply must have George looking his best for the occasion.

The Duke has shown his true nature over the deceased George. The elaborate practical jokes he played throughout his life have in fact been used to cover his passionate side, and to dull the shame that first his father, and then his wife, had instilled in him for not being "man enough". The shooting of deer, which his father introduced and demanded of him at the age of ten, had caused him terrible feelings of guilt. It had affected him almost to the point of despair, though not a soul ever knew. He'd admired the deer, as did Henry. It was a torment for him of which few, if any, were aware.

Over the next two days, while arrangements for George's funeral are being planned, the Duke makes other more exciting and possibly dangerous plans. He mulls over the information George had given him months earlier. It seems with a little too much sherry and a pound note here and there, George had been able to purge some truth out of Bethany Pierce. She had not given away everything, but the old crone had let slip that Rosie mentioned *perhaps going to Australia*. George had only to put two and two together to realise Henry, most probably dressed in disguise, had slipped away the morning the ship docked in Spain, and because of his blood ties with Rosie, she had been his willing accomplice.

On that basis, the Duke had written to Reverend Timms to inquire if any of their party had received any visitors from home, naming Rosie as one. Well, of course, the Reverend could not lie.

> *Yes, my Lord, we were delighted to welcome Rosie and her young cousin, Etta, some months ago now. It seems Sarah and Pierre are more than happy to have them stay forever on their stunning property, if they so wish. They have named it "Mountain View" and it is near the township of Blackheath.*

This was enough to arouse deep suspicion in the minds of the Duke and his faithful servant, but poor George was unable to do any more than die with the question unanswered.

"I will go to Australia alone!" the Duke declares with gusto, as if he is going to war. "Well, not completely alone. I'll take my new personal servant, Roberto," he adds circumspectly. His wife, Cecilia, merely raises her manicured brows.

Roberto is a self-educated man who has worked his way up from pageboy to footman, to first footman, to valet, and to finally become the Duke's new personal butler – not without a decent amount of cunning, it must be said. The news of the Duke's plans makes Roberto so enthusiastic that he begins to read all he can about the colony of New South Wales, and he becomes a great source of information for the Duke. Roberto's heart is full of adventure and stealth; whatever it takes, he will find a way to raise himself in the Duke's estimation. His obsequious manner and humble demeanour will assure his success.

The Duke of Harrowfeild is most impressed with Roberto, especially with his natural intelligence, which is balanced by a good dose of common sense. The Duke, therefore, has no hesitation in leaving all arrangements for their passage to Australia up to Roberto.

"Jolly good, my man! We are all set then, and I must say the more I think about it, the more it makes me feel like a young boy again. Off on an adventure of a lifetime, say what!"

"Yes, my lord, I must agree with you. And I'm sure, just the mention of an adventure takes at least five years off your age. And forgive the impertinence, but I think my lord has lost a considerable amount of weight?" Roberto inquires, with a knowing grin.

"No, no, not rude at all. I'm pleased somebody has noticed." The Duke pats his reduced waistline proudly, taking a quick look over his shoulder to where his wife Cecilia sits, pretending to embroider. He knows for a fact that Milly, his wife's Lady's Maid, always mended Cecilia's embroidery mistakes, finishing the work for it to be admired by all. Of course, the compliments on the handiwork went to Cecilia!

The Duke is more than content with the thought that he will soon be on his journey to Australia, far away from his narcissistic wife. Yes, without any warning to Reverend Timms or Pierre, in approximately three months' time he will simply arrive on their doorstep, completely unannounced! *Ah yes, better than my best practical joke ever!*

CHAPTER 24
HENRY

Rosie and I have been up to our elbows all day, preparing a special dinner for our loved ones and guests. Attending, is Mr Tootle, or "Winking Theobald", as we've come to call him, Teddy March, whose mental condition has yet to show improvement, and Constable Ernie Lamb, Rosie's new beau – no strings attached. Ernie has met our Jimmy MacKay and seems to accept that he is Pierre's new helping hand. *Thank the Lord.*

The dinner party idea is for Pierre's and my need to celebrate before travelling down the mountain in the morning to the Hawkesbury valley, in particular to the Hawkesbury Racecourse. We've rented a stable there for Pierre's colt, Mountain Boy, who has come to hand quickly and, if all continues to go well, Pierre says he will win every race that we place him in. Now there's a brave statement. Nonetheless, I believe Pierre for he is such a skilled horseman and not one to exaggerate. What fun we will have in the next few months! I long to be swanning around and attending the races with the other glamorous ladies in their finest attire. But I wonder – how I will compare? Oh well, Rosie and I have almost finished preparing a delicious four-course dinner, all made with local produce, I'm proud to say. We will start with trout terrine, followed by roast lamb and home-grown vegetables. For dessert, there is lemon tart, created from the first harvest of lemons in our orchard, and served with a good dollop of cream from Jessabelle the cow. Then to finish, it's cheese and dried fruit that we have produced ourselves. We will wash it all down with some lovely wines and a decent drop of port. I cannot explain how proud I am to be a contributing, valued member of our small society, and not being waited on hand and foot as I was before in my gilded castle.

At last, we are finished. I fling my pretty apron to the floor, like a victorious matador does his cape. Sheepishly, I pick it up because I realise we haven't a housemaid who will do it. I have prepared what is set to be a succulent taste sensation. Well, with a lot of guidance from Rosie, I must confess.

"Sarah!" I call, then smack my forehead, remembering she won't hear me. I go and partly open the door to her bedroom where I know she is feeding baby Sascha. "May I come in?" I ask stupidly before pushing the door fully open after she stamps her foot twice – our code to enter. I step into the room and see a vision of tranquillity and beauty. The scene inspires me; I must start painting portraits, I think. My hands move to tell Sarah this and she is overjoyed.

"If only you would, Henry. My great wish is for you to capture the love between my daughter and me on canvas," she signs.

"I will try, Sarah, just as soon as we return from our racing triumphs," I sign back to her.

Now three months old, Sascha resembles her father. I won't say "Thank Heaven", but I'm sure Sarah would agree. The baby, unlike her, is truly beautiful.

"May I?"

I extend my arms to hold the little cherub, cradling her close to my chest. "I do wish I could have a baby of my own. You are so enchanting, beautiful and delicate. I simply adore you, my darling," I murmur as I gaze into the deep blue pools of her eyes.

I tenderly kiss the blond down on her tiny perfect head and notice the silken strawberry blond hair appearing from beneath. The colour will enhance those deep blue eyes with their dashes of silver, the same as her father's.

Reluctantly, I hand her back to Sarah, who mouths, "I will put Sascha down to sleep, so I can help you and Rosie. I will set the table if you wish. I would like to use my best china and cutlery." I accept Sarah's offer with grace, as I wish to bathe and have enough time to look my best.

We sit, as usual, on the front veranda sipping sherry, waiting for Mr Tootle and Ernie Lamb to arrive, as the day's shimmering light makes way for the dark velvet of the night sky. Also invited are Reverend Timms and his wife, Charlotte, but unfortunately, she has come down with a head cold – again! I feel for her not being able to enjoy her first grandchild as much as she'd like; she has so much illness, poor woman.

Before we see their shadowy bulk materialising from the darkness into the light provided by lamps either side of the driveway, the clip clop of the horse's hooves alerts us our guests are approaching.

Rosie can't help herself. She rushes to greet Ernie Lamb with one of her bosomy hugs once he's dismounted, then gives him a smacking kiss on the cheek. She must stretch up on her toes to do so as Ernie is six feet tall, and Rosie a foot shorter. Arm in arm they leave Theobald Tootle to scramble as best he can from the buggy, although I must admit, I wish to greet Theobald with the same enthusiasm as Rosie did Ernie. I am so excited to see him. My painting of Satan is complete, and I can't wait for his review of what I think is a triumph. Now that is conceited, I know, but I shall be disappointed if he does not agree with me, and I am bound to respect his professional opinion.

After chatty embraces, our motely yet harmonious little crew enters the dining room to take our places at the lavishly set table. A silver candelabrum takes pride of place in the middle, holding four flickering candles. Place mats, designed and painted by Pierre's mother, lay before each person. These depict scenes from the gardens at Harrowfeild and are beautifully executed. When I look at them, a feeling of melancholy edges into my heart for a moment before I smile and introduce the menu to our guests.

"Rosie and Sarah will soon be serving the trout terrine and then I, along with Pierre, will serve the following course of roast lamb," I say proudly.

Appreciative sounds are heard, and I smile with confidence.

I appear composed, but I am restless with the need to show Theobald Tootle my impressionist painting of Satan. Should I risk indigestion and hold off until dinner is complete or simply get it over with? Either way, the anticipation or the disappointment will affect my enjoyment of the meal. No, I must control my nerves and wait until dinner is finished as I originally planned. Or should I?

"Theobald," I say with a flutter of my eyelashes. "I have something to ask you."

"Yes, Etta?" he inquires.

I have the distinct impression he knows what I am about to say. "I have finished my painting of Satan and I'm hoping you will want to see it. Perhaps after dinner?"

"My dear young lady, I cannot imagine why you would think I could possibly wait so long." He half stands, excusing himself to the others who are in robust conversations of their own, except Teddy March who, as usual, simply sits and nods at anything and everything.

I grab Theobald by the arm, virtually dragging him to my new art studio, which Pierre has added as an annexe to the kitchen. The poor man is given no chance. We both stand for a moment in anticipation of my unveiling a large span of canvas. "The painting is yet to be framed," I tell him. "I will ask you later, Theobald, for the best place to have one's paintings framed. Ready?" I bend forward and take the silk cover between my forefinger and thumb, tugging if off and saying, "Ta da!" The silk falls to the ground like a discarded nightgown. The look on Theobald's face tells me he is impressed, if not astounded.

"I am speechless, Etta," he says quietly after several moments of contemplation. "It is difficult to find the words to describe this painting without resorting to clichés. It's simply magnificent. What you have created here is what art is all about – capturing the essence of what you are painting. Etta, my dear, through your talented hand I am able to tell exactly what this horse is thinking, what he is feeling, and what lies within his soul."

Theobald shakes his head – in wonder, I assume. He studies Satan's picture closely, silent but still winking, before delivering what I think to be his greatest compliment. "I strongly suggest you enter this painting in the Sydney Art Competition. It's to be held next month, Etta. I cannot imagine any judge in their right mind not placing a blue ribbon on it, not to mention awarding you the hefty sum of fifty pounds first prize money."

I am overwhelmed to the point of feeling weak at the knees. Never did I think his praise would be so high. I hide tears behind cupped hands, such are my emotions. He clasps me to his chest, and because he is a good six inches shorter than me, his head and my false bosoms make contact. My bosoms collapse, and I see his puzzled look when we part. I beat a hasty retreat back to the dinner table. "Come, Theobald," I call over my shoulder, "let us not appear rude. Our first course of trout terrine should be served by now. And I'm anxious for you to convey your opinion of my painting to the others." As he catches me up, I kiss his cheek and drag him back to the dining table where the terrine sits beautifully presented before our guests and our empty places.

"I do apologise," I give a quick embarrassed look around. "I hope you will forgive two obsessed artists indulging in their passion." I see shocked expressions, except from Teddy March. "Oh, how delightful! You all thought Theobald and I – oh, never mind, what I meant to say was, indulging in our love for art. Silly me! Anyway, bon appetit!" I say, a little flushed and still bursting at the seams with pride and wanting to hear again and again the praise Theobald had bestowed upon me.

Throughout dinner, which was a great gastronomic success, I notice Ernie Lamb taking the odd surreptitious glance at James, aka our Jimmy MacKay. Some of Ernie's questions leads me to suspect he knows who Jimmy really is and is in two minds whether to tell us. "Let sleeping dogs lie," I want to say to Ernie.

The story is this, as James told us: the murdered man, Archie Jones, had threatened to have James's friend Peter killed for failing to repay a substantial debt. James had gone to speak with Archie simply to assure him that the money Peter owed him would be paid within the week. James would stake his own life on the promise. However, the evening James arrived at Archie's premises to tell him this, he was welcomed by his housemaid and told to go upstairs, "He's in his office." When James entered, he found Archie lying on the floor with a dagger protruding from his heart. He leaned over the dead body to feel for a pulse and while doing so, the housemaid appeared in the doorway with a tray of refreshments. She screamed and dropped the tray.

"MURDERER! MURDERER," she'd yelled. James tried to explain to her he was not the murderer, but she would not listen. James had been the only person she had allowed to enter the home. The circumstantial evidence looked cut and dried, so James jumped out of the open window, tearing his breeches as he did, and made a run for it.

We all believe James's story without a doubt. He is such a kind and considerate man we feel he could not possibly commit a murder. And to add to the tragedy, James's *so-called* friend, Peter, has abandoned him. Instead of standing by him, Peter has returned to England with the money he'd borrowed previously from James. Now I ask you, what sort of a friend is he? And don't worry. I have asked James the same. He simply shrugs it off with his favourite saying, "Hard to pick your friends sometimes." If the need does arise that we, or I alone, should have to defend our James, it will be to the death! It sounds terribly melodramatic, but you know how I am.

As the evening continues, we sit around the fire burning merrily in the enormous stone fireplace. Its warmth and the sumptuous port we sip soon releases any tension we may have felt. It sets us in the mood to chat.

The first thing we talk about is my painting of Satan. Pierre has just now brought it in for all to view. It is unanimously agreed that I should enter it in the Sydney Art Competition. Their flattery has fuelled my inflated alter ego. I already knew the painting was good. In fact, it is a masterpiece. *I think.* I will have the perfect opportunity to enter it as Pierre and I will be much closer to Sydney while in the Hawkesbury valley. Why, I could even sail with the painting down the Hawkesbury River to Sydney Town! What drama! I can see the headlines now. *Sydney's new talented and beautiful artist, Etta Brown, delivers winning painting via the Hawkesbury River, like Cleopatra down the Nile!* Oh, what fun.

Teddy March's persistent condition is our next topic of conversation. We all have our own ideas on what can, or should, be done to help Teddy return to his normal self. One notion comes from Rosie. She's heard of a man who was hit so severely on the head that he, too, suffered with amnesia – until he received a second blow. From that moment on, he remembered everything, even some things he had forgotten before!

Personally, I believe Teddy has more than amnesia. He seems simple minded as we must care for almost his every need. Fortunately, he does know when he needs to relieve himself or when he is hungry. One of us must keep a close eye on him though, for he tends to wander. Pierre is very patient and treats Teddy kindly, especially when seeking his help with several tasks about the place. Teddy manages to complete these, usually with obvious signs of satisfaction. I give him art lessons, and to my delight, he shows great promise, although his work is what they call in the art world "naïve". Still, there is a market for such a style, I'm sure. I wonder if Teddy will ever regain his senses. I fear if he does, he will surely remember my parting gift to him. No! It's best that he stays the way he is. This reminds me, Pierre and I have planned to travel to Goulburn within the next month, not only to race Mountain Boy there, but also complete the sale of Teddy's property. I will invest the sale money and use it for his care, as I am now his guardian, according to his sister. I therefore have her permission to do as I see fit toward the welfare of her brother's existence.

A reflective mood settles over us. We sit silently, entertained by the dancing flames of the fire. Is this the right time to approach Ernie about James's identity? Should I attempt to clear the accusations of his guilt?

I noticed Rosie has snuggled her glorious curls into the hollow of Ernie's broad shoulder. I see by the look on his face that Ernie is in an expansive mood. With another port under his belt, I'm sure he will be more than open to hear the truth, while still sober enough to believe it. Yes, I think this is a good time to discuss the real identity of "Jimmy MacKay", even though it is a sensitive subject.

Almost dreamily, I begin. "Ernie, I was wondering. Have you heard any more of the escaped murderer, James Howard? Have the police not found him yet?" Ernie sits up straight and coughs twice to clear his throat.

"Well, now you mention it, Miss Etta, I do have my own theories on the matter that have come about through my investigations. I believe with a reasonable degree of certainty that James Howard may be hiding in the Blue Mountains. As I oversee this area, I have made myself familiar with the background of the accused." He gives a wry smile, "You see, I rather fancy myself as being a bit of a detective, not just a police constable."

"Soon to be promoted, I hear." I smile and raise my glass.

He straightens with pride, nodding his thanks at our congratulations, losing Rosie her spot resting on his shoulder. "From what I have gathered, this wanted man Howard has no slurs against his character and he has no previous criminal record. In fact, I could find only attestations to his excellent reputation, which is more than I can say for the deceased. Not to say the man deserved to be killed, mind you, but this is one case I find hard to fathom. My only hope is that I should find this James Howard, before the Sydney police find him, because I have another sneaking suspicion – the city police were into some sticky business with the deceased, now what did he call himself?" Ernie's brow furrows and he scratches his head.

"His name was Archie Jones. Well, at least that is what he called himself," James aka "Jimmy" said evenly and without the Scottish accent.

"Ah, I thought it might be you, Mr Howard," Ernie replies with a raised eyebrow. "Despite having maintained a very good masquerade, especially with your Scottish accent." Ernie smiles, a little relieved it appears, before looking down at his boots. He takes a huge breath and lets it out with a huff before raising his head to look James in the eye. "Now would you care to tell me your story, Mr Howard?" Ernie looks briefly at each of us. "From the calm response from your friends, I think I'm safe in assuming that they all know about you. Now tell me the truth about the murder. I'm all ears, sir."

Ernie sits back relaxed, as if he is about to listen to a good yarn – and he is, although this one is completely true. After James has finished his story we breathe a collective sigh of relief. Ernie's response is positive.

"I believe you, Jimmy... I mean, James. I have more than a slight suspicion that the Sydney police know who the real murderer is, but for their own crooked reasons were happy to let someone else take the blame. I've been asking a few questions and with the considerable help of a detective friend of mine in Sydney, I have some evidence that completely absolves you, James. You can thank 'Billy Boy' Bunting for that," he says, nodding in James's direction. "A more honest bloke you could not find. He detests crooked cops because back in England his father was murdered by one of the bad bobbies, just before he was about to blow the whistle on him." Ernie shakes his head in sorrow.

I can imagine Billy Boy wanting to seek revenge for the death of his honourable father; I would feel the same. Oh my, but this is playing out like a melodrama, one in which Theobald Tootle seems to have little interest – he nodded off to sleep some time ago, in fact. I think it was when our conversation about art ended.

"James, I think it best you keep your disguise," Ernie adds, "at least for the time being. And with any luck at all I will be able to get you off the hook – so to speak!"

Ernie is noticeably proud of himself. I assume his detective work will reap rewards, if not for himself, then certainly for James. Well, for all of us, come to think of it. We have been harbouring a suspected criminal, after all. And on that note, although excited about James's prospects of freedom, we bid each other goodnight. It is too late and too far in the dark to travel home for Theobald Tootle and Ernie Lamb. No guessing who Ernie is sleeping with! Poor Theodore is left alone to sleep on the chesterfield. However, I do lend him my teddy bear to cuddle.

CHAPTER 25
SARAH

Our prayers are answered so quickly that I would not have thought it possible. I have no doubt Constable Lamb will pursue the matter of James's innocence. I will sleep well with the thought that James and I are living free together, to do whatever we want and go wherever we please.

And on this bright summer morning we gathered to bid Henry and Pierre farewell, as they set off on what we hope will be a prosperous journey. Henry is determined to become a person of self-sufficient means. The sight of him in a bright yellow frock, carefully placing his well-wrapped painting in the back of the buggy, then kissing the nose of Mountain Boy for luck made me giggle – he's such a queen! Well, not all the time at least. Henry has become quite useful. He has taken on simple chores around the farm with exuberance. He wants to learn all there was to know about growing vegetables, fruit and herbs, and he helps Rosie to turn them into the most delicious meals I have ever tasted. Multi-talented our Henry has become. I could not be happier for him and Pierre.

I helped Rosie with tidying the house as we were entertaining not only my father for afternoon tea today; a young woman would be joining him. She is to be interviewed for the housemaid's position. Father insisted I take on some help and so he placed an advertisement in the local *Gazette*.

"Now you have a baby to care for, Sarah," I recalled he admonished me, "Rosie cannot be expected to do everything by herself. After all, you have three hungry men to cook and care for. And with what I have witnessed there is not much help from Etta, who appears to be stricken with constant headaches! Just as well she is accompanying Pierre on his racing tour – I think the fresh air and diversion may do her good," Father added in his righteous manner. He has been a little cynical towards Etta, I'm afraid. Dear me, if only he knew.

I am much relieved that my father took matters into his own

hands. However, I was dumbfounded (now there's a pun) that he hadn't yet fathomed who Etta was, even after receiving the Duke's letter. How bizarre it was! He seemed not to have enough sense to work it out. Or was he so naïve he could not possibly envision Henry dressed as a woman?

James is busy building yet another annexe onto the house for our new maid. He began the project with Pierre's help, but now he has assistance from Teddy whom we purposely kept busy and out of sight while Henry left with Pierre. We feared how Teddy may have reacted, for it seemed either because of his current state of disorientation or his previous reality, Teddy remained attracted to Henry. I dare say he will be very upset when he has realised Henri-Etta has left.

Father arrived with a very young woman and from where I stood on the veranda, I suspected she was not yet twenty.

"Sarah, my dearest daughter, I would like you to meet Miss Melanie Muscat. Melanie is excited at the prospect of finding a suitable household in which to be trained as a housemaid. Though, mind you, Melanie is the eldest of thirteen siblings and has been expected to do more than her fair share of the work. There is no doubt she will attend to all your requirements in no time, Sarah." At last he took breath and turned to Melanie with a smile, "Is it not so, Melanie?"

"Yes, sir, "Melanie said meekly. Her voluptuous red hair was tied with a piece of twine, the apron she wore was patched in the extreme, and her shoes, although clean, were worn to the last of the leather. My heart went out to the poor little urchin. Although she was thin and a little careworn, she was quite pretty with her sparkling blue eyes. I smiled kindly at her and communicated with hand signs to my father, who then translated to Melanie.

"Please come inside, Melanie, and meet our dear friend Rosie. We will have some afternoon tea Rosie has prepared. I do hope you will be able to learn sign language quickly, as it saves a lot of time and trouble, not to mention all the pencils and paper I need to write on." Melanie smiled a little uncertainly and followed me into the house.

The interview went well, in between the banging and clanging from James and Teddy, which I could not hear, of course, but about which my father complained. I explained to him, "The room is being built to house Melanie. It is not quite ready, but do not fear, Father, Melanie can stay in Etta's room until the annexe is complete." I turned slightly towards Melanie, "Pierre, my husband and Etta, our friend, should be away for at least three months, travelling the country to race our thoroughbred horse, Mountain Boy." This information Father relayed to Melanie on my behalf, as Father was already aware of these events.

Melanie was shy but well-mannered and I could see she had been brought up properly. After our tea, she gathered her meagre belongings from the buggy and waved goodbye to Father. As a doting grandfather, he reluctantly handed Sascha back to me before making his way back to Blackheath.

CHAPTER 26
HENRY

"I will hate to leave our beloved mountains, Pierre," I say wistfully. We rattle and bump our way to the Hawkesbury valley with Mountain Boy tethered to the back of the buggy, contentedly clip-clopping slowly behind. "We must now take into our memory the majesty of it all," I say with arms spread wide. "Light beams dance like silken angels flying between our perfumed gum trees. Oh dear, there I go again, I'm claiming this wondrous land to be all ours. Tell me, Pierre, do you think as I do that the mountains hold such magic?"

"I do, *mon petit chou,* but I'm not the romantic you are." He glances sideways toward me with a smile deep enough to show his dimples.

"No, I suppose not. Still, one of us must remain grounded," I concede. "But still, I think for a person with good business acumen and great vision, the Blue Mountains would become a prodigious tourist attraction. Especially with the hot springs discovered near Medlow Bath and the overwhelming abundance of wildlife to be seen throughout our spectacular surrounds. Not to mention breathing in such cleansing air, while walking or hiking through the bush. It gives such great pleasure and is different from any other country, I'm sure. Why, I think the Blue Mountains must be nature's gift to mankind. Apart from everything else I wish to achieve, Pierre, I would like to find a business partner who shares the same dream as me. I want to create a grand hotel, catering for those who wish to maintain a state of wellbeing in both mind and body and to offer treatments for those who wish to attain it," I say with even more animation. *If possible?*

I look sideways at Pierre. He has a faraway look in his eyes, and I feel my descriptions are boring him. "You seem somewhere else, Pierre. Please tell me, is something bothering you?"

"No, not at all, *cheri*, I'm just thinking about my own dreams, breeding and racing the very best horses." He turns to me, smiling.

"That is also part of my dream, Pierre. To see you successful and content could not possibly please me more. That reminds me," I say, changing the subject somewhat, "do you think it safe for me to travel alone to Sydney with my painting? I'm not sure if I can trust anyone else to deliver it for me."

"Don't worry, Henry. I'll go with you, just as soon as we settle at the racetrack and find a reliable stableboy to care for Mountain Boy while we're gone." He gives my knee a little squeeze and I gently stroke the nape of his neck.

Happy with Pierre's promise, I relax to enjoy our necessarily slow trip down the mountain. However, with Constable Ernie Lamb's warning of bushrangers potentially lurking behind boulders and trees ready to attack us, I remain alert, but ponder about Rosie and Ernie. They seem such a perfect match, I think. I guess Rosie would be about five years older although she certainly does not act so in his company. In fact, she behaves like a much younger woman. I delight in knowing that Rosie has at last found her true love. And I'm not concerned at all by Mrs Lamb's position in the matter, should Ernie choose Rosie above her. After all, the woman has been a shameless and deceitful slut! My, my, but that's a little harsh, Henry. Oh well, I must speak the truth sometimes, harsh though it may be.

CHAPTER 27
THE DUKE

"Never in my wildest dreams could I imagine what utter agony it would be to sail through a continuous barrage of thundering waves and ferocious winds! And worst of all is not being able to stand still long enough to piss in my chamber pot!" the Duke yells as he sways, penis in hand, trying to direct his stream at a sliding porcelain pot.

"If I may be of assistance, my lord," Roberto offers as he immediately scoops the pot up and holds it under the Duke's wavering flow.

"Thank you, Roberto. I must say I don't know where I would be without you. Your assistance has been most invaluable."

After shaking his old boy and wiping the drips with the cloth Roberto handed him, he sits heavily on his bed, mellowing a little after his exertions.

"How long did the Captain say we had to endure this agony before landing in Sydney? I'm not sure if I can last another day, Roberto. I'm feeling sick to the stomach and homesick as well. Even facing my unloving, unattractive wife seems a blessing compared with this relentless torment," the Duke claims miserably, his spirit almost broken by the horrendous voyage.

"If I may, my lord?" Roberto bows slightly and sits beside the Duke, placing his arm, tentatively at first, around the Duke's shoulders. The Duke relaxes and rests his head on Roberto's shoulder. Together they rock with the heaving of the ship as Roberto consoles him.

"The Captain did say this morning, Sir, we were to arrive no later than three days hence, and if the seas are favourable, the voyage should take less time. I do hope my lord feels better in the morning and I shall pray for calm seas." Roberto turns the bedclothes down for the Duke and makes him comfortable.

Roberto's prayers are answered. They awake in the morning to a

121

cloudless blue sky, the sea shining silver with the brightness of sunlight. The Duke of Harrowfeild rises to greet the day with a changed attitude.

"Good morning, Roberto. The Good Lord must have heard you. What a magnificent day it seems," he says cheerfully, opening the porthole to view the full splendour. "Close to land we must be, Roberto, because the seagulls are out in force. Scavengers of the sea, my father would say, though I tend to like them myself," he adds with a smile, admiring the little white forms swooping to find food or sitting like tiny sentinels on the rigging.

"I'm pleased you are in good humour and obviously feeling much better this morning, my lord," Roberto comments as he places the breakfast tray on the table in the centre of the cabin. The two of them had taken most of their meals there because the Duke was often not up to joining the Captain at his table. Like his father before him, the Duke was not inclined to treat his staff as being beneath him, and he and Roberto had dined on opposite sides of the table in the two captain's chairs. Nor did the Duke address his servants by their surnames, as was the habit of the aristocracy. His staff were more like subjects taken into the realm of a kindly, albeit gruff at times, ageing monarch.

"Roberto, I have been thinking," the Duke begins, his eyes lowered and fingers fiddling with his napkin. "If we are unsuccessful in finding Henry, I would like to be assured that my daughter, Gertrude, is married to a suitable and trustworthy man. No need for me to find a man of money or breeding. I have funds to provide at least four generations with a most extravagant lifestyle." The Duke suddenly looks up. "Do you understand what I am offering you, Roberto?"

Roberto has the good grace to look a little embarrassed, though his excitement is hard to quell. Not that he finds Gertrude attractive in the slightest, but the money – that is a different story.

"If I am to understand correctly, Sir, you *are* offering to me your daughter Gertrude's hand in marriage? I am your faithful servant, Sir. Nevertheless, other than your employ, I have no means to support Gertrude in the manner to which she is accustomed."

"For goodness sake, man, did you not listen?" the Duke snaps, his fork halfway to his mouth. "I am offering you not only my ugly daughter but my handsome fortune as well! You must consider this offer, Roberto. I have raised and educated you from a young boy and I trust you will follow my wishes to the end should we not find Henry or, more to the point, in the event of my own death," the Duke says with a shudder.

Deep in thought, Roberto stands and begins pacing the cabin. After a long moment, he pauses to look the Duke in the eye. "I am truly sorry for hesitating, my lord. I have never dreamed of such an incredible thing happening to me." *Like hell I haven't.* He scratches his head roughly and shakes it, as if to be rid of the thought that this might be yet another one of the Duke's practical jokes. Roberto had been the victim of a few small jokes but nothing that had hurt or humiliated him in the extreme. But this? Well, he wasn't sure. *I should go along with the offer and see where it leaves me. Wealthy, I hope!*

Roberto straightens his shoulders, takes a small bow, and says formally, "I am honoured, Sir. I will gladly marry your daughter, if you so wish. I will adhere to your every command, be it in life or death." Roberto bows deeply before his Duke and future father-in-law. "However, am I to understand that if Henry is found alive, I will not be required to marry your daughter, Sir?"

The Duke coughs and splutters, not expecting Roberto to be so quick on the uptake.

"Well, yes. In that event, the marriage will not be necessary, as Henry will, of course, inherit the family fortune. I trust you understand why I do not want my wife to have power over Gertrude. God knows what would happen if she were to oversee such a fortune. However, I do know one thing. You, Roberto, and all the others who work for the Harrowfeild estate, would be treated with utter contempt if my wife were left in charge. Therefore, I need to make plans, just in case. You see, I trust you Roberto. I wish you, with your suave Italian charm, to soften my daughter's attitude and refine her femininity. Hopefully, you will be able to resurrect any traces of compassion she may have left after her mother's influence. I'm sure, Roberto, you would have witnessed my wife's deeply rooted scorn and distrust of everyone around her. I sometimes wish there were a pill I could give her to sweeten her sour nature." The Duke sighs and smiles sadly at Roberto.

Roberto had often dreamt of becoming a wealthy man, especially being Lord of the Manor at Harrowfeild Castle. But only in his dreams, mind you. Sometimes, just the inkling of such an idea coming to fruition can cause a vast change of mind in a previously mild-mannered person. Not only cunning, as is Roberto's nature, but ruthless they may become.

CHAPTER 28
HENRY

Our journey to Windsor went without bandits harassing us, nor any other problem that may have spoilt our pleasure. We have now been staying for three nights – in separate rooms, of course – at the Macquarie Arms Hotel. Mountain Boy is stabled with a fellow trainer-cum-jockey whom Pierre says he trusts because he is the son of an Anglican Minister. I suppose it's a good enough reason, but I also agree with Pierre, as Timmy Smith strikes me as being a young man of good character. He is straightforward, he looks you in the eye when speaking, and has a firm handshake, albeit a small hand of a man small in stature. Maybe he could double as Mountain Boy's jockey?

**

With all details settled and taken care of, Pierre and I travel all the way to Sydney Town under threatening clouds that provide the occasional shower. There, we will enter my painting in the competition and stay one night in the Grand Hotel. Just how grand, we will soon see.

Comfortable and suitable is how I shall describe *our* room. Yes, our room. We dare to book in as Mr and Mrs Boyar. With no apparent suspicion, we are ushered to our boudoir that contains a double bed. It could not be any better in Heaven, especially when I see the look on Pierre's face. I smile at him seductively and think maybe God will get it right next time and I won't have to pretend to be who I should have been in the first place. One huge mistake, dear Lord.

Our evening is filled with fine dining and fine romance. We gaze across the dinner table, in public, mind you, into each other's eyes which seem to dance with the gentle flicker of candlelight. Our candour is amazing; we are finally able to live our dream of loving each other in the company of strangers, albeit with me in disguise. I wonder if there will ever be a day when men can show their love for each other in public, and without the threat of punishment by the law. To be locked up for what?

For simply loving another person. Oh well, I'm sure the day will come. Yes, when I'm dead and buried.

After a brisk walk next morning and as we are about to enter the building where I am to leave my paintings for judgment, I see Theobald Tootle walking towards us carrying a large parcel shaped like a painting. He's winking – as usual.

"Mr Tootle, what a wonderful surprise! How lovely to see you!" I exclaim.

Theobald nods to us. "I would tip my hat to you, Miss Brown, but as you can see my arms are full." His smile crinkles into a thousand lines, resembling the London railway tracks. *What a nasty thing to think, Henry*, but Theobald has frazzled my nerves. Surely, he is not entering his magnificent painting "The Mare and Foal"?

"You are forgiven for that, Mr Tootle. Though I may *never* forgive you if you are entering your masterpiece," I say lightly, nevertheless I am filled with dread.

"I am sorry, Miss Brown. Alas, I shall have to find a way to live without your forgiveness for I am in fact entering my work. However, I am embarrassed to be putting it alongside your painting. I am only hoping for second place next to your portrait of Satan. It is indeed a *chef-d'oeuvre*."

"That is most kind of you to say, Mr Tootle," I reply graciously, a little mollified by his praise.

After filling in all the appropriate forms and inviting Theobald Tootle to share morning tea with us, which he declines, Pierre and I decide it is time to return to Windsor.

"Oh Pierre, I was so excited with the thought of maybe winning the competition, but now Theobald has entered his painting, I'm downhearted. I'm sure his painting will win. I know I would choose his above mine, if I were a judge," I say petulantly on our way back to the hotel. Pierre takes my gloved hand and raises it briefly to his lips.

"Let's not worry too much, *mon coeur*, after all it's only one person's opinion, unlike Mountain Boy who must be physically first past the post to win. That is much fairer, *n'est-ce pas?*"

I agree with Pierre and try hard to put my reservations to rest.

The following morning, Tuesday, we return to Hawkesbury Racecourse where I stand beside Pierre to watch Mountain Boy have his final gallop before his first race this coming Thursday. He looks to have worked well within himself, going to the line strongly in his gallop. Timmy Smith soon returns to us aboard Mountain Boy, whom we have nicknamed, The Boy.

"I kept a good hold of him, Pierre," Timmy says. "I hope not too many onlookers noticed how easy he was going. I thought it best to save his energy for the race. This horse has untapped talent, I know, because I used only a quarter of it this morning and he still felt like a champion. His top speed should leave 'em standing on Thursday. I'd like to ride him for you, Pierre." Timmy grins wide as the sky and slaps the horse's neck affectionately.

"*Mais certainement*, Tim!" Pierre asserts. "There are not too many jockeys I would trust with this horse and, of course, I am honoured for you to ride him. Besides, I can see you have a special *rapport* with The Boy," Pierre says as he strokes the horse's nose.

**

How exciting it is to be finally at the races and to be dressed in my new champagne-coloured silk frock, topped with an extravagant hat to match, and be surrounded by women who seem to have the exact same idea as me – to be the most glamorous lady at the races. I'm pleased to say the English tradition of dressing up when attending horseraces appears to have worked its way into the fabric of life here in the colonies.

It is a bright, early summer day with a soft south-easterly breeze cooling the air to a low seventy degrees, I guess. The Blue Mountains surround the racetrack on the western side, presenting a distant but lovely backdrop. The racetrack looks to be in excellent condition. All amenities are satisfactory, as are the food and beverages. Yes, I'm thinking this race club has potential. Although it is quite a way from Sydney Town, it does possess a certain country charm and is sure to attract many city racegoers. In fact, the whole area has a steady stream of new settlers arriving by the boatload.

Butterflies begin a dance in my stomach when I see The Boy prancing alongside Pierre as he leads him into the mounting enclosure. I am left alone to speak with our jockey, Timmy Smith.

"I'm assuming you have a plan on how you will ride him, Timmy? From the front or the back?" I suddenly realise my *double entendre* and laugh a little too boisterously for a lady. Heads turn, and I cough delicately behind a gloved hand. "I mean, do you think The Boy will want to lead, or do you think he will relax behind the field at first?"

I ask as I regain my composure.

Timmy frowns. "I'm not sure, Miss Brown, but I can tell you one thing – I'll have him where he's happy, whether he comes from the back or the front!"

Once again, I find it hard to contain my laughter. At such times, an oversized fan proves to be most useful. The riders are called to mount and Pierre and I leave The Boy in Timmy's capable hands.

The six-furlong race is to start on the south-west side of the course, parallel to where Pierre and I stand on the north-east side, near the winning post. This means when the sun begins its decline in the west, it will bathe all attendees in its excessively warm glow. Why, I wonder, didn't the designers build the grandstand the other way around, leaving the crowd cooling in the shadows of the afternoon and not in the blinding light and heat of the afternoon sun? Oh well, it can't be helped now I concede as I unfurl my parasol.

The race stewards holding the starting string call the jockeys to the fray. "Take control of your horses, boys. Line up – line up, steady now!" The horses snort and prance, nostrils wide and ears flicking. I can feel my heart pounding in my chest, and I hold my breath.

A moment later the string pullers allow the field to race away! They're off in a good line! Dashing to the front is our beloved Mountain Boy. Sitting second comes – daylight! Not the name of a horse, it's just that The Boy is so far in front I can see only daylight between him and the next horse, which is some five lengths behind. *Clever analogy I think Henry.*

Mountain Boy rounds the first bend, clinging to the fence as he's been trained to do. He strides effortlessly over the ground, revelling in his speed and strength. And now as the field is approaching the home turn, Mountain Boy lengthens his lead even though Timmy still has a good hold of him. Into the home straight, Timmy releases his hold and gives The Boy an encouraging swipe with the whip. Oh, no! Mountain Boy has never been hit with the whip and reacts to this affront by swerving out and running off the track! Timmy stands in the stirrups, struggling to steer his recalcitrant mount back towards the fence while the others are catching him, catching him, catching him! But NO! The Boy is far too good. He crosses the line and manages to win by two lengths, albeit on the outside fence. I suddenly realise I am jumping up and down on the spot, screaming like a girl! Pierre grabs me by the shoulders and plants a smacking kiss on my lips, which helps curb my senses. I must say, the excitement of the win has overwhelmed my emotions. Hardly unusual for me, I must confess.

Timmy triumphantly trots our horse to the winner's circle where Pierre stands, full of pride. He graciously congratulates Timmy on his ride before embracing Mountain Boy. I see tears of joy in Pierre's eyes; it confirms that Pierre is a man of deep feelings. Thankfully, he is not like me, with everything on exuberant display. He is so stoic and strong.

We collect our winnings and lead The Boy back to his stable situated on the opposite side of the track, where the grandstand should be. Once there, we pay Timmy Smith for his care of The Boy and his winning ride. Timmy accepts the generous handout with one of his most delightful smiles. His eyes disappear into thin dark lines, his yellow teeth flash big as a horse's, and his prominent ears seem to wiggle.

"I really appreciate your faith in me, Pierre," Timmy says humbly. Turning to me he adds, "And you too, Miss Brown." He lowers his gaze momentarily then looks me in the eye. I'm almost certain I know what he is about to ask. "I was wondering if you would do me the honor of accompanying me out to dinner one evening, Miss Brown?"

I use my fan to hide my embarrassment and my five o'clock stubble. I flutter distractedly as I try desperately to think up an appropriate excuse. Pierre, damn him, is enjoying my discomfiture.

"I would love to, Timmy, but I'm afraid I'm engaged to someone else. He – he's coming here from England. He – he should be here next month. I do hope you understand?" I say, my voice quivering with regret at having to tell yet more lies.

"Yes, of course I understand, Miss Brown. Well, perhaps we three could go out tonight and celebrate our win?" he asks.

Pierre nods in agreement with Timmy's proposal and with a cheeky grin, leaves to feed Mountain Boy.

"What a splendid idea, Timmy," I concur, "and this evening will be just the start of many celebrations, wouldn't you say?"

"I would definitely say so, Miss Brown!" Timmy grins at me, his eyes full of puppy-like adoration.

It is settled; we will dine at the Macquarie Arms Hotel in Windsor, just a short buggy trip from the track.

CHAPTER 29
THE DUKE

Since Roberto learned of the Duke's plan for him to potentially become the Duke's son-in-law, Roberto has catered tirelessly to the Duke's every need, even greater attention to detail than before.

"No need to fuss like an old hen, Roberto. I'm not about to change my mind or my plans. Relax man, I'm quite capable of mounting a railway carriage step! Why, I am still able to mount a sixteen-hand stallion without help. For God's sake man, unhand me!" The Dukes says testily as he extracts himself from Roberto's grip. Roberto does as he is ordered and steps aside, allowing the Duke to enter the first-class cabin on the Blue Mountain Steam Train express – unassisted. Once settled, the Duke barks an order to the cabin steward. "Your finest Scotch whisky and a large Cuban cigar!"

His every wish is the Chief Steward's command; never before had the New South Wales railways carried a Duke. The first-class carriage has been reserved for the sole use of the Duke; such is the honour the Railways of New South Wales feels obliged to bestow.

"I say, Roberto, this should be a bit of fun, hey what? Who would have ever guessed I would be travelling on a steam train to the Blue Mountains in Australia?" asks the Duke, having regained his good humour.

"No, Sir. I, for one, would never have guessed it. And more to the point, I would never have dreamed I would be the lucky servant to accompany you." Roberto smiles in a self-satisfied way.

The Duke chuckles as the train chugs away from the station, and they settle back against the soft leather upholstery of their seats, glad to be on their way to search out the Reverend Timms and the elusive Henry. The whisky finally takes its toll and the Duke duly nods off to sleep, snoring gently. This gives Roberto time to think exactly what he will do about Henry – if they find him.

This is a once in a lifetime chance. How can I allow Henry, whom I'm quite sure is happy with his lot here, to return to take over the family fortune? I know I don't have it in me, but somehow, I will find a person who, for a large sum, is willing to do away with Henry, or perhaps kidnap and keep him until the three years has passed. No, I will not miss this rare opportunity. I must do it.

"Sir, Sir," Roberto ceases his reverie and gently taps the Duke's knee, "we have arrived in Blackheath, my lord."

"What? What?" the Duke sits up, rubbing his face. "Oh, yes. Good show, Roberto. Gather my things, there's a good chap." He steps down from the carriage and looks with interest at the scene before him. The one and only commercial horse and carriage, owned and driven by local man Marcus Manning, is there waiting to be of service to the Duke. Marcus is a master builder of fine carriages, and supplies the odd coach run for the right price. Word was given to the Mayor that the Duke will be arriving in Blackheath on this day at 2pm, and not wanting to overwhelm him with a crowd, the well-informed and sensible mayor has hired Marcus to be on call for the Duke.

"If you would allow me, my lord, I am at your service." Marcus says, respectfully bowing his head and holding open the carriage door. The coach impresses the Duke, and he takes time to closely inspect the craftsmanship before entering. He admires the golden scrollwork running artfully across the high gloss black paint of the carriage. Inside, the seats are upholstered in plush burgundy velvet, studded with buttons covered in the same fabric. He tests the cushioning with his hand and is surprised to feel the resilient spring of the seat.

"I say, do you know who built this carriage? What is your name?"

"I do apologise, m' lord. My name is Marcus Manning. I built this carriage and many more like it, all of which I have sold," Marcus tells him.

"Well, I must say, you have done an excellent job, Mr Manning. If I were to remain in Australia, or even decide to visit more regularly, I would employ you to build the same for me."

"I would be honoured, Sir," Marcus says with another bow. "I must apologise to you again, Sir. Exciting news has a way of getting around a small country town. I believe the Reverend Timms wishes to see you first, m' lord? The Reverend would have been here to greet you personally, however, he is giving the last rites to an elderly lady who has been a faithful parishioner since the Reverend held his first sermon." Marcus removes his hat and holds it over his heart. "I hope you understand, m' lord?"

"Yes, Mr Manning. I have no doubt about the Reverend Timms's faith, or his compassion."

"In that case, Sir, I will take you directly to the Reverend Timms's home. I know that Mrs Timms, with help from the ladies of the church committee, is preparing afternoon tea for Sir." With that, the Duke and Roberto climb the carriage steps and settle into the plush seating.

After hearing the carriage approach, Charlotte Timms and five ladies of the church committee line up outside the vicarage. They stand to attention in their Sunday best dresses and broad smiles to match. Charlotte's garden abounds with glorious colour, and the white picket fence perfectly frames the spectacular display. The scene impresses the Duke.

"My dear Mrs Timms," he says, bowing slightly and shaking her extended hand. "Firstly, I must say how wonderful your garden looks before I give my apologies for arriving here – unofficially announced. However, it appears the carrier pigeons have done their job and my visit is not the surprise I had planned." He smiles benevolently at the little group of women who are plainly awestruck by such a regal personage. When Duke kisses Charlotte's hand, her cheeks turn the same scarlet as her beautiful roses. She giggles before introducing the Duke to her associates.

Roberto remains outside with Marcus as the Duke is escorted into the delightful cottage by all six ladies, each pressing to be close to his eminent presence. They jam briefly in the doorway as it fails to cope with the rush. Once inside, the Duke spies a modest rosewood table covered with delectable delights – chicken sandwiches, tiny meat pies, cupcakes, lemon meringue pie, and apple pie.

"A feast fit for a king!" he declares, his gaze transfixed by the inviting cuisine. "And, I'm sure, for his subjects, too." He turns to the simpering group. "Ladies, would you mind if my manservant, Roberto, and Mr Manning, the coach driver, were to join us to indulge in such fine fair?"

"We would be most pleased, my lord," Charlotte says with a curtsy.

They exchange many pleasantries over several cups of tea and savour the home-baked goodies until the Reverend Timms arrives, appearing somewhat distracted and saddened by the passing of his most faithful parishioner. The ladies know it is time to clear the table and leave the room, but not before Charlotte pours Timms his tea exactly the way he likes it and presents him with a plate full of treats. Roberto also realises it is time to take his leave with Mr Manning, and they continue their discussion outside. The Duke and Timms are left alone.

"I am sorry I need to talk so seriously at such a sad time, Timms. I do give you my sympathies, although from what I hear, the lady had had a damn good innings and she had lived an exemplary life. I would imagine she'd be on her way to Heaven as we speak. Cheer up, old man. We all have to go sometime," The Duke reminds the Reverend, patting him on the back.

"Yes, quite right, Duke, silly of me really. I for one should be celebrating her life and not feeling quite so sorrowful. It's just that some people touch you deeply and Maude was one of those. She never thought of herself, only others. She was our model of charity and good will. It is difficult to be happy when people like Maude leave us, even for Heaven." He takes a sip of tea and sighs, "Selfish, I suppose."

"Yes, quite right, man. And now I would like to get on with the business for which I have come such a long way. Do you think Rosie's cousin, Etta, could possibly be my bro… I mean Henry?"

Timms nearly dropped his cup of tea in shock and took a moment to calm himself before answering. "My lord, I have no idea! To me, Miss Etta seems quite genuine, albeit a little unwell at times. I have not seen much of her since she arrived with Rosie. It seems she is plagued with debilitating headaches and spends a lot of time in her bedroom. There has been so much happening in my parish, I haven't really had the time to investigate Henry's whereabouts. However, I cannot imagine Henry dressing as a woman, even with my knowledge of his particular interest in the same sex."

"Perhaps you are a man of *little* imagination, Timms?" the Duke asks mildly.

"No doubt, Sir. I cannot deny your claim. However, I would be most surprised if Etta turned out to be Henry in disguise," Timms says mulishly. "I can only tell you that Etta and Pierre have taken the first colt by Satan out of Cheval D'Azure to race at Windsor, and from there they intend to travel to Goulburn where they have further business to attend to. And then enter the colt, Mountain Boy, in another suitable race there."

Timms's small speech leaves the Duke nodding thoughtfully. "It would appear then that Pierre has done well. With the stallion and mare, I mean. Would you care to fill me in a little more, Timms? I'd appreciate anything you can tell me. It may help with Henry's whereabouts. After all, it is coming up three years since he's vanished, and we all know what will happen in the end. Henry will be known as the *late* Henry Harrowfeild."

The Duke gives Reverend Timms a steadying look, urging him to concentrate. Timms thinks back on the events, trying hard to remember every detail from his arrival up to receiving Rosie's letter in which she claimed to be in Sydney with her cousin Etta. Was her request to visit him, along with Pierre and Sarah, a little strange, given that Rosie and her cousin went straight to Pierre and Sarah's home first? He tells the Duke how things have unfolded thus far. "As to what has happened, my lord, this is as far as I can recall."

"I thank you, Timms, for your information and your hospitality. Now I must ask Mr Manning if he would drive us to see Sarah. Perhaps she will accommodate us overnight. If not, then we shall return to Blackheath where, no doubt, you will have made a tentative reservation for rooms for Roberto and my good self?" The Duke proffers his hand to Timms, who shakes it solemnly.

"I would be honoured to do so, Sir. I'm sure you will find Sarah most pleased to see you and to show off to you her darling baby, Sascha." Timms's eyes light up like a beacon at the mention of his granddaughter's name. "I must tell you, my lord, she is the prettiest baby I have ever seen, even more so than her mother."

He chuckles and misses the Duke saying under his breath, "I certainly hope so." More audibly he adds, "This is splendid news, Timms!" and smacks him heartily on the back. "I knew my decision to send you to the colonies was the right thing to do. So, there you have it, man. Pierre and Sarah have a baby! Well, well, what do you know?" The Duke's smile abruptly disappears. "But why, I ask you, has Pierre taken Rosie's cousin Etta with him around the countryside? It seems a bit odd. Unless, as I say, Etta may be Henry in costume?" he proposes, furrowing his bushy brows.

"I'm sure I can answer your question satisfactorily, Sir," Timms says with confidence. "You see, Miss Etta has completed a fine painting

133

of Satan, the stallion you gave Pierre. Etta went to Sydney with Pierre to place the painting in the Sydney Art Competition. Then they were to travel to Goulburn where Etta is to arrange the sale of a property belonging to Mr March…"

"Who's Mr March?" The Duke asks, butting in and a little bewildered and only vaguely registering the fact of Etta being an artist.

"Well, let me explain," Timms says, and proceeds to relay the entire complicated story, complete with such animated descriptions it's like a game of charades. At the conclusion, the Duke falls into contemplation once more and silence reigns for a long moment. Finally, the Duke tells him, "Well, I think it best I take my leave now, Timms, before any more problems arise. And no doubt I will meet Mr March. Teddy, you said his Christian name was?"

"Yes, Sir, Teddy March."

Mmm, the name rings a bell. The Duke rises from his armchair and shakes his head in an effort to clear the many thoughts circulating within. Unobserved, Timms takes the opportunity to have a closer look at the Duke.

The Duke certainly has lost weight and seems to be quite enjoying his role as detective. He looks quite a few years younger than when I last saw him. Perhaps getting out and about is agreeing with him? Or maybe it is simply being away from that shrew of a wife. Forgive me, Lord, but she would test even Job's patience! I think he is on a wild goose chase with finding Henry. I do hope he concludes that poor Henry is, in fact, deceased and Etta is simply accompanying Pierre for her own purposes and business and, of course, to place her painting in the competition.

It is only when the Duke has settled himself in the carriage for the next leg of his journey that it suddenly dawns on him. *A painting of Satan, did he say? Ah ha! Another clue pointing to Etta being Henry!* He congratulates himself, smiles fondly at Roberto, and calls to Marcus, "To 'Mountain View', Manning!" He settles in to enjoy the trip.

Half an hour later he stands on the veranda of the property he'd funded. Wiping her hands on her apron, Rosie opens the front door and gasps at the figure standing before her. "Oh! Duke Harrowfield! What a most unexpected – I mean, a pleasant surprise!" Rosie exclaims, suppressing an involuntary shudder of nerves.

"Rosie, my dear woman, I must say you look positively radiant. It appears the mountain air has done you good," the Duke says, taking

Rosie's plump and still-damp hand and raising it to his lips.

"My lord, I cannot explain how happy I am. Please, come inside and sit down." She ushers him into the living room and seats the Duke in the best armchair. Rosie turns to Ernie who has followed Rosie to see what all the fuss is about. "Duke Harrowfeild, I would like to introduce to you our dear friend, Ernest, or Ernie, Lamb. Ernie, this is the Duke of Harrowfeild." The Duke takes note of Ernie's massive frame in its police uniform.

Ernie isn't quite sure how to greet the Duke. He's never had such an honour before. He bows his head before proffering his massive hand.

"Pleased to meet you, Duke… I mean, your Lordship. I've heard plenty about you, Sir."

The Duke accepts Ernie's hand and raises his eyebrows. "All good I hope, Constable?"

"Yes, Sir. Indeed, Sir, extremely good. But if I may correct you, Duke Harrowfeild, it's actually Detective. I was promoted – today, in fact," Ernie says proudly, his enormous chest puffing out like a rooster. "I'll be wearing a different uniform as from tomorrow, Sir."

The Duke notices the pleasure and pride Rosie shows in relation to this information as she adds with enthusiasm, "Yes, m' lord. Ernie here – I mean, Detective Lamb, has just dropped in to give us the good news of his promotion." As a pink flush appears on Rosie's cheeks, she lowers her head to hide it. "I shall go and fetch Sarah now, m' lord. She should be finished feeding baby Sascha by now, and what a bonny wee thing she is. This is all so exciting. Who would have ever imagined you being here, Sir, and our Mr Lamb being promoted, all in the same day? Although he did deserve it after…," Rosie stops abruptly, drops a quick curtsy and hurries off to tell Sarah of the Duke's arrival.

The Duke turns his attention to Ernie sitting opposite. "Now, Ernie, if I may call you that?" Ernie nods his approval. "Would you have any idea what Rosie was about to say? Your promotion must have been due to an outstanding accomplishment. You must tell me about it – it sounds fascinating," he says, thinking that he himself was quite like a Detective in his endeavours to find Henry. Ernie is more than pleased to tell the Duke about how he went about overturning the charges for a man who'd been wrongly accused of murder. He does not let on that it is James, whom the Duke will surely meet in time but, thank Heaven, not today. James happens to be in Sydney where a magistrate is clearing his record of all criminal charges. By the time Ernie has told his story, Sarah enters with baby Sascha in her arms.

"Dear Sarah, how delightful to see you again! And, may I say, what a beautiful baby!" The Duke stands and leans over to study the baby's features, noting the gurgling baby bears no real resemblance to either Sarah or Pierre. "You must be very pleased, Sarah."

Sarah smiles and hands the four-month-old baby to Melanie, who is hovering at her elbow and who is now an indispensable part of the family at "Mountain View". With her hands free, Sarah writes a note for the Duke, welcoming him to their home and expressing her pleasure at seeing him. *As my hand is shaking with excitement,* Sarah adds, *I will ask Rosie to introduce you to Melanie, our new housemaid, and Mr March, whom we now care for after having had an unfortunate accident.* She smiles sweetly, handing the note to the Duke, but not before Rosie has a quick peek. Rosie introduces a blushing, wide-eyed Melanie, then a vacant Teddy who, with his head lowered coddles the Duke's outstretched hand. The Duke gives Teddy a strong look of disapproval. However, Teddy continues to wear the same bland expression regardless of what's happening around him. Even if the house was burning down, Rosie is sure Teddy would simply stand still, staring into space, blissfully unaware of it all. She knows Teddy is their responsibility, but sometimes she wishes she had enough courage to give him another hard whack on the head, just to see if it will bring him back to reality. One day, Rosie thinks to herself, she just might give it a go. He is no problem today though, and they watch a little relieved as Teddy walks slowly towards his room. Sometimes he chooses to remain there for days at a time. The Duke scratches his chin in thought.

It can't be the same Edward March I am familiar with, can it?

Then with a hurried mixture of notes, sign language, lip reading and Rosie interpreting for both Sarah and the Duke, they engage in a long conversation, catching up with the news from England and being introduced to Roberto, the Duke's new personal butler.

"Poor Georgie passed away," the Duke tells them with a tremor in his voice and a tear in his eye. "But young Roberto here is a splendid chap. And he's doing an excellent job," he adds warmly. Roberto says nothing but tries hard to look modest. Finally, it is decided that all three – the Duke, Roberto and Marcus – will stay overnight, and Rosie hurries off to prepare the Duke's room. Marcus and Roberto will sleep in the small cottage attached to the barn.

The following morning after a hearty breakfast, Sarah and Rosie escort the Duke around the property. He shows particular interest in the horses, most of which Pierre has bred, apart from the few he's purchased. Rosie explains Pierre's plan to breed the best racehorse possible.

"Pierre has now had two breeding seasons completely booked out for Satan," she says proudly. "And now with Mountain Boy being the first of his progeny to race and win, it will surely place him as first choice for the thoroughbred breeders in New South Wales, if not the whole of Australia. If Satan can produce winners, then breeders are sure to send their mares to him, no matter how many miles lie between them," Rosie proclaims like a sideshow spruiker.

"A very impressive delivery, Rosie. It seems you too have been charmed by the dream of a successful stud. I mean a horse stud!" He smiles at her discomfort with his innuendo. He has noticed, with some amusement, the affectionate looks Rosie and Ernie exchange, and is sure he heard some stifled giggles coming from the kitchen earlier that morning. One would have to be blind not to see their blossoming romance.

Meanwhile, Roberto is still doing his own investigative work with Marcus.

"The Blue Mountains, so they say, are renowned for hiding criminals. The caves and hidden gullies are almost impenetrable, giving safe harbour to bushrangers and the like. Is this true, Marcus?"

"Yes, we do have our fair share of outlaws. Most of them are caught eventually though," Marcus says with a shrug.

"Have you had any dealings with these criminals, Marcus? Do you know in what area they choose to hide?" Roberto tries to keep his tone light and conversational.

"Yes, I do, but I keep well enough away. Though my mate, Andy, says they aint so bad, well, most of them aint. They're just blokes who've been in the wrong place at the wrong time. A few are escaped convicts who hate being flogged or locked up in some stinking prison for something they didn't do. Me mate Andy has run into a few of them and says he supplies them with a bit of food and grog. They've formed a gang and they must rob coaches or steal things to keep alive. Some of them get caught. But they never dob in their mates, no matter what the troopers do to them. You know, honour among thieves," Marcus finishes with a smile.

"I'd be interested in meeting this group of men. You see, my father was wrongly accused of a serious crime back in England and he rotted in jail for it. I have great sympathy for these men. I, too, would like to help them. Is this possible do you think, Marcus?" Roberto's lies slip easily off his tongue. He thinks it will be a clever way to meet the band of thieves. Perhaps there is an assassin among them who would be happy to be paid for his skills.

The Duke has enjoyed his guided tour and is appreciative of Sarah's hospitality and her warm welcome, but he is waiting for an opportunity to talk privately to Rosie. He finds himself alone at last with her as she brings in some tea and cake. He knows he can no longer summon her to him as he would have done at Harrowfeild; he is not the Lord of the Manor here. It is with some surprise he realises he quite likes this more egalitarian approach.

"So, Rosie," he begins without preamble, "you must know I am here to find Henry." Rosie's expression gives nothing away and she continues to pour the tea. The Duke presses on. "I have heard rumours that Henry may have escaped the ship in Italy, dressed as a female." He looks searchingly at Rosie; whose face betrays no flicker of emotion as she offers him some cake. He is frustrated by her composure but keeps his voice mild and his manner calm. "I would appreciate the truth, Rosie, as it is coming up three years since Henry's disappearance and I'm sure you know what that means?"

Rosie takes a deep breath and her eyes glisten with unshed tears. "M' lord, with all due respect, you don't know how tortured my poor Henry's life has been living in that castle, being raised without any love from the woman he thought to be his mother. Not to mention being considered a criminal simply because of his sexual urges." She blinks away some tears before she mutters an afterthought. "Mind you, I think half the English aristocracy is that way inclined."

"This is where you are wrong, Rosie. Not about the aristocracy, but about me. I *do* know about Henry and what he has had to endure," the Duke says with a bushy eyebrow raised, "and I do feel for him. But can you blame me for trying to head him in the right direction? Meaning, to have him married and produce heirs to carry on the name of Harrowfeild? For Heaven's sake, woman, what do you think will happen to the family name and fortune if Henry is not there to carry on and produce an heir?

My wife is a self-absorbed narcissist, to put it kindly. My daughter, well, she will eventually become her mother's double, unless I can find a good man who is willing to be her husband and follow my wishes to the end. Do you understand me a little better, Rosie?" He reaches across to take Rosie's hand in his. "Please understand, Rosie, I have woken up and I now know where my heart lies. I need to see Henry, in a frock or not. I have forgiven him, and I need him to come home."

Rosie sniffles and dries her eyes with the corner of her apron. "The rumour you heard about Henry dressed as a woman is true, Sir. Before he left England, I booked Henry's passage for him from Italy all the way to Australia. Henry, I assure you, was unaware I would be waiting for him on the ship in Italy. I can't tell you how happy he was when he saw me in his cabin. And then, when I told him the truth about me being his natural grandmother and all, it was like a heavy weight had been lifted from his heart. I showed him the picture of your father the Duke and my darling Emily. He saw his resemblance to her at once. He was most pleased about it, I can tell you," Rosie says, nodding her head emphatically.

She tells the Duke the entire story, from when she and Henry arrived in Australia, up until the most recent events, that being when Henry and Pierre waved goodbye on their way around New South Wales.

"So, there you have it, m' lord. I'm sure they will be in Sydney Town by now. The winner of the Art Competition is to be announced tomorrow evening, after the Grand Banquet at the Town Hall. And then the next day, Pierre and Etta – we call Henry – will take Mountain Boy and travel slowly to Goulburn. If you leave by train this afternoon, you will surely catch them."

"Thank you, Rosie," the Duke said sincerely. "We'll leave straightaway. Please give my heartfelt thanks to Sarah and tell her I'm sure to see her again soon. And look after that policeman, or should I say Detective, of yours," he adds with a wink.

Without further ado, the Duke summons Roberto, who is not at all pleased about having to dash back to Sydney. His own plans must now be put on hold. However, he consoles himself with the thought that there are sure to be scoundrels in Sydney willing to take a risk for a large amount of money.

CHAPTER 30
HENRY

"How do I look, Pierre?" I ask, twirling around in my red silk evening gown. A fashionably high lace collar contours down to the dense silk bodice, which allows my false breasts ample coverage.

"Stunning, Henry, I mean Etta, *ma belle*. I think you look far more attractive as a woman than as a man. Come here and give me a kiss." Pierre grabs me by the waist and holds me close. Our eyes lock in a moment of unquenchable love. "Never will I stop loving you, *cheri*. I don't care what happens to me, I don't care if they lock me up, hang me, or starve me to death. I vow, I will love you always!" he declares passionately.

"Please don't make me cry, Pierre. My eyes will smudge. I love you too, my darling, and will do so until the day I die. And then who knows? We may meet again in Heaven."

"If God takes our type in Heaven," Pierre murmurs into my neck.

**

The Sydney Town Hall is decked out splendidly. White linen table cloths give contrast to the silver cutlery and fine crystal glasses which shine in the candlelight, vases of red roses sit as centrepieces. On every wall hang the paintings entered in what is considered to be the most prestigious art prize in Australia – providing you don't ask the Melbournians. They tend to lay claim to be the home of all things cultured and prestigious.

Pierre taps my shoulder. "Look, Hen – I mean Etta – Theobald's painting is next to yours, and they are nearest the stage. Do you think it means anything?"

"Yes, of course, Pierre. It means they are next to each other – and nearest the stage!" I say curtly before I apologise. "I'm sorry, Pierre, my nerves are frayed. I really have no idea."

A waiter glides by with a tray laden with tall flutes of champagne and small glasses of sherry. I choose the champagne, swill it down, and grab another.

"Etta, that's not very ladylike," Pierre whispers.

"I don't care," I whisper back. I feel another tap on my shoulder and I turn quickly with nervous anticipation, spilling my drink over Theobald Tootle.

"I am dreadfully sorry, Theobald," I say as I brush the bubbles from his lapel.

"No, please, Etta, I'm sorry. I didn't mean to startle you. I say, you do look beautiful this evening. I can't imagine how Sarah can trust her husband to escort such a beauty this evening. Not to mention travelling around the country with him."

I feel like punching his winking eye, but I compose myself. "You are a naughty man, Theobald! Fancy thinking such a thing. We both have business to attend to, and we're helping each other in the process. I'm sure you realise Sarah, and baby Sascha being so young, could not possibly accompany Pierre though I don't know why I feel the need to explain the matter to you. Good luck this evening, Theobald. I'm sure you have produced the winner."

I turn away with my nose in the air and I take several paces. I hear Pierre apologise for my behaviour before I feel his taut body against my side, guiding me to our table, his strong hand in the small of my back. Thank Heavens Theobald is not seated with us.

To say I am nervous is a gross underestimation. Competitions unsettle my normally outgoing nature. When I was much younger, I was sure I had a delightful singing voice and so I entered a local competition at the village fair. Much to my horror when my turn came to stand on the stage, I was struck dumb by nerves. I was unable to sing a single note – I opened my mouth but not a sound came out. It was so humiliating, and I swore I'd never enter another competition of any sort. And yet here I am waiting for my painting to be either ignored or awarded a prize by someone who probably doesn't have the faintest idea what good art is. *Shut up, Henry, just have another drink!* I tell myself. So, I do, I have several, in fact.

Ah, this is much better. I relax and giggle at everything and everyone. Dinner is served. I can only say it was acceptable, but as the courses come and go, I am so preoccupied that I eat without tasting. Once the tables are finally cleared, the band strikes up, and Pierre takes the opportunity to dance with me in public for the first time – oh, how we danced! For hours it seems, with Pierre's strong arms holding me tightly as we waltz around the floor, I am lost in the moment and forget my cares. My elation subsides, and my nerves return when the music stops, and the President of the 'Sydney Art' Committee makes an announcement.

"Ladies and gentlemen, may I have your attention! The Committee of 'Sydney Art,' has only just this minute been made aware of the presence of an eminent guest. We are honoured to have here with us this evening a peer of the realm who will do us the honour of presenting the winning artist with his – or her – trophy and a bank cheque for fifty pounds."

"My goodness, who on earth could it be, Pierre?" I ask excitedly.

"Shush, Etta!" he whispers. I scowl and smack him on the hand with my fan.

The President continues, "Ladies and gentlemen, it is with great pleasure I introduce to you –" here he pauses for dramatic effect, "– the Duke of Harrowfeild!"

The crowd cheers and I faint. Someone thrusts smelling salts under my nose, and Pierre very gently slaps my cheek. When I sufficiently regain consciousness, I can see the Duke on stage, scanning the room, obviously looking for his son, or perhaps the woman he thought to be his son – ME! When the applause dies down, the Duke is handed a card that bears the name of the winning artist. He opens it with care and studies it for what seems an eternity before he speaks.

"The Committee of the Sydney Art Show Competition has obviously had trouble deciding which painting deserves to be the outright winner. I see two names here." The Duke shows the card to the President, who says something then nods to the Duke. "Well, this is unusual. I'm afraid the prize must be split. The artists who have shared first prize are – Miss Etta Brown for 'Satan' and Mr Theobald Tootle for 'Mare and Foal'."

As the applause erupts, I find I cannot move. What am I to do? Pierre holds me tightly and whispers, "Please, Etta, you must go through with this. Just smile and accept the prize. The Duke will never know. *Please, Etta! Walk to the stage!*"

Theobald comes to my rescue and escorts me – well, almost carries me to the stage, helps me up the steps, then supports my swaying body so I do not fall. One look into my brother's eyes is all it takes, and

I break down and weep. The Duke reaches his hand to me then suddenly grabs at his heart before dropping to his knees. All hell breaks loose, and he is immediately rushed to the Sydney Hospital with a suspected heart attack.

I turn to find Pierre at my side. He thinks it best we leave and go straight to the hospital to see the Duke, but I am in a dither at what to do and I insist we first return to our hotel. It is obvious the Duke has made the pilgrimage to seek me out. Just how far he's gone and what he's found out we do not know. However, the fact he's shown up at the last moment at the prize presentation leads us to believe he has been well advised as to where he could find me. He must know, or at least suspect, I am who I am: Henry, and not Etta Brown. What are his intentions? Can I trust him to keep my secret and not let the law know what I have done and who I am? I have never been able to trust him entirely; everything is just a game to my brother. Why did he even bother to call me his son my entire life instead of telling me the truth? What does he hope to gain from me? Why does he not simply accept that I am lost to the world, and leave his fortune to his daughter? It is all a mystery to me.

"Oh, dear Pierre, I don't know what to do. I really don't know!" I tell him tearfully.

"I think we should visit the Duke anyway, Henry. He may have a perfectly good reason for seeking you out – it may not be what you suspect. Please, give him the benefit of the doubt, *cheri*. And after all, it may be the last time you see him. If he's had a minor heart attack, there may be more to come. Please, *cheri*. And I think you should dress as Henry, not Etta, when you see him. Maybe the shock of seeing you in a frock brought this on."

"What would I do without you, Pierre? You are so… so *normal*. And I'm such a fool. I follow only my heart. My head seems to take a back seat in everything I do. I love you so much and yes, you are right. I should go and see my brother, especially since he has travelled such a long way to find me. And if I think about it, the three years are almost up. It's time to make important decisions, Pierre. Will you please come with me to the hospital?"

"You'd better borrow one of my suits, Henry." Pierre goes to the wardrobe and begins to organise clothes for me.

"Oh, Pierre," I wail, "Not *that tie, please!*"

CHAPTER 31
THE DUKE

The Duke lies awake in his hospital bed, feeling bewildered.

"Did you see her – I mean, him – Roberto?" The Duke asks feebly, a pleading look in his eyes.

"I did, m' lord. Is it any wonder you had a heart attack? The shock of seeing your son in a frock, especially on a public stage accepting first prize in an art competition. Scandalous, m' lord!' Roberto is enjoying the opportunity to display some moral outrage.

"Shut up, Roberto, it wasn't all that bad. I thought Henry looked most attractive. He seems to have fooled everyone with his charade." The Duke laughs weakly. "If my heart hadn't given way, I would have been proud to kiss his hand. I can see the humorous side of the entire episode." He gasps a little for breath and coughs. "I say, I'm rather tired now, Roberto, so best you let me sleep."

"Certainly, m' lord. I will be here for you when you wake. I will not leave your side." Roberto tucks the bedclothes in and moves the chair closer to the bedside.

"No need for that, man. Go back to the hotel and get some sleep yourself." Closing his eyes, the Duke flaps his hand in Roberto's general direction.

"As you wish, m' lord." Roberto wastes no time, using this opportunity to seek out a couple of nefarious characters as he walks the streets of Sydney Town. He has every hope of finding a willing accomplice. It isn't long before he comes across two ragged men loitering in a dark alley, looking like they are ready to pounce on some unsuspecting passerby, perhaps someone very much like Roberto. However, he is looking for them. They shoulder together and block Roberto's path.

"Got any money, mister?" asks the shorter one, sniggering and rubbing his nose along his sleeve.

The taller one adds, "Yeah, sure you got money! Look at ya. All dressed up like a bleedin' toff. Give us y'money, or you'll regret it!" He grabs Roberto's lapel and is a little taken aback to see Roberto smiling.

"Now, gentlemen, there is no need to threaten me. I'm sure I'm able to pay you more money than you pair of ill-mannered louts have ever dreamed of – providing you follow my instructions. I have been looking for two, ah, bright and industrious gentlemen such as yourselves." The compliment goes down well with the pair, and they noticeably straighten their shoulders. "I need help to be rid of someone who is a particular nuisance to me. Do you understand?"

"Yeah, we understand, don't we, Sam?" The taller one, Freddy, looks down at his mate, who nods up at him. Freddy lets go of Roberto's lapel. "How much y' payin', mister, and what do y' want us to do?"

Roberto unfolds his plan while the men listen. The amount of money Roberto is offering would allow the two murdering thieves to realise their dream of buying their own tavern along the road to Parramatta. They have had this plan for quite a while but have never gotten around to stealing sufficient funds because most of what they got went straight down their throats. To this pair, Roberto's offer is too good to refuse.

"You're on, mister. You can trust us, can't he, Sam?" As Freddy looks down, he digs his elbow into Sam's ribs. Sam's smile reveals toothless gums.

"Here, take this money. Go now and have a bath, a shave and a good feed," Roberto says as he shoves a pound note into Freddy's hand. "And buy some new clothes while you're at it. You will return here tomorrow morning at eight o'clock and I will give you the firearm. If you do not show, I will search you out and shoot you myself!" Roberto has no intention of doing any such thing, but he knows he should act tough when dealing with criminals.

"No worries, mister. Eh, what's y' name, *Sir*?" Freddy thinks it wise to show a little more respect.

"My name, my good man, is no concern of yours. You will simply do as I say, and in return you will receive a very generous amount of money. Understood?"

"Yes, Sir! Understood, Sir! We'll do exactly as you say," says Freddy obsequiously as he pockets the pound note. Roberto gives them a curt nod, turns on his heel and walks briskly into the night.

The Duke has nodded off to sleep, dreaming of Henry. He thinks he can see Henry standing beside him, smiling. He is dressed in a rather dapper light grey suit, and a golden bowtie brings out the highlights in his topaz eyes. He is clean shaven and is looking as handsome as ever in a boyish way.

"Henr... Henry..." the Duke's voice trails off weakly.

Henry bends over and kisses his brother on the forehead. "I'm here. I'm right here."

The Duke blinks, trying to focus on what he thinks is an apparition. "Henry – is it really you, Henry?"

"Yes, it is I, *brother*," Henry says before realising another shock may deliver the Duke a final heart attack. He gently takes the Duke's hand, as the Duke softly speaks.

"You know everything, Henry. Rosie told me; you know everything."

"Yes, I do, and I forgive you. I understand why you did what you did. Had your wife been a sweet-natured woman, our life together would have been much better. I just needed to come and tell you in person. You must let me live my own life the way I wish. Will you give me licence to do so, dear brother? I don't want or need the family fortune. Give it to Gertrude."

"No, Henry! I will not!" the Duke states emphatically, placing a hand against his chest. "Please do not upset me. I feel my heart racing again; it may take me out next time. Come back tomorrow after I have rested, and we will talk."

"I promise I will. Now rest, brother, knowing I love you," Henry says before kissing the Duke's forehead twice. The Duke sighs and settles into his pillow, a tired smile on his face.

**

The following morning brings heavy rain and the need for umbrellas as Henry and Pierre walk back to the hospital. Unbeknownst to them, Roberto and his accomplices are following. Hiding behind carts and ducking up alley ways, Roberto and his thugs tail them until they are certain they are following the right men. Once satisfied, Roberto leaves his assassins with instructions to trail the unsuspecting pair for the remainder of the day. Then, when daylight is failing, they are to ascertain the perfect time and location to shoot and run. Their getaway will be made easier under the cover of night.

"Henry!" the Duke calls happily upon seeing Henry and Pierre

146

walk into his private Hospital room. "I'm feeling much better this morning. The doctor has just left after giving me good news. He said I had more of a shock to the heart than an actual heart attack. I didn't tell him, but I think the travelling and rushing around, not to mention seeing you," he drops his voice to a whisper, "*in a frock* was what caused the problem."

The Duke's cheery mood is not shared by Henry. Indignantly, he replies, "I take no blame for your ill health, brother. As I said, I have a right to live my own life. You are not my father and, although I do love you, I am not duty-bound to do as you say."

"Henry, my dear boy, I feel you should think more clearly about what you plan to do with your life here in Australia." The Duke is trying to placate Henry but then decides to change his tack. "I am in a mind to expose you." He can tell by Henry's expression the words have immediately incensed him. "If you do not come home and take up your rightful inheritance, there is no possibility that I will be able to leave this earthly realm and rest in peace knowing that Cecilia will have total control of the family name and fortune. You must marry and sire an heir, Henry. I insist!"

Henry is speechless with rage, his hands unconsciously clenching into fists. Pierre gently enfolds him into his arms and comes to Henry's defence. "M' lord, you cannot possibly expose Henry. Where, pray tell, would that leave you? I'm sure you know it would result in Henry being imprisoned or committed to a mental asylum. Therefore, you would defeat your own purpose of having him return home," Pierre says with some satisfaction.

"You are correct, Pierre! But it would not stop me from revealing *you* as a homosexual!" the Duke counters.

Henry looks levelly at his brother. "I didn't think you would stoop so low. You disappoint me, Sir," he says, his voice barely above a whisper.

"You have left me no choice, Henry. Don't you realise how important it is that you return home? Would it kill you to sire a child, hopefully a boy who would then carry on our family name? It saddens me deeply. We are the last of our line and I have a duty to uphold the family name, Henry, as do you, my brother."

Henry has the good grace to hang his head and think for a few moments about the Duke's proposal. However, Henry can do only what he's knows in his heart and soul is right and proper.

"It seems, Sir, that despite everything you know about the person I am, and despite the fact that you profess to love me, you are still trying to force me to go against my heart. For a second time, you want me to sacrifice my love for Pierre, merely to carry on a name that in the greater scheme of things is of no real consequence. You see, I do not place such importance on names or family trees. I believe we are here on earth to love one another and nurture the wonders God has created. Do as you will, but I will not be returning to England. I have made my home here in Australia."

"It doesn't matter where you live, Henry, you would be living a lie!" the Duke snaps, his hand clawing the bedclothes in agitation.

"Yes, that may be so, but the lie I'm living here makes me happy." Henry gives a sidelong look to Pierre and smiles. "But the lie I would be living at Harrowfield would eventually destroy me. Now, for the final time, brother, there you have it. I pray you live a long and healthy life and leave this earthly realm knowing you did your utmost to carry on the family name." With Pierre by his side, Henry turns to depart, however, before he does he peers steely at his prostrate brother, 'Why don't you sire another child, you may be lucky, it may be a son!

'Unfortunately, Henry, my sperm seems to have given up the chase.'

The Duke, alone once more, stares at the ceiling and ponders his future. He sighs heavily and speaks to the empty room. "I wonder if life really is how Henry sees it? Do we place too much emphasis on the generations to come, rather than focus on our own happiness and satisfaction while we are here on this earth? He could be right… we have so little time in our lives, maybe we should simply enjoy it while we can. And perhaps this is the place to do it, in a new country that is not weighed down by the traditional ways of thinking." With that lingering thought, the Duke drifts into a fitful sleep.

CHAPTER 32
HENRY

Pierre and I stand outside the hospital for a moment, while I try to clear from my mind the thought of returning to England. I look Pierre in the eye and ask, "Do you think the Duke would report me – or you – to the authorities? Do you think he would be so cruel? Pierre, you know he takes delight in deceiving others, and now he knows I won't be returning to England, maybe he won't care if I go to prison, or both of us, for that matter. Oh, Pierre – I don't know what to do," I tell him miserably.

"Let's walk, *mon cheri*. We'll think of something, *sans doute.*"

As the rain clouds dissipate, and the sun shines warmly upon our backs, we venture closer to the harbour. Tugboats chug to and fro, their horns blowing loudly. Sailors sing as they scrub their fishing trawlers, while wool bales are being unloaded onto the wharf. The scene captivates me – I wish I had my easel and paints.

"I have come to love this country, Pierre," I say, sighing. "I cannot possibly return to England. I do love Harrowfeild for itself, but not for the memories it holds. Since I have been in Australia with you, Sarah and Rosie, my life has become a dream come true. I think we should leave for Goulburn right now and cast caution to the wind. Let us see where fate leads us. If anything terrible happens, we will always have our memories to cherish," I tell him, feeling better to have made a decision.

Pierre's smile shows the dimples in his cheeks, and he squeezes my shoulder as we quicken our pace towards the hotel. A brisk southerly breeze feels fresh against my face and the raindrops clinging to the surrounding trees scatter about. My feeling of dread is washed away and in its place is a sense of unfettered freedom. I have at last confronted my brother; I have stated my case, and now it is up to him to do as he wishes. I no longer care.

"Henry," Pierre asks in a low voice, "Do you have a feeling we are being followed?'

"Why no, Pierre. What makes you think so?"

"Maybe I'm imagining it, but I thought I saw two men following us before we went into the hospital. They disappear then reappear every now and then. And now, the same two men have been walking behind us since we left. But when I look back, they stop and turn the other way." He sounds concerned.

"How intriguing! I wonder if we should stop and ask them what they want of us."

"The Duke may have put a tail on us to see where we go. Do you think he would?"

"No doubt. He's not going to give in without a decent fight, I'm sure. We'll have to outsmart them and make a run for Goulburn through the back entrance of the hotel," I tell him decisively.

As we approach the hotel entrance, I make a point of standing still and saying loudly enough so our followers are sure to hear, "I really am quite tired, Pierre. I should take a long nap before we return to the hospital. I do hope the Duke will stay alive until then. I would hate for him to die before I see him once more. So sad." I shake my head, feigning sincere sorrow.

I'm sure they've heard me. I can see the two leaning against a hitching post nearby. How amateurish! As if we'd not realise they were trailing us. Fools!

With haste, I throw our belongings into a valise while Pierre goes downstairs to pay the bill and give the clerk extra money to keep our departure quiet. Pierre gives the clerk instructions to say, if anyone inquires, we have booked for another two days stay. Hopefully, we will get a head start on the two men my brother has hired to follow us. I'll be damned if he is going to outsmart me.

CHAPTER 33
SARAH

I feel a little guilty for not missing Pierre or Henry as perhaps I should. I have not received word from them since the Duke left our company two months ago now. I hope they have been able to reconcile their differences. I am anxious to receive a letter from either one, just to let me know what has transpired. I really wish there to be a satisfactory outcome for all, especially after such a time lapse.

My life at "Mountain View" is happy and full, especially with baby Sascha starting to crawl. At one time she stood all by herself, hanging on to the furniture. I'm sure she will be an early walker, though I think it best she does not walk until she is at least twelve months old. A few days ago, I realised I was pregnant again. I told James the news this morning and he was overwhelmed with joy. Ever since his conviction of murder was dropped, James has become a contented soul. I thank God every day for my blessings.

Rosie adores baby Sascha and when not minding her, or helping me, she appears happy to be Sergeant Lamb's mistress, although that word conjures up a more glamorous image than our stout and dependable Rosie. She confesses to me that Ernie is in the process of divorcing his wife and he has promised to marry her next summer. Why they are waiting until summer, I don't know. Maybe it is because she mentioned taking their honeymoon by the sea. Whatever they choose to do, I could not be happier for her.

Melanie is a gem. I'm sure she is grateful for the lighter workload here compared to keeping house for her parents and caring for twelve younger siblings. She is blossoming into a beautiful young woman. I don't know how long she will stay with us, as she has spoken of one day going to Sydney to find work. I suppose her marital chances are slim here in the sparsely populated mountains. And as I said, she is certainly blossoming and seems to have marriage on her mind. She often asks questions about married life. I am sure she is relieved to know that not all marriages involve the ceaseless toil and poverty her parents are enduring.

Teddy March remains the same, only more physically active. He can thank James who keeps Teddy working about the place on all sorts of chores that Teddy completes with efficiency and pride. However, from time to time, I see him casting looks of frank appreciation at Melanie. I keep a close watch on them. After all, they are both handsome. And no doubt, as young men do, Teddy's manly desire will make its presence felt around Melanie.

Yes, I have my fair share of work and organising to do so that all things flow smoothly within the household and in our massive vegetable garden. Life is very busy! My dear friend Amy Watson joined us for afternoon tea. We discussed my taking up her earlier offer as teacher's assistant. I had been excited at the thought, especially as Rosie and Melanie were quite capable of running the household and caring for Sascha in my absence but having another baby has changed my mind.

CHAPTER 34
HENRY

Afternoon brings more showers. We travel in damp discomfort until we find a coach stop along our first leg to Goulburn. Luckily, Pierre is able to hire stables for the horses and a room for us. As our followers expect to be looking for two men, I decide it would be safer to be dressed as a woman. I choose a travelling frock of beige calico and a brown dust coat. I do not look as glamorous as usual, but the outfit is eminently suitable for the muddy roads.

Upon entering the coach stop, I notice my attire doesn't seem to dampen the innkeeper's admiration.

"Will that be one room or two, Mr Boyar?" he asks Pierre, his eyebrow raised in a suggestive manner towards me.

"One room, thank you, sir. This is my wife, Mrs Boyar," Pierre says with pride.

I blush as I fan my pretty face. Although having been told many times I am beautiful, it seems having Pierre refer to me as his "wife" thrills me more than any compliment possibly could. Pierre shakes his head in fond amusement at my girlishness.

At the risk of our devious shadows catching us, we relax and share a delightful meal of Irish stew that contains a greater ratio of lamb chops to potato, I'm glad to see. If we were in Ireland, it would be the other way around. The hot damper is perfect for soaking up the gravy. With dinner over and the horses attended too, we retire to our room for a good night's sleep in a clean, warm bed.

The early sunrise glows fuchsia, sending an unearthly glow over the quiet landscape.

"Red sky in the morning, a shepherd's warning," I quote as we set out on our way to Goulburn.

"At this slow pace, it should take us about six days to reach there," Pierre calculates. "I hope the weather favours us, Etta, and your prophecy isn't fulfilled," he says, looking worryingly at the sky.

As the sun rises higher, a sleepy breeze stirs but before too long it gathers force. We brace ourselves against a howling gale. Long strips of bark and leafy branches ripped from giant trees hurtle through the air, lashing us and the horses. The fierce wind whips up red dust and confetti of small stones, stinging me with such force I cover my body and face with a horse blanket. Fortunately, the gale soon abates and by sundown, the wind's fury is all but exhausted. Bruised and battered, we pull off the road into a sheltered clearing and make camp for the night.

The following day, the wind picks up again and we trudge on relentlessly through the leafy debris, determined to make up time lost. By the third day, the wind loses its ferocity and Mountain Boy jogs happily along behind, resting when we do and staying physically sound throughout our ordeal. This is a blessing as Pierre plans to race him two weeks after we arrive at Goulburn.

After seven days of some good – and some horrid – weather, plus comfortable coach stops and stables for Mountain Boy, we arrive intact and safe. Goulburn is, surprisingly, a well-established town. Most buildings and premises, I notice, are built of brick and stone, giving the town a feeling of strength and solidity. Firstly, Pierre and I need to find a place for us to stay, and stables for the horses. We ask a few locals for their advice on the best accommodation, also inquiring if they know of an Edward, or Teddy March, the owner of "March's Run". We are surprised to learn Teddy's property is not too far out of town and it would be best to go straight there. This information is conveyed to us by a scruffily dressed man sporting a most unflattering bushy beard that he smooths down with a soiled hand as he speaks. His name, he tells us, is Jackeroo Joe. We, in turn, tell him about Teddy's unfortunate accident and our intention of maybe selling the property on Teddy's behalf.

"The overseer's a good bloke. I'm sure he'd put you and your horses up, specially seein' you're here to give him the news," Joe says, his large hand stroking his beard. He scratches his head. "Y' know, my boss, Barry Night, he's been interested in buyin' that place. Do you want me to tell him y' here to sell it for Mr March?'

"What a good idea, Joe. Tell your boss, if he's still interested in the property, to meet us tomorrow at the Royal Hotel for lunch. As our guest, of course," Pierre says with authority.

We decide to make haste to March's Run and meet with Teddy's overseer, Bill Goads. However, upon our arrival we are overcome with disappointment when we find the place deserted – not a soul in sight. The timber house is open and swarms of flies' crawl over every surface. The home is sparsely furnished. It's neat, but not clean; a thick layer of dust has accumulated throughout. It looks like it hasn't been lived in for some time.

"What do you think, Pierre? Do you think Mr Goads has done a runner?" I ask.

"I don't know, *cheri*. But I do know I'm hungry and thirsty. The horses are too. I'll tend to them while you find us something to eat." Pierre goes outside to tend to the horses while I roll up my sleeves and get to work. I clean, dust and scrounge around looking for anything edible. Thankfully I find ample flour, sugar, tea, some lard and potatoes. I build and light a fire to heat the oven and whip up a damper in a wink and put the kettle on top to boil. I grate the potatoes to make a German potato cake, which I fry in lard until golden brown. I stand to attention when Pierre enters.

"Please sit, my love, I have excelled – I hope." I watch a trifle nervously as he devours my attempt at pleasing him.

"Henry – I mean Etta – this food is delicious, you are a fine wife, my love," Pierre winks at his joke.

I blush once more, thinking of how right it sounds, and with us living and loving together, I should be Pierre's wife, or marital partner at least. I cannot help but feel my bitterness rise when I think that in the real world, our loving relationship is not even tolerated, let alone recognised. However, I am becoming accustomed to quelling the anger, learning to live in the moment to enjoy every blessed minute spent alone with Pierre. My thoughts and feelings are consoled by the fact that we will be sleeping together that same evening. It brushes away my insecurities and fills my loins with desire. Oh, naughty me!

The following morning presents a clear blue sky, but no Pierre. He must have risen early to tend the horses. I rise and put my dustcoat over my white cotton nightie and as I make my way to the front door, I hear voices. I look through the window to see Pierre talking to a stranger at the end of the veranda and, to my delight, alongside him stands Timmy Smith, our jockey-cum-stable boy. Excitement overcomes me as I run and almost tackle Timmy. He grabs his hat while accepting my rough embrace with good humour.

"I didn't think you'd be so pleased to see me, Miss Etta," Timmy says with a chuckle.

"Of course, I am, Timmy! We've missed you. Haven't we, Pierre?"

Pierre nods in agreement and says formally, "And now, Etta, I'd like you to meet Mr Bill Goads, Mr March's overseer." I stand, more than surprised. I really thought he'd done a runner.

"I'm so pleased to meet you, Mr Goads. I've heard only good things about you," I say. Suddenly, I remember I haven't shaved and with no fan for protection, I make a hasty retreat. "You must excuse me; I feel ashamed meeting you in my night dress." I bound off like a young deer, perhaps a gay one, while Pierre laughs.

"Don't mind Etta. She's oversensitive to such things. She likes to look her best for strangers." I am in the bedroom and can hear their conversation clearly through the open front door.

The good news is that Timmy wishes to be Mountain Boy's permanent jockey, so he has tracked us down. Bill Goads explains to Pierre he has been out mustering sheep for a week and has only just returned early this morning with a mob of over three hundred to be shorn. The sheep are penned near the woolshed and the shearers will be arriving at any moment.

"We could do with a hand, if you could spare the time," Bill asks Pierre.

"No doubt we will help you, Bill, though first I must meet a Mr Barry Night. He's a local grazier who's interested in buying 'March's Run'," Pierre explains.

"I know Barry Night," Bill returns sourly. "He's an ex-convict and I wouldn't trust him as far as I could throw him. Don't let yourself be duped by him. And I tell you, Mr Boyar, I wouldn't stay here working for a man like that. Mr March was a real gentleman. It's such a shame what's happened to him and all. Tell me, what do the doctors say? Has he any chance of recovery?"

"There are many theories as to how Teddy – Edward – may recover, Bill. One of course is time, though if he has permanent damage to the part of his brain that holds his memory, then recovery may never happen. It's been a long time now and still Teddy is unable to remember his past. We have been teaching him trade skills and Etta has been able to interest him in painting. Etta is quite an accomplished artist, you know."

"Yes, I do know. I read in the paper how Miss Etta won the Sydney Art Prize, and as I said before, Mr March is a gentleman. He's always treated me fairly. I feel I owe it to him to keep the property going and to make a profit. I'm not much of a housekeeper, I know, but I don't want to spend extra money on hiring a woman to do it. I reckon if I maintain the outside structure, the inside can be easily cleaned."

"I think you will be surprised, Bill. I'm sure Etta will be cooking us breakfast in your now clean kitchen. Etta got to work when we arrived yesterday," Pierre says with a smile, slapping Bill on the back.

"Sounds good to me. I'll go fetch some lamb chops for Miss Etta to cook. I killed a sheep yesterday and I've got it wrapped in canvas," Bill tells him as he starts walking towards the lean-to on one side of the house. Pierre reaches out and grabs his arm.

"I'd wait if I were you, Bill. Remember, Etta likes to look her best in company."

"No worries," he smiles at Pierre and nods. "I have a bit of work to do first."

"And I also have work to do," said Pierre ambling off to the stables with Timmy.

CHAPTER 35
THE DUKE

After a few days rest in the Grand Hotel in Sydney, the Duke is feeling refreshed but a little forlorn when thinking about Henry. He knows he cannot possibly report to the police that his brother was impersonating a woman, not to mention committing a carnal sin with his lover, Pierre Boyar. They would both be locked up, probably in a mental asylum, or worse, hung by the neck. He could not allow that to happen, apart from the fact that it would also mean the Harrowfeild name would be disgraced. Henry, he reluctantly acknowledges to himself, has won.

"My plan, Roberto," the Duke tells him sadly, "is to return to England next week and a short time after our arrival, you will marry Gertrude." He dabs at the moisture clouding his eyes. "I must say though, I do like it here in Australia – I feel free and adventurous. If only I had a happy marriage. Returning home wouldn't feel like I was returning to jail. Part of me would very much like to remain here." He sighs heavily.

Roberto has other more immediate concerns. The two men he's hired to kill Henry are, as far as he knows, still on his trail via the Goulburn Road. The plan is for the shooting to look like highway robbery but now that will be no longer necessary. *How am I going to get word to them to call off the hunt?* Roberto wonders. *I must think of a plan.* Roberto has paid his accomplices half the money promised to track Henry and Pierre to Goulburn and hopefully do the deed somewhere along the way. The other half he will pay when the job is done. Roberto figures the men may be in Goulburn by now, if they haven't already committed the crime. He prays they haven't.

"M' lord, don't you think it a shame to have come all this way to Australia and not see more of the countryside? I thought perhaps you may like to have one last chance to convince Henry to come home. Goulburn isn't far away by train," he suggests to the Duke.

"Very thoughtful of you, Roberto, but I need to go back to

158

England where, it seems, I belong, despite the fact that I must concede defeat before the arrogant Cecilia. I can hardly bear the thought. No, there's nothing and no one to keep me here any longer."

"I have a feeling, m' lord, that Henry may accede to your wishes, if only you would try one more time. The fact you have gone to such lengths to come to Sydney and then follow him to Goulburn will surely tug at his conscience?" Roberto waits impatiently as the Duke considers this proposal.

"You may be right, Roberto. However, I don't feel up to the journey – train or no train."

"Would m' lord permit *me* to have one last try at convincing Henry? In the meantime, you can relax and recover your strength for the voyage home. This is a fine hotel and the food, I think, is splendid. The ship back to England won't be leaving for another week. It would give me time to speak with Henry in Goulburn and return well before the ship sails." Roberto arranges his features into a look of sincerity.

"I don't know what to say – or what to think, Roberto. I thought perhaps you would be thrilled to live the life of the gentry – as my son-in-law. Why don't you leave Henry be, as I am now prepared to do? I have made up my mind to tell the press that Henry has been found but has made a new life for himself in the colonies. He has forfeited his right to be heir and refuses to return to England. For the life of me, why won't you accept this fact as I have, Roberto?" the Duke asks testily.

"It is simple, m' lord. I like Henry and feel unworthy to take his place." Roberto delivers this statement with a slice of humble pie big enough to choke a donkey.

The Duke is impressed. "I say, that is most gallant of you, Roberto. I'm pleased to say it confirms my high opinion of you. You are a decent young man and you will be a worthy successor."

If Roberto doesn't feel guilty now, he never will. *I must put a stop to the murder. I do hope I'm not too late.* His conscience has awoken, and he is stricken by the potential consequences of his criminal actions – albeit a little late.

"I am honoured to be considered worthy enough to be the next Duke of Harrowfeild. However, I beg you to allow me the opportunity to speak with Henry before we return home. I would not feel my actions to be honourable unless I do." Once again Roberto hangs his head for effect.

"Personally, I think you would be wasting your time. But if you insist, Roberto, I give you my permission. Yes, go to Goulburn and do your best with Henry. I shall wait here in comfort for your return. You'd best leave straightaway, man, because there is not one hour to waste. If you do not return before the ship sails, I shall depart without you and the marriage is off. Do you understand? And by the way, tell the manager on your way out that I will need a personal assistant while you are gone."

Roberto can barely contain his relief and elation. "Yes, m' lord, I understand, m' lord," Roberto says, walking backwards and bowing simultaneously until he bumps into the door. "Oops, silly me!" He opens the door then closes it gently behind him.

"Naive young man, really. I can't imagine how he will ever talk Henry into returning to England," the Duke says to himself, chuckling at the thought.

CHAPTER 36
HENRY

"Thank you, Bill. These lamb chops will be a perfect partner for the eggs I found yesterday. It's so nice to see chickens roaming free. They must be happy," I say with my most charming giggle.

"Well, actually they should be locked in their pen. I forgot to do it before I left. The foxes usually kill them all if I don't lock them in. You're lucky, Miss Etta, as it seems some must have escaped the carnage. I think you'd better crack the eggs in a cup first. They may be rotten. I've been away for a week and they don't last too long in the heat," Bill says with furrowed brows.

"I found the eggs just a little way under the house. I could see the chook sitting on them, so I shooed her away. Do you think they'll be alright? They were in the shade," I tell Bill, this time a little concerned because I am so looking forward to chops and eggs, as are Pierre and Timmy.

Bill laughs. "We'll soon see."

I crack the first egg in a cup – it is fine. I transfer it to the sizzling pan, then crack another. I have seven eggs, and all are good so far, except one yoke has a slight drop of blood. *Oh well, it will cook out, I suppose.*

"This is the last one." I hold the egg up for all three men to see. "I found this one under a shrub near the house, I remember as it was the only brown one."

I crack the shell and almost pass out with the explosion of rotten gas. A skunk could not have reeked worse, I'm sure. With horrified gasps and hands over noses, we all run from the kitchen.

Once outside, there is a loud cracking sound and Timmy grabs at his leg. "Shit, what was that?" he yells, looking down to see blood oozing through his trousers.

"It sounded like a gun shot," Bill says, peering around anxiously.

A moment later a whistle of hot air whooshes past my earlobe.

The bullet continues through the windowpane behind me. I shriek and throw myself to the ground. Another shot misses Bill by the slimmest of margins then pierces the front door. Crouching like hunchbacks, the men shield my trembling body and drag me inside the house. Our nerves unravel amongst the rotten egg gas. Which is worse – the bullets firing at random, or choking on stinking fumes?

"Pardon my French, Miss Etta, but who the fuck would be trying to kill us?" Timmy asks nervously.

"I haven't got a clue," I say, shaken and breathless.

"Whoever it is, he isn't a good shot, thankfully. Do we have any guns, Bill?" Pierre asks in his usual calm manner.

"Yes, I have a rifle in my cupboard and a shotgun under the bed." Bill smiles at me. Noticing my surprised expression, he adds, "You never know who you may run into, Miss Etta, especially living on your own." He gives me a wink.

Was I to assume Bill was yet another admirer? Or was he simply enjoying the cowboys and Indians game we seemed to be playing? I say "cowboys and Indians" because I actually went to see Buffalo Bill's Wild West Show in London about three years back. It was an amazing show of horsemanship, shooting, and American Indians firing bow and arrows. I remember laughing at the sight of Prince Bertie hanging over the balcony, cheering with unbridled excitement. *Oh, now that has taken my mind off my worries.*

Just when I think the shooting has stopped, another racket fills the air. It sounds like an army of horse-drawn wagons accompanied by loud husky voices.

"Don't tell me they've called for the cavalry?" I whimper.

Bill throws his head back and belly laughs, and I tell him sharply, "I don't think it's amusing to be shot at and almost killed!"

"It's the shearers, Miss Etta. I'd better go warn them we have a sniper on the property." Bill regains his composure, but my nerves are frayed.

"Surely, they'll leave if you tell them that, Bill?"

"Nup, I reckon they'll join the fight. If I know shearers, they're a tough crew."

Bill's eyes glisten, but whether with fear or excitement I can't tell. His stride is determined as he fetches his shotgun and edges his way out the back door. I hear him yell.

"Hey, Harry, it's Bill here. Watch your backs, we've got a bloody sniper on the property. He's a crook shot, but he's aiming to kill! Take cover, then give me a hand to hunt him down!"

Pierre follows tentatively with a .22 calibre rifle, his finger on the trigger. I fear for his life and mine, especially if I were to lose him.

"Pierre, please come inside. I don't want you killed!" Sobbing, I beg and beg again.

"Don't worry, Etta, I'll be fine. Remember, I'm an excellent shot."

His matter-of-fact attitude reassures me. Gathering my senses, I go about bandaging Timmy's leg which, thankfully, is only grazed. I then slide snakelike under a bed where I haven't had time to sweep. Ugh! I am filthy, my favourite house frock grey with dust, dirt and cobwebs. I think about how it might look when I am saved. Am I a coward of a man or a defenceless woman? I decide on the latter and console myself with prayer.

"Dear Lord, please help us! Whoever is trying to kill us must be a madman, so he will need your help – in Heaven – not here! It is we who need your help now. You know, the righteous ones. I pray we will be saved. Amen." *That's a bit tricky, Henry.* Will the Lord decide I am not *righteous* because of my sexual longings? What a dilemma! I am terrified but my fear for Pierre's safety is greater. Oh, my God, the suspense is killing me. I must see if Pierre is alright.

"Timmy, where are you?" I call from my hiding place.

"I'm in the kitchen, sitting on the floor having a cuppa."

"How can you enjoy a cup of tea in such a life-threatening situation, Timmy? How's the smell? Has it faded?" I demand, incredulous.

"Well, I did get a real shock, Miss Etta, with my leg and all, so I made myself a cuppa with plenty of sugar. They say sugar helps with shock, and yes, the stink aint so bad now," Timmy says calmly.

"Then you'd better pour me one, too. Thank you, Timmy." I crawl out from under the bed over to Timmy. We have enough good sense to sit with our backs to the wall, sipping our hot sweet tea as the battle rages outside.

It seems an eternity passes before, finally, the shooting stops. My immediate relief soon turns to anguish. *What if Pierre is lying out there somewhere, dead? What if the sniper had killed them all and I am left alone with Timmy, who doesn't seem to be the bravest man I've ever met?*

What if – what if? Stop it, Henry, and pull yourself together!

The front door flies open. From where we sit on the kitchen floor I can just see a large man lumber in. He stands in front of us, a rifle at his hip. He looks every bit a villain who was about to shoot us, Timmy clings to me like a leech, our teeth chattering in unison; we are terrified. I try to scream but not a sound passes my red lips.

"Good! You're both alright then," he says with an almost toothless grin, then crinkles his nose. "What the hell is that smell?"

I've lost all sense of smell, or perhaps we were used to it. "Ye – yes, we – we are. Thank you – Mister? And that was a rotten egg," I stammer.

He proffers his large hand to help me up off the floor. His nose twitches in discomfort. "Me name's Harry. Harry Webb. I'm the shearer's boss. I'm pleased to meet you, Miss Etta. Pierre says to tell you he'll be all right; it's just a small hole in his arm, really. He's in the barn with Bill and me men. One of the snipers is dead, and we've tied the other on a horse. Bill's going to ride him into Goulburn and turn the bludger over to the police."

"Did you ask why they were trying to kill us, Mr Webb?" I ask tremulously.

"Yes, we did Miss Etta, and he said they'd been paid to do it. He couldn't tell us the name of the man who'd hired them. Said he wouldn't give his name, but we got a good description. Our shooter said he was a real stuck up toff, English an' all."

I too feel shot by this news, as much as I would be if it had been a real bullet. *No! It was not possible! The Duke would never hire men to kill us, surely not.* I am shocked to the core and I feel the blood leave my face.

"Let me help you to a seat. You look a bit pale, Miss. It must be a real shock for you. I wonder if Bill's got any brandy in the house." Harry takes me gently by the elbow. He leaves me propped at the kitchen table while he searches for brandy.

Timmy pulls a chair close and holds my hand.

"Do you know who it might have been who hired the killers, Miss Etta? Is that why you look so pale? You look like you've seen a ghost!"

"Yes, Timmy, I do, though I find it hard to believe. I would never have dreamed the Duke capable of such a thing!" I shake my head trying to free myself of such a terrible thought. I suddenly realise I've given too much information away.

"The Duke? You mean the Duke who was in the newspapers, who came to Australia? Why would he want to kill you, Miss Etta?" Timmy asks, a deep frown creasing his large forehead.

"No, no, it's just the pet name I gave to a friend," I extemporise. "Well, it seems he's an enemy now! He's no relation to me – just one of my jealous admirers!" I am pleased with my quick thinking. *What a good answer, Henry!* I only hope Timmy believes me.

"I can imagine, Miss Etta. A beautiful lady like you would stir the devil up in any man," he says seriously.

"Really? Do you really think so, Timmy? It is not my intention to do so. I am an innocent young lady." My dreadful vanity even in these circumstances causes me to flutter my eyelashes; it seems the fashion has finally caught me. I smile sweetly. Suddenly, I am acutely aware of my dishevelled state and feel my wig slipping. "You'll have to excuse me, Timmy," I say, raising a hand to my head, discreetly securing the wayward hairpiece. "I need to go to the ladies' room."

Timmy chuckles, "I wouldn't call that hole in the ground, surrounded by fallen timber, a lady's room, Miss Etta."

"Nevertheless, I need to go!"

"Oh, Christ!" Timmy yells. "The bloody kitchens on fire!"

With the preceding panic, I've forgotten the lamb chops frying on the stove, and now a spitting fatty fire rages.

"Quick, get some water, Timmy!' I yell, one hand still trying to push my wig back into place. He limps outside, yelling, "Help! There's a fire in the kitchen!"

Just as I secure my wig, Harry returns with the brandy, and a group of men come charging through the door with buckets of water and wet hessian bags. Thankfully, with their major effort, the fire is soon smothered.

"Oh dear, what a mess!" I wail, before the burly young men offer gentle sympathies.

"We'll help you clean up, Miss Etta," Harry says, even more solicitously.

"Thank you, I would appreciate it, Harry. But will it keep you from shearing the sheep?"

"No, not at all. We'll get stuck into cleaning the kitchen right now and it'll be done by nightfall. We'll start shearing in the morning," he assures me.

Pierre, having remained in the barn to help Bill secure the villain upon a horse, now stands in front of me, his arm oozing blood.

"I'm sorry about the kitchen, Etta, but could you spare a moment to tend my arm?"

"Of course, Pierre, and don't worry about the kitchen. These nice young men are going to clean it up for me." I flash them a beaming smile. "Come out to the veranda and I'll look at your wound," I tell him, welcoming the excuse to talk.

We huddle close on the veranda as Pierre removes his shirt. "Do you know who sent those murderers to kill us, Pierre?" I whisper.

"The one Bill took into Goulburn, he said —", Pierre starts but I interrupt.

"I know what he said, Pierre, and I feel sick to the stomach, thinking it could be the Duke who hired those men. How could my brother harbour so much hate for us? It doesn't make sense, not at all! He wouldn't come all the way to Australia to try and talk me into coming home and then have such a dramatic change of heart as to want to kill me because I refused. I simply cannot accept it. The whole thing just does not make any sense at all."

"I agree. I just wasn't sure if Harry had told you the story."

I give a deep, sad sigh and begin bandaging Pierre's arm. The bullet has missed the bone and lodged itself in the bicep. It will take a long time to heal and he must be very careful not to let infection set in. Luckily, in my search for food, I've found a large box containing all things needed to disinfect and bandage a wound.

"Are you feeling up to the journey to Goulburn, Pierre? Remember we are to meet Mr Night. And you will need to see a doctor to have the bullet taken out. I couldn't possibly do it," I tell him sternly as I finish bandaging.

"Yes, I know," Pierre says, his sensuous lips parted in a brave smile. "I'll be fine, Etta. I'll wash up and if you could manage to bring me some bread and jam with cup of strong black tea, I would appreciate it."

"Of course, Pierre. I won't be long." *Lots of sugar – yes, lots of sugar – for the shock.*

I walk back into the kitchen where Harry and his men are up

to their elbows cleaning and scrubbing the soot off every surface in the kitchen.

"Thank you so much, Harry. I can't tell you how much I appreciate this," I say, gazing around at what had already been accomplished.

"It's alright, Miss Etta. Though one day soon, maybe you could cook us a cake? That would be a nice thank-you."

"I most certainly will. But now I must go to Goulburn with Pierre. He needs to see a doctor and I have made an appointment to meet Mr Night who, from all accounts, is interested in buying March's Run."

"I wouldn't trust that bloke, Miss Etta," Harry says, frowning.

"I know, Harry. Bill has told us the same thing. But do not worry yourself, Pierre and I are not fools."

We are soon on our way, bumping along the potholed road in our horse-drawn buggy. After a bone-shaking twenty-minute ride, we reach the town of Goulburn.

"I say, Pierre, this town seems to be thriving. The women here are all quite well dressed. They appear prosperous, so no doubt they own some of the enormous mobs of sheep and cattle we've seen on our way. And the pasture is so abundant that I think Goulburn must sit within a rain belt."

"You sound like an educated grazier, *cheri*," Pierre says, smiling fondly at me.

"I simply observe my surrounds. Artists have to, if they want to paint scenes depicting the truth, and not merely an impression."

"I'm sure you're right, Etta, and I hope you take the time to paint a picture of the homestead on March's Run. It would be nice to take home for Teddy. It might just jog his memory."

"I don't know if I want it to jog his memory, Pierre. Anyway, we may be doing the wrong thing in selling his property. Perhaps we should not sell. I could ask Bill Goads to stay on as manager. After all, he's done a wonderful job so far. And if Teddy does come to his senses, he may not be happy to learn it's been sold. What do you think, Pierre?"

"I think you may be right, Etta," Pierre says, twisting himself in half, looking back at a man he thought he'd recognised. "Quick, Etta, look over there! Isn't that Roberto, the Duke's personal butler?"

"Why, yes, it is!" I say, looking in the direction Pierre nodded. "I wonder what he's doing here?" My mind is whirling. "You don't think he had anything to do with the men who tried to shoot us do you, Pierre?

Remember, the man said it was a toff from England who'd hired them?"

"Now that's a thought, Etta. Though why on earth would he want to kill us?"

"No time to speculate. Oh Roberto, Roberto!" I call, just as he is about to walk into the Royal Hotel.

He turns, squinting into the sun, obviously trying to recognise who it is calling his name. He sees me waving from the other side of the road.

"Yes, my name is Roberto. May I ask who you are, Madam – Sir?" He calls, looking from me to Pierre.

"It's Pierre, Roberto, from Harrowfeild, England!" Calls Pierre, laughing. "Don't you recognise me?"

"Pierre, you're –," Roberto starts, and immediately crosses the road. He seems unexpectedly relieved, then when he comes closer to me, he is smiling broadly. "And you must be Etta!" he says excitedly. He tips his hat, bowing low. "I am so relieved; I mean so happy to see you both." Why, I ask myself, is Roberto so deliriously happy to see us?

"You are correct, Roberto. I am Etta Brown. Now may I ask, what business brings you here to Goulburn?" I ask stiffly.

"I have come here on the behalf of the Duke of Harrowfeild. He wishes me to speak with Henry. I am to have one last attempt at talking him into coming home with us. Do you know where Henry may be?' A hint of a smile curls his lips. *He knows who I am!*

"I most certainly do, and I can assure you, Roberto, you would be wasting your time – again – trying to talk Henry into returning to England. However, there is another matter which I need to discuss with you, if you would be so kind as to lend us your ear. Perhaps in the park, away from the crowd?"

"I am your servant, Miss Etta."

Like hell you are! My instincts immediately tell me Roberto is the toff who hired those men to kill us. But why?

We tie the horses up to a hitching rail and walk over to the park where we find a lovely spot to sit under a struggling weeping willow next to the manmade lake – or to be more exact – a muddy dam.

"Roberto, firstly, I must ask, how is the Duke? His health, I mean. Has he fully recovered from his turn?"

"Yes, he has, Henry - Etta. Oh dear, what do I call you?" Roberto asks, embarrassed.

"Etta, if you don't mind!" I tell him sharply. Pierre merely raises his eyebrows and looks amused.

"Well, then I must ask you, Etta, because the Duke desperately wants *Henry* to return to England. If you, I mean if *Henry* does not, then the Duke will be forced to tell the authorities that *Henry* is dead and therefore his entitlements will be forfeited." He looks searchingly into my eyes to gauge my reaction to this news.

"We know this, Roberto! I have lost count of how many times *Henry* has told the Duke he will not be returning. *Henry* has relinquished all rights to his inheritance. *Henry* is more than happy with his life here in Australia. So, you can just hop on board the nice train back to Sydney. I hear its whistle blowing. I pray you both enjoy your voyage back to England. However, there is one question I need to ask you. Has the Duke offered you compensation in my absence, Roberto? For instance, will he adopt you, so you can take my place?" I ask him bluntly.

"I must be honest with you, Hen – Etta. The Duke wishes me to marry Lady Gertrude. We are to produce heirs, so the family name will continue. And yes, I am to assume the courtesy title 'Lord Harrowfeild', but it is Gertrude's. Our eldest son will become the next Duke. It's all quite complicated," he says, smiling apologetically.

"So, tell me, Roberto, did you at any stage in your search for *Henry* think it possible that *Henry* might, as heir apparent, return to take up his rightful place and his title? Which, of course, would have left you remaining in your position as manservant, and no more?"

The ace up my sleeve is knowing that Roberto apparently knows nothing of what has just taken place out at March's Run, though he does keep gazing at Pierre's bandaged arm.

"Yes, I did wonder about that. But I am a humble man and I had trouble at first accepting I would become the heir to a fortune," he confessed.

I fix him with a steely look. "You said 'at first'! What do you mean, Roberto? Did you ultimately become seduced by the vision of a carefree luxurious life, with your every whim catered for by servants? Especially young chambermaids?"

Roberto has the good grace to look contrite. "I must be honest. I did think about all that, Hen – I mean, Etta. But I changed my mind. I couldn't do it. I feel so ashamed, so please forgive me." He hangs his head, his emotions in turmoil once again, I'm sure.

"You couldn't do what, Roberto?" I ask him pointedly. "Hire men to kill me, just to make sure I never returned to lay claim to what is rightfully mine?"

"No, no! I could never –" he protests.

"You mean you could never kill me, or you could never hire men to do the dirty deed?" I ask him coldly. I turn to Pierre who, if his expression is any indication, is enjoying my interrogation immensely. "I think it's time, Pierre, to see if Roberto is telling the truth. Do you agree?"

Pierre nods emphatically, "*Absolument!*"

"I am telling you the truth, Henry!" Roberto says, horrified. "Why do you not believe me? And how do you know someone was out to murder you?" Roberto asks, then realising what he has just said, gasps and looks terribly guilty.

I am furious and do not hold back. "How do I know? You stupid man! We were ambushed at March's Run this morning in actual fact! It was just as well the shearers arrived in time to help Bill Goads and Pierre hunt the culprits down. As you can see by Pierre's bandaged arm, he was almost killed in the process!" I poke Roberto sharply in the chest. "One of *your* accomplices was shot dead. The other degenerate is in the Goulburn jail right now! It's unfortunate for you, Roberto, that the captured man was able to give a description of who it was that hired him to kill me," I finish triumphantly.

With that, Roberto breaks down sobbing. We wait for him to compose himself.

"Roberto,' I continue seriously, "I'm truly sorry it has come to this. We will now take you to the Goulburn jail, where my would-be assassin will no doubt identify you. As an accomplice to attempted murder, you cannot be let off lightly. Nobody should."

Still sobbing, Roberto pleads with me. "I'm so sorry, Hen – I mean, Etta. I promise I will never do anything like this again. I came to Goulburn to try and save you. I was praying they hadn't killed you on your way here. I was so happy to see you both alive. Surely you could see how happy I was when we met? Please don't send me to jail. I promise I will serve your father faithfully until I die." Roberto's pleading look changes in an instant, becoming quizzical. "Is the Duke your father, or your brother, Henry? There has been a rumour going around the castle…"

"I shall squash the rumour, Roberto. The Duke is my brother, and Rosie is my grandmother, so there you have it. Now continue to beg!" I demand imperiously. Much to Pierre's amusement, Roberto does – pathetically and unrelentingly – until I began to grow weary of his performance. "Please help me out here, Pierre. What should we do with this feeble excuse for a man?" I shake my head, both in dismay and disgust.

"Well, I always look at the big picture, Etta. Remember, Roberto has struggled all his life with having to please your difficult family. Therefore, I can imagine how he would be tempted to secure the rewards the Duke promised him. And because I truly feel Roberto has repented, I think we should offer him a compromise." Pierre looks lovingly towards me. "Providing Roberto agrees to send you a certain amount of money each month, Etta, just to assist us with the life we have created here, *and* if he promises to never tell a soul about our relationship or your penchant for dressing as you do, then I'm sure we can trust him to return to England with the Duke and take up his generous offer."

"This is the perfect solution! How clever you are. I am so pleased I have you to solve our problems, Pierre." I snuggle into his shoulder and plant a smacking kiss on his cheek.

To his credit, Roberto does not flinch at my display of affection. He is probably being much more circumspect about what he says and does right now, given that his freedom depends upon it. When he speaks, his voice is husky with emotion. "I thank you from the bottom of my heart, Pierre and Etta. Your secret will be safe with me; I swear on my mother's grave! Even if I were to be tortured, I would never say a thing about the way you live together. I swear on the Bible I would not! As for sending money, you must simply name the amount, Pierre, and I shall organise it with the bank – once I am married to Gertrude, of course, and receive my allowance." Roberto proffers his hand to Pierre who shakes it firmly.

I offer my gloved hand to Roberto who sheepishly raises it to his lips. *Etta: one. Roberto: yet to score.*

"Now you'd best go, Roberto, and be a good boy from now on. If I hear you have committed anymore skulduggery, I shall return to England and you will face the perils of my wrath! Do you understand?"

"I certainly do, Miss Etta, and I will be forever in your debt. I can only say that I hope you and Pierre will be very happy in your life together. I must add, I cannot imagine how anybody here could think you were a man, Henry – I mean, Etta."

"Very kind of you, Roberto," I say graciously. "Now we must hurry. The train will be leaving soon, and Pierre needs to see the doctor. And we have a luncheon engagement."

We return to the horse and buggy, and Pierre drives as fast as safety allows for us to arrive just in time for Roberto to catch the train. We wave goodbye to him with an enormous feeling of relief. "Do you understand why we had to let him go, Etta?" Pierre whispers.

"I do, Pierre. The whole sticky business would have been – well, it would have been disastrous. It was the only way to handle the situation. I am pleased you came forward with the right answer – as usual. I do adore you. Not only for your body and soul, but also for your intelligence, and especially for remaining calm in situations that need clear thinking."

"*Merci beaucoup, cheri!*"

"And as for our meeting with Mr Night – what do you think? Should we sell 'March's Run'? Or should we keep the property just in case Teddy comes to his senses?"

"I've been thinking the same, Etta. Considering Bill Goads is a genuine man and takes excellent care of the property, I think we should leave well enough alone – for a while at least. Besides, it would be a good place to come and stay when wanting to race our horses in this area. We don't need the money just yet. I say we leave things as they are. Besides, I should concentrate on Mountain Boy now. The race is next week."

"Excellent idea!" I concur. "Now, off to the doctor with you!"

CHAPTER 37
THE DUKE

The Duke's sense of duty and loyalty to his family title are seriously challenged from the moment he sets eyes upon his temporary personal assistant, Miss Lily White. Love and freedom are most powerful persuaders, and now the scales begin to tip in their favour.

Lily had heard from the manager about the Duke needing a personal assistant while his manservant was away. She'd convinced the manager that there was no candidate more suitable than herself to attend the Duke and cater to his needs in a professional manner. She was, she told the manager, the only one who could possibly attend to the Duke's demands with discretion and decorum. *Decorum indeed!*

At lunch in the hotel dining room, the Duke confesses, "If you don't mind me saying so, Miss White, you are the most beautiful young woman I have ever seen. May I call you by your first name? I would be delighted if you were to call me Albert."

"You flatter me, Duke Harrowfeild. I am not as young as you may imagine me to be, just well preserved. And yes, you may call me Lily. I should like it, Albert." Lily lowers her eyes and blushes prettily.

"I wish we'd met some years ago, Lily. My heart has never felt so strong, so joyous. To think only that two days ago, you came to my hotel room to offer your services as my personal assistant. I couldn't believe my luck. I was bedazzled by your captivating eyes," the Duke tells her dreamily.

"I felt the same, Duke…, I mean, Albert, seeing we are now on first name terms." Lily gazes into the Duke's eyes as she thinks, *Well, it's about time fate dealt me an ace or two.* Her long elegant fingers caress his as she contemplates the possibility of becoming the Duke's mistress. After all, he isn't *completely* unattractive. "I have often entertained the idea of returning to England, you know. However, I do enjoy my job here in the hotel as assistant manager. It pays well, and I have a comfortable room. It's more than I ever had in England."

"If you agree to return with me, Lily, I would purchase you a fine apartment in London. You would never have to lift a finger. Your every wish would be met. I beg you to consider my offer." The Duke raises a bushy eyebrow. "Perhaps you could consider my offer and let me know of your decision over supper this evening – in my room? Never in my life have I felt this way about a woman. I am your servant, my dear," the Duke tells her, his voice husky with desire.

Yes, you will be. And you won't be the first man I've had at my beck and call.

"I will think about your generous offer, Albert, and I do appreciate your attentions. I must admit – the feeling is mutual, although I confess it has taken me by surprise," Lily giggles coyly and squeezes his hand. "I shall meet you in your room, say, nine-thirty this evening?" Lily's sensuous smile sends shivers down the Duke's spine. Entirely aware of her power over him, she rises gracefully from her chair. "Until then, dear Albert."

The Duke uncharacteristically stands and escorts her to her office in the hotel. His heart pounds with the thought of at last finding a woman he truly loves and lusts after. Lily has ignited a flame he thought had flickered out long ago. *Fancy finding such a beauty in Australia.*

Later that evening the Duke excitedly paces his room, stopping only to occasionally twist the champagne bottle nestling in a bucket of ice. Dishes full of oysters and black caviar sit to one side. A pyramid of succulent strawberries is piled high on a silver plate, a generous bowl of whipped cream alongside. He cannot help but visualise Lily licking and sucking the cream off each strawberry – the thought causing his manhood to stir energetically inside his trousers, something that had happened only rarely after the initial, forced attraction he felt for his wife petered out once he came to know her true personality. Certainly, he'd had the odd bit of skirt over the years, though none had set him on fire – not like Lily. In fact, most wenches had been required to work hard to earn their money. The idea of making love to Lily was driving him to distraction.

Finally, I have found my one true love. Please come to me, Lily. Come to me now!

His prayers are answered when a gentle knock echoes on his door at nine forty-five. The Duke opens it to see Lily, looking like a vision and smiling seductively. She slinks past him, coming tantalisingly close to him and leaving a subtle trail of perfume in her wake. She looks around the room and turns slowly to face him. With the determination of a lioness viewing her pray, she fixes her gaze on him.

"My, but haven't you gone to delicious extremes, m' lord? What a feast! I *adore* oysters – and champagne." Lily lifts the bottle from the ice and views the label appreciatively. "My favourite – Veuve Clicquot. Goodness me, what a celebration! I am flattered once again, m' lord."

"Albert – call me Albert," the Duke reminds her. "No trouble at all, my dear Lily, you are worth your weight in gold. As I promised, your wish is my command." He bows low and kisses the fingers of the hand she languidly extends.

The Duke pops the cork and the champagne fountains over the lip, tiny bubbles cascading over his hand. Lily giggles and gazing into his eyes, brings his champagne-doused hand up to her full lips and sucks each finger. What little remains of the Duke's composure departs.

"My darling Lily, how can a man control himself when such beauty confronts him? I am a slave to your charm. May I kiss you?"

"You don't have to ask, m' lord." She loves saying "m' lord". Never had she made love to a Duke before, or anyone with any title, come to think of it. "Do as you wish. I am yours alone to love."

The Duke, six inches taller than Lily, lowers his head and kisses her moist lips with virile sensuality. It surprises her. *Mmm, not bad – quite arousing.* She had not found the Duke unattractive, a little old perhaps, but now with his passionate kiss, her excitement is stirred. She kisses him back with increasing urgency. The Duke's erection joins the party.

"I cannot wait a moment longer, Lily. I must make love to you!" he murmurs roughly in her ear.

"You must! My dear Albert, indeed, you must!" *Perhaps this is not going to be as unpleasant as I first thought.* She is quite surprised to feel her own desire mounting quickly in response to the Duke's frenzied caresses.

Quite some time after, both parties are favourably surprised at having had a totally satisfying experience. The Duke is bewitched by Lily's ardent participation, and Lily is impressed by the Duke's skilled performance. They lie together wrapped in each other's arms, neither wanting to rise from the bed. However, much fine fare awaits, and they choose not to waste it.

Wrapped in a soft blanket, Lily sits at the dining table, savouring the oysters and sipping champagne while she listens to her own strategy emerge almost word for word from the mouth of her lover boy.

"I love you, Lily. I need you. You supply the energy to my being; you are my life force. Say you will stay with me. Please say you will accompany me to England."

My God, I could almost have written that script myself. Lily is impressed by the Duke's eloquence.

However, Lily White, alias Maud Stenning, has one small problem with the Duke's plan. She had escaped the London authorities some years past, when a simple robbery went wrong and resulted in an unfortunate death. She was lucky to escape and trick her way on board a ship she thought was leaving for America, when in fact it was heading for Australia. In this instance, her mistake worked in her favour due to the open admiration of the captain for a pretty young woman travelling on her own.

"Oh dear, I must have the ships confused and have made a dreadful error. Kind Sir, could you please tell me where I am to board my ship to America?" she had asked the dashing captain, who was only too happy to come to her rescue. He easily convinced her (so he thought) that the colonies were a much safer place for a young lady to set up business.

"Too many murdering redskins in America, Miss. They'll take you captive and when they've had their heathen way with you, they'll skin you alive." He had thought he may have been laying it on a bit thick, but Lily knew an opportunity when she saw one.

"Oh no! How ghastly! Oh, what am I to do?" she had implored the captain, taking a step closer to him and laying her hand on his uniformed chest. He arranged a transfer to a cabin far from steerage and rather closer to his, and a grateful Lily repaid his kindness in full. They arrived in Sydney having spent a very pleasant time together, and Lily happily disembarked, ready to make her own way in the new world.

Now, she wonders if ten years will have been long enough for the London authorities to have let the case go. Would her new identity be enough to keep her criminal past at bay? While she had not been responsible for the death of her robbery victim, she could still be considered guilty of manslaughter. Could she take the chance?

"I suppose, my dearest love," Lily asks sweetly, her fingers stroking the nape of the Duke's bullish neck, "you would not consider living in Australia?" She sighs and pouts her plump pink lips. "It's so terribly cold in England and we could start a new life here – together."

The Duke looks at her with adoring eyes, still slightly glazed from his recent blissful experience. The way she had pleased him, well, more than pleased him, was unprecedented. She was all of Heaven and more, wrapped in a soft adorable bundle – a bundle he could now not live without.

"If saying 'no' meant losing you, Lily, I would agree in a heartbeat. However, I have much to organise in my life before I could live here. As you can imagine, my business dealings in England, for one, would have to be sorted. I'm sure, when I ask for a divorce, I will have a very sticky time with my wife." The Duke lowers his eyes for a moment before looking steadily at Lily who, with hedonistic pleasure, raises a whole luscious strawberry to her rosebud mouth and slowly sucks off the whipped cream. It is enough to stir him underneath his silk dressing gown. "Oh, my dear Lily, I cannot deny you a single thing. Wherever you wish to live, I will be by your side forever more. Just say you will marry me and never leave me – and the world is yours."

Lily is taken aback by this fervent declaration. *Marriage! My goodness – he is serious! But am I? Do I want to commit myself to this man? I don't know!*

"I'd like to think about it, Albert," she replies softly. The disappointment on his face unexpectedly strikes her heart. *It seems I do have some feeling for him – he is such a sweet man!* She tries to repair the blow she has so clearly delivered. She says quickly, "What I mean, Albert, is I'd like to think about where we should live, not about marrying you, dear Albert. It is without a doubt our meeting was meant to be. Of course, my answer is 'yes'! I *will* marry you – if possible."

"Anything is possible for you, my dear Lily. We shall return to England together and I will divorce my wife immediately." The Duke's face is wreathed in smiles and he clasp her slim waist in his beefy hands. "The only reason I married her was to get our estate out of a spot of bother. I have never loved her. You must believe me when I say you are the only woman I have truly loved."

Lily raises a sculpted eyebrow and tips her pretty head to one side. *I have him by the short and curlies.* "Are you aware, Albert, that a divorce can be obtained via correspondence? Your lawyer in England must simply draw up the document and then hand it to your wife. Cecily, is that her name?"

"Yes, it is." He's even forgotten his wife's name – Cecilia. "However, my estate is vast and complicated, and it will take months to complete the legalities satisfactorily for both parties."

"I only suggested doing it by correspondence, because when I first travelled to Australia by sea, I near *died* from a most terrible seasickness. I would be most reluctant to again expose myself to such a debilitating experience, Albert." She offers him a tremulous smile. "But I'll risk my life for you – if you want me to, dear Albert."

Another lie.

"Of course not, my darling! I cannot even contemplate the possibility of losing you. No, definitely not! I shall write to my lawyer and ask him to handle my divorce. However, I will not mention you, my dearest Lily. I will say my health has weakened considerably and the doctors recommend that I remain in the warmer climes of Australia. I will tell Cecilia that unless she is prepared to leave everything behind and join me here, I will have no other choice than to divorce her. She will be left with more than ample funds, of course. That should do it! My lawyer will do my bidding. He gets paid handsomely enough; God knows!" The Duke takes Lily's hands in his. "We shall remain here, my love, never to be parted. Well, only when I must return to the estate to execute my ducal duties. And perhaps one day, there may be a medicine that will prevent you from being seasick, dear Lily, and then together, we will be able to travel the world." The Duke leans forward to place a kiss on Lily's cream-covered lips. "Delicious, my love, simply delicious."

She giggles, letting the blanket slide off her shoulders to reveal her perfect breasts.

The Duke moans. "My God, but I must have you again, my sweet treasure."

And he does.

CHAPTER 38
SARAH

I have come almost to the last page of my journal. It makes me realise how far we have come to establishing not only a stunning horse property, but so many genuine friendships with people who are more than willing to help us in any way possible. Yes, we have a very caring community in the Blue Mountains.

I was sure Henri-Etta (as I call Etta only because Henry was still there underneath all the fluff and frivolity) would be home soon, safe and sound with Pierre and Mountain Boy in tow. I do so hope they will make it home in time for Rosie and Ernie's wedding. We have worked industriously in the garden to present it at its best in early December, when the wedding will take place.

Ernie's wife was quite happy to give him a divorce. She packed her belongings as soon as the papers were signed and left early the next morning with her younger lover. I cannot imagine any mother doing so, but she left the children with Ernie. Rosie has helped to care for the six little ones, and she doesn't seem to mind at all. However, I have come to rely more and more on Melanie, as has Teddy, it would appear. He was forever asking her to help him, either to gather wood from the surrounding bush, or to muck out the stables, which I was sure he was quite capable of doing by himself. I have had to put a stop to his interfering with her daily chores as it was most annoying when I called for her and she was nowhere to be found. I wondered if there was a romance blossoming. I have decided to question Melanie when I get an opportunity.

Later I have taken up my pen.

Well, there was no need to ask Melanie. During this afternoon, Rosie rushed into the kitchen, giving me a start. My hands immediately flew to my heart in shock. She placed her hands upon my face and looked me in the eye, speaking so quickly I found it hard to keep up with what she was trying to explain.

With signs, I relayed, "Please slow down. What is the problem?" Rosie took pencil in hand and scribbled urgently.

Teddy is in the barn with Melanie, and he's making her do unthinkable things with him!

Where is James? I wrote.

He's gone to Blackheath to get some stores. Quickly, Sarah you must help me.

Together we hurried to the barn where I saw through a crack in the wall Teddy March energetically having his way with Melanie, whose expression was unreadable. My anger explodes. Melanie was my responsibility – I had to stop them immediately! I grabbed the first thing I saw – a short but solid plank of wood. I ran towards Teddy who was mounted on top of Melanie and going for his life. Before Rosie could prevent me, I struck him on the head with such force it sent vibrations through my arms. With that, Teddy immediately fell unconscious to the floor. Interestingly, his penis took a little longer to react! Melanie sat up slowly, covered her bare breasts and stared blankly at us. Rosie knelt and felt Teddy's pulse. My body shook with anger and remorse. What had I done?

Rosie looked up at me. I could read her lips. "He's alive, Sarah, don't worry. I'll handle things from here. You go and put the kettle on, and I'll be there in in a minute."

I could barely move my feet; why did I hit him so hard? Was it because I couldn't yell at him? I had never felt such anger, but how could I do such a thing?

I did as Rosie said. Slowly I walked to the kitchen and put the kettle on the stove, then sat down at the table, nestling my head in hands – mortified. Before too long, Rosie appeared with Melanie in tow. Melanie apologised in writing, *I truly love Teddy – and he me. He has told me so. He wants to marry me. He said I should let him do it, you know. I was scared.* My anger subsided as I held Melanie's hand.

I'm so sorry, I mouthed. I knew it had been Teddy who had initiated the whole thing.

A bedraggled Teddy staggered into the kitchen with one of James's horse bandages wrapped around his head. He sat opposite and laid his head on the table, looking pale. Melanie and I sat studying him.

Rosie soon placed a pot of tea on the table, along with her delicious fruit cake and my finest china plates and teacups. A celebration?

No! This was a very serious matter – Teddy must marry Melanie. There was no way out of it. We had the tea and cake in silence before Rosie spoke with Melanie.

I stayed out of their conversation. I felt terribly guilty, along with feeling like a washed-out rag doll. Besides, I had to go and check on my sleeping child. Thank Heavens Sascha slept well. I stood gazing at her, wondering if I would ever have the same problems with her about her choice of men. I prayed not. I returned to see a bewildered Teddy pacing the room. It seemed the hard whack on his head had cured his amnesia but had obliterated his memory of the past months spent here in our care.

"What am I doing here? I was on my way home to Goulburn," he said, holding his bandaged head. "What happened to my head? Why is it bandaged? I have a terrible headache; I feel quite ill." He sat down, and with a puzzled look he asked Rosie, "Please explain, Rosie. I cannot fathom what has happened."

Rosie did an excellent job, remaining calm when speaking to Teddy and simultaneously translating in sign language to me. I suddenly saw a funny side to this awful state of affairs and laughed. Unfortunately, I could not laugh out loud. My body simply shook with the effort. Rosie's suggested cure had worked! My hitting Teddy on the head had brought him to his senses. Well, what do you know? I'd felt terrible for what I'd done, now I felt like I had done him a favour. Teddy was back to reality, thank the Good Lord. He was beginning to be such a worry, prowling around Melanie, and now, with their act of fornication. Oh dear! What about poor Melanie – what would happen to her now? I wondered if Teddy would remember what he did to her. He was like a stray dog rutting with a bitch on heat. Would he remember the proposal of marriage Melanie said he had made? I was assured of this when he pointed at Melanie and asked, "who is she?"

I looked over to see Melanie swallowing convulsively before suddenly bursting into a torrent of tears that flowed down her cheeks, dampening her dress. Obviously, Teddy had no idea of his interlude with Melanie. I felt for the poor child. A satisfying experience it may have been for him, but to her, if there was no offer of marriage, it simply meant a ruined reputation. Though on reflection, I wondered why a young, industrious, intelligent woman would think marriage was the be all and end all. These days, and particularly in the colonies, hundreds of women were making their mark in a man's world, opening businesses on their own and earning just as much money as men, and sometimes more. I would do my best to console her. However, if Melanie found she was pregnant by Mr March, then I would surely lay down the law!

CHAPTER 39
PIERRE

"Whoa, boy, take it easy. Save your strength for the race," I whisper into the wind as I watch The Boy work. I couldn't be happier with the way he's settled in at March's Run. He's certainly developed into a magnificent horse; his coat gleams like a jewel and his eyes are bright and full of life. Even though I would prefer to work him among the hills at home, the flat ground here has given him an easier time, especially after his long haul from the Blue Mountains. Obviously, the hills are not needed to have him fit for the mile race tomorrow. He's spot on, I reckon.

"How did he feel, Timmy?" I ask. "Is he ready?" I'm feeling blessed to have Timmy join our team. He is the final spoke in our wheel of fortune.

"He's a firecracker, boss. Did you see him pulling on the bit? It took me a while to calm him down. I reckon he's as fit as a stud bull. We should let him run as he pleases tomorrow. No holding him up, otherwise he'll just pull himself into the ground. If I let him have his head, he'll win for sure." Timmy could hardly contain his enthusiasm for the horse.

I nod agreement just as Etta rings the bell for breakfast.

"Good, I'm starving. Can you look after Mountain Boy, Tim, before you come in for breakfast? I'll save you a chop."

"No thanks, boss, I'd better keep it light for tomorrow. Don't want to weigh The Boy down." He dismounts, landing lightly beside the horse, and leads him off towards the stables.

I kiss Etta on the cheek, "Thank you, *mon petit chou*, I could eat a horse and chase the rider." Etta giggles, and I love the sound.

"Now, Pierre, I don't want to worry you, but Mr Night has sent yet another note to say he will pay even more than his last offer for March's Run. What do you think? I wonder why he wants it so badly. There's plenty of other land to be purchased around this area."

"It might be the spring-fed creek, Etta. A permanent source of good water is a real asset. I think we should send word to Sarah and ask if there's any change in Teddy's condition. If not, perhaps we should sell. The money would come in handy for more stables at home and we could fence the last paddocks. Maybe we could even buy more land."

"Well, that settles it. At least I can give Mr Night an answer. I'll say we should wait to hear how Teddy March is faring with his amnesia. But if his condition does remain and we must care for him forever, perhaps we should accept Mr Knight's offer. When we're in Goulburn tomorrow, I'll send a telegram to Blackheath for Sarah. Her reply should arrive in a day or two."

"I'll let you handle it, Etta. No doubt we'll also see Mr Night at the races tomorrow. The races are a big attraction here. Everyone lays down tools to attend. I like this part of the country. I could quite easily live here. What do you think, Etta?" I say in between mouthfuls of lamb chop.

"I would be deliriously happy wherever you are, Pierre. I love you more than life itself."

When Henry speaks of his deep love for me, the unfairness of our situation, for want of a better word, hits me like a blow to my heart. My longing to love a man – not a woman – has me wondering when and how it all happened. Though, I must admit, Henry's womanly disguise does please my eye. Perhaps it's this charade that keeps our love for each other inoffensive to others and therefore, when Henry is dressed as a female, I feel safe to outwardly admire his beauty. Women have such an advantage over men; they have licence to camouflage or enhance their appearance with cosmetics and fine couture. Not that Henry needs any enhancement. He's magnificent either way.

"And I, you," I reply, standing to wrap Henry in my arms.

As night falls, I become anxious about the race tomorrow, and I'm unable to sleep due to nervous energy. *Will he win? What if he doesn't? YES, he'll win!* The morning light brings some relief. I have convinced myself Mountain Boy will win again and be on his way to champion status. At least I hope so. Maybe I'm setting my goal too high, wanting to breed the fastest horse in Australia. I would like to go down in history as being the breeder and the trainer of a champion, and if I don't give it my best shot, I shall never know.

I dress quickly and go to the stables. "Timmy, are you up? How's our Boy this morning?" I ask him.

"He's fine, boss. He slept a damn lot better than I did. I kept hearing strange sounds all night, thinking it was someone coming to put a stop to him racing today."

"Why would anyone want to do that, Timmy?"

Timmy smiles at my naivety and explains about the influence of gambling, especially the amounts that can be wagered before the race day. This gives underhanded people reason to back a horse, then put a halt to his rivals by administering drugs to prevent them running at their best.

"Thank you, Timmy. I now know the reason you insisted on sleeping outside his stable."

"Yeah, well, I didn't want you to worry too much, boss."

The morning progresses smoothly. With all preparations complete and with The Boy's needs met, we are ready to leave. Etta is looking ravishing in her new mauve silk organza frock with a picture-book hat to match. We set off and arrive an hour before the first race, duly tethering The Boy in his allotted stall. We take time to view the large crowd steadily making its way into the racecourse. It certainly is a popular day out with the locals.

The surrounds have been established with marquees selling food and beverages, some private and the others public. A grand carnival atmosphere pervades, escalating the crowd's enthusiasm. The bookies set up their boards near the saddling enclosure and stand on wooden boxes to scroll down the odds for each horse. Mountain Boy is three-to-one. The local horse, a huge chestnut named Goulburn Flyer, stands favourite at even money. The rest of the field are decent each way bets. On paper, it looks to be a race with only two real contenders.

My only concern is that Mountain Boy, like any full-blooded young male, is at the mercy of his hormones. Each time a filly walks by, he whinnies and makes his intentions quite clear, much to the horror of the more delicate female racegoers. The men just look on with either admiration or jealousy. Goulburn Flyer, a gelding, will have his sights set only on winning, not on the fillies that race alongside him. I must have a word with the race committee. In my opinion, they should hold separate races for fillies. It is not fair for stallions to be tempted by the fairer sex during a race; it's a major disadvantage. My hopes of winning are now fading.

Timmy makes his way to the jockeys' room while I remain

brushing Mountain Boy. His coat is already gleaming, but it helps me stay calm and perhaps take The Boy's mind off romance. Many racegoers stop in their tracks to admire him. He has perfect conformation, a deep girth and a muscular rump, which, I always say, is the engine of a horse. He has the most beautiful head one could possibly wish on a stallion, with doe-like eyes set well apart on his broad forehead. His luxuriant black mane and tail would serve for two horses. He is almost the image of his father, a magnificent specimen of equine beauty. I become a little bored with answering the punters' questions and smile when I see Etta in the distance. She is in her element, sailing through the crowd, accepting appreciative glances and compliments. She returns to see if I need anything.

"A drink or something to eat, Pierre?" she asks in her girlish voice, which is a key or two higher than Henry's.

"No thank you, Etta, I'm fine. We'll celebrate once The Boy wins," I say with a confident smile, not wanting her to know I am feeling anything *but* confident at this juncture. "Could you stay with the horse now while I go and get the saddle from Tim?"

"Yes, of course. Though I must tell you, I spoke with Mr Night a moment ago, and I told him we are waiting for a reply from Sarah to see how Mr March is progressing. I told him if Teddy remains the same, we will probably sell the property. He seemed most pleased. We must stop at the post office on our way home to see if the telegram has arrived."

"Good. We'll talk about it later, Etta. I need you to come and stand right here. Please keep The Boy calm. Tell him if he wins, he can cover one of those fillies he's been eyeing off."

Etta giggles. "How funny, Pierre. Do you think he'll understand?"

"I can only hope so. But more to the point, I hope he doesn't get mad at me for telling him a fib." I give her a wink and leave.

To say Mountain Boy was excited in the mounting enclosure would be shying away from the obvious. He was beside himself, prancing and showing off. I suppose it had to happen; he was rising three. I wish he was a mild-mannered stallion like his father. Perhaps I'll have to geld him. It is the last thing I wanted to do but we will soon see if he can keep his mind off the fillies and on the job.

Timmy needs no instructions on how to ride the horse. However, Mountain Boy needs a good talking to. There again I am lucky to have Timmy calm the horse by singing, albeit out of tune.

The starting string has been pulled into position at the mile post. Horses are moving up quietly to take their place, except Mountain Boy. He's rearing high. Oh damn, he almost throws Timmy off! Nerves burn my stomach. Wait, now he settles. He walks forward – just as well. The line is steady, steady – they're off! The horses charge forward to the thunderous roar from the crowd. Mountain Boy flies to the lead and maintains it easily for the first four furlongs. I pray he'll stay there, but wait, here comes Goulburn Flyer. He cruises up to join Mountain Boy, who then pulls away, I assume to show The Flyer whose boss. But can The Boy sustain this astonishing pace to the line? He has many challengers now; half the field is trying for the lead. He keeps a neck in front, just to tease them. The field has remained in the same position for the first six furlongs, and now into the home straight Goulburn Flyer is trying to run The Boy down – but he fights back! Over the final fifty yards, The Flyer seems spent. The Boy forges ahead to win by two lengths. Yes! Jubilation, ecstasy – no words can explain how I feel. I jump about like an idiot. Etta is beside me jumping for joy.

"Pierre, what a horse! There was no catching him. He simply dominates all rivals!"

"Yes, at this stage he does, Etta. Let's wait and see what The Boy can do when he races in stronger company," I say a little breathless, trying to maintain some sense of reality.

After Timmy dismounts and unsaddles the horse, the first person to appear and congratulate us is Mr Night, a middle-aged man, well-groomed, but coarsely spoken – from a common background, I would guess.

"Great win, Mr Boyar, very impressive," he says, proffering his hand. "I've a mind to give you my team to train. If you stay in Goulburn, that is."

I take his enormous hand and feel the rough callouses in the weakness of his grip.

"Thank you, though I don't think it will happen, Mr Night. I must return home. I need to tend to my stallion and mares."

He raises an eyebrow, mischief in his beady eyes. He says, "Why don't you lighten your load, Mr Boyar. I'll buy Mountain Boy, relieve you of your baggage, then you can travel home by train with your charming companion here." He nods towards Etta. "It's a far better way to travel for a lady."

He gives Etta a lascivious grin – I almost give him an uppercut. I don't like this man. Our first meeting at the hotel had unnerved me. I wonder what it is about him, apart from his aggravating arrogant personality that puts me on my guard.

"Mountain Boy is not for sale, Mr Night, and neither is March's Run," I tell him bluntly.

"So, you've heard from Teddy, have you? He's back to his old self then. He's a bit of a devil. Comes across as a gentleman, he does. Though mind you, he's no grandee when he wants somethin' – or someone. You know what I mean?"

Etta can see my discomfort, especially as I am trying to lead a fractious colt back to his stall and talk at the same time. She chimes in.

"Mr Night, with all due respect, we wish to be left alone now. We need to tend to Mountain Boy. As I have told you, I will not know about Mr March's condition until I receive word from home. However, Pierre and I have been speaking about the property and we see no reason *not* to keep it running the way it is. The manager is doing a fine job. He would have been here today, only he had far too much work to do. He's so industrious and trustworthy. You can be assured; we will be in touch when a decision is made – one way or the other."

Etta flutters her fan furiously, throwing him a haughty look. He just laughs.

"I won't give up easily, Miss Etta. Oh, and by the way, Pierre, how's your deaf and dumb wife? Has she missed you yet, or more to the point, have you missed her?"

If I hadn't been leading Mountain Boy, I would have punched him in the nose.

"Keep walking, Etta, and ignore him. He's not worth getting upset about," I whisper. Etta turns to face Mr Night, determination planted on her pretty face.

"We do not appreciate your company, or your vulgar comments, Mr Night. We wish for you to leave us alone. Enough has been discussed about the sale of March's Run. We will contact you if it is, in fact, for sale. Goodday to you, Sir!" And with that, she turns on her heel, dismissing him and coming swiftly to my side. "What a disagreeable oaf!" she says, loudly enough for Night to hear, as was her intention.

We can hear Mr Night's loud grunt and muffled curse as we part company. From then on, I ask Etta to decline any more offers for

Mountain Boy. They came from an assortment of people; one was from a woman dressed like a man. Etta finds it hard to keep a straight face when explaining no sale to this unusual person. Etta smiles behind her fan as the woman dressed in baggy man's pants and boots, topped with a presentable lady's blouse struts away.

"Sensible attire for women in Australia, I think. After all, we are expected to work as hard as men," Etta remarks in all seriousness.

However, I see the funny side and smile at the paradox. But do I have the right to comment, when I nearly always refer to Etta as a she, when Henry is dressed and behaves like Etta? Now I think about it, our life is one huge paradox.

I am pleased to be on our way after having to explain again and again to interested parties, "No, Mountain Boy's not for sale."
We reach the post office in time to collect the telegram. Etta reads it aloud.

"Teddy March has his memory back. Please return at your earliest convenience."

Etta's recollection of the day when Teddy fell from the buggy shows in her distressed expression, and her body tenses like a child who knows it is about to be slapped.

"I know what you're thinking, Etta. But I wouldn't worry too much. I'm sure he'll remain dazed about the incident. Look on the bright side. At least we won't have to care for him any longer. Teddy will be able to resume his life in Goulburn and we won't have the concern of selling his property, or dealing with Mr Night," I tell her in an attempt to cheer her up.

"You may be right, Pierre, though I have another opinion of Teddy March. Let us return home and face the fray, shall we?"

I can only hope there is no fray to face, I think dismally. My attempts at lightening the load, as Night had put it, are to no avail.

"I've heard the railway may be attaching a stock carriage to the Sydney-bound train, Etta. I'll check at the station before we return to March's Run. We should try and get home the quickest way." Etta nods with a worried look.

CHAPTER 40
THE DUKE

Roberto returns to the hotel and is immediately stunned by the Duke's exuberant love for Lily White. He is almost speechless. "But Duke Harrowfield, do you think it wise to be so… so ardent? Your heart may not stand the strain!"

"Dear Roberto, if I die now, I'll die deliriously happy. For the first time in my life, I have found my one true love. And to think I've had to travel to the end of the earth to do so has given me more faith than I could have ever imagined."

Roberto says nothing, but he is observing. *The Duke's face, though still ruddy, seems thinner, and his frown lines, once predominant, have all but disappeared.*

"I have to admit, Duke, you do look positively radiant. I, for one, have never seen you look so happy. But on a different note, I must now give you bad news. Henry has refused your request. He said, 'For the last time, tell the Duke I will not return to England'. He said he relinquishes all rights to his inherited fortune." Roberto lowers his eyes and asks sheepishly, "Does this mean I am to still marry Gertrude and be adopted by you, m' lord?"

"Frankly, Roberto, I don't give a damn what happens to my conceited twit of a daughter, or my bitter-as-a-lemon wife! I have joined Henry's ranks. I have found true happiness and fulfilment. I now know money or station cannot replace what I feel for my beloved Lily. Who was it who said, 'My kingdom for a horse?' Well, they were damned right! Yes, now I remember. It was King Richard 111."

"Lily? Lily? You don't mean Lily who works in the hotel office?" Roberto asks, aghast.

"Yes, the one and only, beautiful, charming, delightful Lily, who has elevated me from being the dictatorial, power-hungry, empty man I was, to a compassionate, caring human being," the Duke explains.

The Duke's weighty and self-satisfied exhalation fills the room like a momentous breeze, and with a similar inhalation, the Duke continues to wax lyrical about his beautiful Lily. All the while, Roberto watches and listens, a knowing smirk curling his lips. *Mmm, one door shuts, another door opens.*

"I couldn't be happier for you, m' lord. But how, pray tell, will you go about explaining this situation to the Duchess? It's none of my business, I know. Although one minute I was to become the heir to your estate and now, well, I'm not sure if I even hold my position as your personal butler?" Once again, Roberto injects the proper amount of humility into his words.

"Never fear, Roberto. You will remain my personal butler and because of my recently enhanced generous nature, I will increase your wages, along with one full day off a week. How do you like those lollies, Roberto?" the Duke asks, pleased with his own munificence. He gives Roberto no time to answer. "Mind you, we may be staying here. In Australia, I mean. You see, Lily suffers dreadfully with seasickness. She almost lost her life on her voyage here," the Duke adds gravely.

"I understand, m' lord," Roberto says. *I'm sure it wouldn't have been the first thing she'd lost.* "May I ask once again, how will you go about settling your personal and business affairs in England, Sir? I would assume it will take a lot of doing."

"Yes, quite right, Roberto. However, I have a most valued and trustworthy firm of solicitors and accountants at my beck and call. Once they receive my telegram, the wheels will be set in motion. However, I do have more than a little fear that my wife may cause the most trouble. But if I am generous and kind, I'm sure she will understand my change of heart. Besides, she knows I have always loved Henry, albeit at arm's length. And there's another reason, Roberto. I dread to leave him behind. He is my only brother and now, it seems, our hearts are similar. Passion versus wealth and position. Whoever would have thought, hey?"

The cogs of Roberto's devious mind begin to turn. The thought of blackmailing Lily with the information he knows about her past immediately comes to mind. *Sending Pierre and Henry money – how ludicrous! They will pay me to keep my mouth shut, and I will pay the stool pigeon in jail a little money to keep him quiet and provide a clever lawyer. Serving this overstuffed, pompous idiot for the rest of my life is the last thing I want to do. I don't mind this new country; plenty of opportunity for an ingenious mind. Yes, with a little conniving, a life of leisure will be all mine.*

"Roberto, you're daydreaming. Wake up, man. We have work to do and letters to write. From this very moment, I bid farewell to my old life and welcome the new!" he announces happily, but immediately pauses and rubs his chin contemplatively. "I do trust Henry will be pleased to hear I will be living close by – well, most of the time. Maybe we can kindle some degree of real affection for each other. After all, he is my younger brother. I shall send a letter to Sarah. I would like to introduce Lily to her – to everyone, really. Perhaps we could have a jolly weekend at 'Mountain View' on Henry's return. What do you think, Roberto?"

"Absolutely, m' lord. What an interesting array of characters to place together in such a beautiful location," Roberto adds facetiously. "A real cause for celebration, don't you think?"

"Quite right, Roberto."

His sarcasm is totally lost on the Duke.

"Now I need some more writing paper. Oh, and some ink. I'm sure you know the way to Miss Lily's office; she will be happy to oblige." The Duke says mildly as he begins getting his papers in order.

No doubt she'd oblige anyone – for the right price. "Certainly. Straightaway, m' lord," Roberto says walking backwards, bowing twice. *What a perfect opportunity!*

Roberto knocks loudly on Lily's door, to which she responds, "Do come in, I'm not deaf, whoever it is!" She looks up distractedly from behind her desk. "Oh, it's you, Roberto. I'm sorry I can't help you with your frustrations anymore – you know what I mean. And if you are not already aware of it, the Duke has fallen madly in love with me, so my philandering days are over, and I am now an honest woman. Actually, I'm quite fond of him," she says with a ring of surprise in her voice.

Roberto laughs, loudly and disbelievingly – he can't help it.

"I came only for writing paper and ink. It's for the Duke. He needs to write farewell letters. But since I'm here, Lily, I'd like to discuss an idea." He walks forward and places his hands on the desk, leaning towards her. "In the unfortunate event of the Duke finding out about your illicit past, Lily," he says menacingly," what would you do then? It would be a terrible shame to have to give up the opportunity of a lifetime, wouldn't it, my dear? On the other hand, trust a friend to keep your secret and protect you from other untoward rascals with bribery on their mind would be a good idea, don't you think? What would you be prepared to pay?" Roberto tilts his not-so-unhandsome head to one side and smiles smugly, waiting for Lily to digest his proposition.

Lily's eyes flare like a bull about to charge. "You lowdown gutter snipe," she hisses, "I can't believe you're capable of such a thing. You paid me fair and square for my services. I even did it once for nothing! I thought you were a gentleman. Now I can see what you really are. I have a good mind to tell the Duke you're trying to blackmail me, and what you're saying is nothing more than a pack of bloody stinking lies!"

"Now, now, Lily. Let's not lose your ladylike composure. You see, I have grown up in the Duke's household, and yes, there are sides to him I genuinely like, but also many I don't. I've always been rather envious of his lifestyle. No doubt you'll find out about that in time. Anyway, I have ambitions other than having to bum-wipe a fat, pompous ding-a-ling for the rest of my days. I am young and good looking, with a smart mind for business. I wouldn't mind enjoying a bit of the high life with not too much hard work attached. So, dear Lily, it would be in your interests to pay me for my silence and when you tire of the old Duke's lacklustre performance, I'd be happy to oblige you with a bit of youthful virility – at a cost, of course!"

Lily throws a book that misses Roberto's head by inches. "Get out of here, you despicable worm! And for your information, the Duke is more than capable of satisfying me!"

"Oh, I've forgotten the ink and paper for the old fart, thank you, *sweet* Lily," Roberto says sarcastically, accepting the items Lily thrusts towards him. He turns and makes his way to the door and pauses before turning the handle. "You'd best think about what I've said, Lily. I'll give you until tomorrow afternoon." He closes the door quietly behind him while Lily slumps at her desk, forlornly wondering how to deal with the mess she is now in.

CHAPTER 41
SARAH

My hand is still shaking with anger; it is a wonder I manage to write a note to Teddy.

> *You must stay here until you feel well enough to travel to Goulburn. Also, there are more pressing matters to consider, namely, your seduction of Melanie and your proposal of marriage to her. I am assuming you had in fact asked her to be your wife before you forced your attentions upon her. You have Melanie's innocence and reputation to consider. If she is found to be pregnant, you will have a duty to uphold! I will make sure of it.*

I pass the note to Teddy, who remains sitting at the table nursing his head with one hand. With a huge sigh, he takes the note in his other hand and reads. His brow creases, and his generous mouth droops. This is not the response I hope for. He scribbles words that are hard for me to decipher.

> *Dear Sarah, please forgive me. The man I now am is completely unaware of any advances towards Melanie, nor of any intentions to marry her. I was not of stable mind before; I was someone else completely. I cannot take any responsibility for my actions while suffering under some sort of trance or state of amnesia. Any court in the land would support my claim.*

Rosie stands, peering over his shoulder. Before the ink can dry on the last word, she grabs the note. Her fingers work fiercely, shredding it to bits, her anger rising to boiling point. She grips Teddy's shoulders and shakes him. I try to translate what she yells at him.

"I've a good mind to give you another hard whack, you rascal! You will remain right here, my lad, until Henry and Pierre return." She turns swiftly to Melanie. "Get some rope so I can tie him up. Hurry!" Rosie tightens her grip on Teddy. "I'm not takin' no for an answer, lover boy!" Teddy struggles to stand, but Rosie pushes him down. "Quick, girl, run!"

I scurry to help Rosie hold him down just as James walks in.

"What on earth are you ladies up to?" he asks, surprise and amusement evident in his expression.

Rosie quickly explains the entire episode, while I watch with interest as anger clouds James's fine features.

"I'm not so surprised at all," James says when Rosie has finished. "I've had to put a stop to him following Melanie into the scrub on more than a few occasions. But to think one hard whack on Teddy's head has brought him back to his senses – it's truly amazing. I've heard about that, though never thought it possible."

James leans forward, locking eyes with Teddy.

"So, Teddy, what do you have to say? Can you honestly deny fucking Melanie and not remembering a thing about it?" *A little uncouth, my love, I think.*

"I most certainly can. I don't remember anything! And if you don't let me go, I will have you lot locked up for kidnapping!" Teddy says petulantly.

This statement wounds Melanie, it seems. Her body slumps, and she hangs her head, looking devoid of hope. Poor little mite, I think, as I behold this beautiful young woman. I immediately enfold her in an embrace as she sobs uncontrollably. Teddy March remains completely unmoved by this heartbroken display. I throw him a scornful look and think to myself – I'd rather have the amnesia-struck Teddy. I couldn't imagine what sort of man could be so callous – or could I? Memories resurface of a few rogues my birth mother had the displeasure of doing business with.

James shifts his attention from Teddy to Melanie and then to Rosie, who stands with a cast-iron frying pan at the ready. "I think we should let Teddy leave of his own free will, Rosie. It is obvious this situation cannot be resolved by forcing him to remain here. Though I am sure he would like to reimburse us generously for his care, and board and lodgings, while he was unable to care for himself." He looks directly at Teddy, his eyebrows raised.

Mmm, very clever, James. A little dowry for Melanie if she is pregnant.

"Unless of course, Teddy, you would prefer to face rape charges and bear the consequences. After all, two well-respected witnesses were present. They even rescued Melanie from your untoward advances, Teddy, old chap! You'd have no chance of defending yourself, especially when the ladies say you'd regained your memory only moments before the unfortunate event," James says, slapping Teddy on the back – hard.

Teddy's demeanour changes to dour. Is it because he knows he is beaten, or is he still not feeling well? He looks terrible.

"I must admit," he says, confirming my suspicions, "at this very moment I would not be capable of travelling alone to Goulburn. I feel quite ill and extremely tired. I will rest here, if I may, until I'm able to think straight and be rid of my headache. If you don't mind?"

"We don't mind at all," says Rosie, with a mischievous grin. "Come, let me make you comfortable. You need a good long sleep, that's all, then I'm sure you'll come to your senses." Rosie winks at us as she helps Teddy from his chair.

James makes Melanie a concoction with a liberal amount of rum to help her sleep. "It'll settle her nerves," he says, as she swallows between sniffles. I then lead Melanie to her washroom before tucking her under a comforter, clean from the intrusion on her person. I kiss her on the cheek and gently stroke her back until her sniffling stops and she sleeps at last.

Sascha wakes with perfect timing. I find her chatting to an invisible person, her cupid red lips moving quickly. Little chubby arms reach up and I hold her close to my heart, her legs dangling over my baby-filled tummy. When I swing her over my hip and rub my belly, she leans down, mimicking, before her angelic eyes fix on mine. "Baby," she says, holding my face and kissing me with wet lips. Oh, how I adore her, my precious darling. I am blessed. Suddenly, my thoughts turn to Melanie. How would she cope with a man who has obviously deceived her in the cruellest possible way, then left her to carry her burden alone? I can only pray she has not become pregnant.

Three days pass, with each of us quietly resolved. Yes, we hold our own opinions about what should, or should not, happen. I have changed my mind about forcing Teddy into marrying Melanie. From what I see of the other side of amnesia, he will only treat her badly. To add to my consternation, I had witnessed Teddy's clear attraction to James – most inappropriate. I had seen him touch James's hand, and place a guiding hand on his lower back, rather too near his buttocks for my liking. However, I am sure James will strongly deter Teddy from making any real physical advances. I wonder if I am correct in likening Teddy's behaviour to that of Pierre and Henry. I've become tired of the continuous puzzle and look forward to their return, although James, I'm proud to say, has the property running like a wheel, and caring for the horses meticulously. We simply need a rest, especially from Teddy.

It is yet another cloudless morning while I sit in my favourite chair on the front veranda. I then observe a haze of dust begin to rise from the road, which can only mean the postman or visitors are approaching. With any luck, they will provide some pleasure to alleviate the misery that surrounds me. Teddy sleeps most of the time or sits forlorn whenever James is not around to please his eye. Melanie mopes about, only half doing her duties, and James seems perpetually weary, maybe even a little depressed. Rosie spends most of her time caring for her adopted family and I don't blame her. I am pleased she has found love at last. The garden we have nurtured into abundance is now wilting under the early heat of late November. And my excitement at Rosie's coming wedding is fading like a rainbow end without the gold.

Suddenly, from the dense foliage of a giant red gum, a mass of white wings bursts upon the cloudless blue sky. The cockatoos swoop then hover as a low cloud to surround Pete, the postman. Whenever he carries produce in spring, this always happened. His arms wave about madly, shooing the pesky thieves away – a losing battle, it seems. I hurry as best I can, but so heavily pregnant I can barely move, let alone run to help Pete repel his attackers. Suddenly, the birds fly away and for a moment, my eyes strain skywards. I wonder why until old Pete shows me a craggy smile and James – shotgun in hand – grabs my arm. I jump slightly. It is such a bother to be deaf!

I urgently take the mail from Pete, while James chats with him. The first letter I open is from the Duke. How exciting! He would like to come and stay, along with his friend, Miss Lily White.

Roberto will remain in Sydney for a well-deserved rest.

I do believe you will be welcoming Pierre and Henry
home soon. I wish to be there for their homecoming.
Please telegram if this is not convenient. Otherwise I
shall see you in two days' time.
With fondest regards,
Duke Harrowfeild.

Never has the Duke signed a letter, "with fondest regards". In any case, I thought he'd left for England. I wonder what is so important that he has changed his plans – or mind. Could it be the Miss Lily White he mentions? How interesting! I wave my letters to farewell Pete, and notice more dust rising down the road. I squint beyond the cloud of dust and see a buggy with a horse tethered behind. I am delighted when I realise it is Henry and Pierre.

CHAPTER 42
HENRI-ETTA

I could never have imagined how much I would miss Sarah and all who live at "Mountain View", especially my darling Rosie. I hug and kiss Sarah over her enormous stomach, while James hurries to shake Pierre's hand.

"Dear Sarah, I don't wish to be rude, but are you having twins? You're not, are you?" I ask, my head tilted to one side.

Sarah's body wobbles with silent laughter, probably shaking the poor baby inside. She pats her tummy firmly and lifts her hands to explain.

I am so overjoyed to see you both home safe. There is so much I need to tell you. And I'm sure you have wonderful news to tell us, hopefully it's all joyous, unlike our recent events.

Sarah turns away, gazing into the distance, I'm sure, to hide her sudden tears.

James interrupts to pump my hand so vigorously in a "welcome home" gesture my picture hat almost falls off. We four continue to the homestead where the mood is sombre. This is particularly apparent when meeting Melanie. The pretty and happy young lady we'd waved goodbye to months ago is now drooping with sadness. I wonder if she has had her heart broken by some callous swain. I learn later that this is the case – the callous swain being none other than Teddy March. I am most fortunate to be sitting down as I listen to what has taken place between Melanie and Teddy, otherwise I would have surely fainted to the floor with a thud.

We all gather around the kitchen table over a large pot of tea. Sarah signs the whole sordid story, while James helps by whispering embellishments to the horrifying facts. I am at the point of needing a stiff whisky when the despicable Teddy March enters the kitchen, obviously having just woken from his morning nap. His sleepy, blood-shot eyes peer from behind his tangled hair, most unlike the well-groomed Teddy I knew.

"Teddy," I say sternly, showing him no mercy. "I've been told by James they finally found the perfect means of bringing you back to normal – if I could ever say that." I curl my lip in a scornful smile.

Yes, I am correct. There is nothing normal about Teddy. His personality has more than a touch of Jekyll and Hyde.

He tells me wearily, "I'm unable to remember anything, Etta. They say I was forcing myself upon Melanie. It was why Sarah had to use such dynamic tactics. But I can honestly say that I cannot remember." He brushes away a lock of hair from his eyes, then smiles widely. "I must say, Etta, you look positively radiant. The journey has done you good."

"I am extremely well, thank you, Teddy," I tell him stiffly, "and I would like to tell you all," I continue, glancing around my friends who wait in anticipation, "what a wonderful adventure we have had and how much success and fame Mountain Boy has achieved. Not to forget my success in winning the Sydney Art Prize." My false bosoms swell with the extent of my pride. "Although I will not divulge another word, not until I have heard the entire story about what has happened here. Which reminds me; as from tomorrow we will have another guest staying with us."

"You mean the Duke and his lady friend, Lily White?" James interrupts with a radiant smile.

"What? No! I was *not* referring to the Duke. Has he not left for England? Of course not. Not if he's coming here to stay. With a lady friend, you say. Are you able to offer more information, James?" I am intrigued.

"No, I can't, Etta. Sarah received the Duke's letter just before you arrived. That was all it said. That he and his lady friend are to be here in two days' time. Which, come to think of it, might be today or tomorrow. Oh, yes, he said Roberto would not be accompanying them as he needed to rest."

"For Heaven's sake, the silly old fool. Anyway, Timmy, Mountain Boy's jockey, will be coming to live with us soon, so we'd better start building a bungalow, or perhaps he can occupy the barn cottage? Yes, that will do it."

Pierre sits down beside me; his arm soothes my shoulder and his butterfly kisses on my neck send a shiver through me. I notice Teddy's pained expression.

200

"Can someone tell me what is going on here?" Teddy yells. "Aren't you married to Sarah, Pierre? If so, unhand that man, I mean woman. If I remember rightly, before my accident, Etta, you agreed to marry me!" Teddy shouts, his face scarlet with fury.

I stand and wallop my fist on the table with devastating effect. Teddy is immediately quiet. "I most certainly did not agree to marry you, Teddy." I measure my words carefully. "In fact, even if you were the last person on earth, I would *never* marry you! You, Sir, are no gentleman!" The colour drains from Teddy's face. He clearly knows what I mean and, apparently, so does everyone else.

Pierre and James look daggers at Teddy. Melanie screams hysterically and charges from the room. Sarah is on her tail until she collides with Rosie who's just opened the front door and stepped inside with two of Ernie's youngest. I must say, they look unusually clean and well dressed – the other four older ones are obviously at school. Which reminds me again, I wonder whatever happened to Sarah becoming a teacher's assistant to Miss Amy Watson? Never mind, all in due course.

I ignore the mayhem around me and go to Rosie. "My darling grandmother," I cry, clasping her to my breast, suddenly realising *it feels like only half of Rosie remains.* I hold her from me to view her newly formed figure. "Rosie, you've lost weight. You look amazing! What an elegant bride you will be. I cannot wait! I want to be your bridesmaid so much!"

"There is no one else I'd rather have, Etta." As our tears flow, our embrace reflects the years of love and happiness this kind, adorable woman has given me. No more words are needed.

Meanwhile, James and Pierre firmly escort the irate Teddy March from the house, heading towards the barn. It is a perfect time to speak with Rosie. Without delay, we settle down at the table to discuss all that has transpired in my absence to form both sides of the penny. I regale her with my tale first, her eyes wide with shock.

"What an adventure, Etta! I wish I'da been there," Rosie says when I finish, one hand clasped to her cheek. "Fancy, hey, a shootout just like in the wild west of America! Remember the show we went to see a few years back in London? Fancy a boat load of redskins, gunslingers, including women, coming all the way from America to England. And that included their horses!" Rosie shakes her head chuckling, but nothing wobbles anymore; she is in fine shape and looking ten years younger.

"Yes, I do remember, especially those dashing cowboys, ooh la-la." My hands go to my blushing cheeks and I look humbly at Pierre, who simply smiles, bless him. "It was most similar I can tell you, Rosie." I realise I should comment on Rosie's new appearance. "I'm so proud and happy for you, Rosie. Look at you! You're a vision of joy and loveliness, not that you weren't always. But your happiness now shines from within. And shedding those unwanted pounds, well, it makes you look so young and glamorous. Where did you buy your frock? I simply adore it!" The youngest Ernie begins to cry; I think it is because his brother has hit him on the head with a wooden spoon.

Rosie gives him sympathy, the other remonstration, then fruit cake in equal measures, and peace is restored. We resume our conversation that includes the news about Mountain Boy winning yet another race at Hawkesbury – his third. We'd caught the train to the lower mountains, bought a new buggy, having sold the other in Goulburn, and backtracked to Hawkesbury racetrack. There, The Boy had won by six lengths. My confidence was skyrocketing.

"He is going to win the Doncaster Handicap at Randwick on Easter Saturday! It's a Group One race. And then, my dearest grandmother Rosie, he will go on to be a champion! I will stake my life on it." I proclaim enthusiastically.

"Please don't kill yourself over a horse, Etta. It would break my heart, it would." She quips.

Our laughter, it appears, is loud enough for even Sarah to hear. Ha-ha! No – I must not joke about Sarah's deafness – *naughty Henry*. However, she does enter the kitchen smiling as if she'd heard us, then with signs she tells us:

I have managed to calm Melanie down with a promise that if she is pregnant with Teddy's baby, we will care for her here at "Mountain View" and nobody will know. Melanie has made it clear she does not want the baby. She will adopt it out. What she does want is to open a milliner's shop in Sydney Town. She works industriously in her spare time, creating the most beautiful hats imaginable. I will show you, Etta.

Sarah hurries away and soon returns with several examples of what I can only call millinery masterpieces. Feathers and bows abound upon fine straw and folded chiffon; all are fashioned in different colours and spectacular shapes.

"How magnificent, Sarah! I will buy the lot. What a clever

young lady. I wonder where Melanie's talent comes from. Is her mother a seamstress perhaps?"

"No, she isn't," Rosie speaks, "and her mother was not happy with Melanie leaving her alone to care for the other twelve siblings. Poor woman never gets a break from cooking, cleaning, and waiting on a lazy husband. Is it any wonder Melanie wants nothing to do with having babies, and wants to make a life for herself? She told me she would have children only if she married a rich man who could afford to pay for a nursemaid. Otherwise she's determined to run a successful millinery business. She's saved every penny she's earned here, apart from buying material to make her hats."

"I must congratulate Melanie later!" I say, clapping my hands and noticing that the backs of them are getting a *little* hairy! Damn hair, it should know better than to grow on my otherwise feminine hands and my dimpled chin. Anyway, back to the matter at hand. "It's all settled then. We will be rid of Teddy March post haste! It would be well if he were gone before the Duke arrives. Let us pack Mr March's bags at once, ladies!"

CHAPTER 43
THE DUKE

The Duke gently brushes Lily's inner thigh, his fingers inching closer to her rosebud, as he calls it. She gives him her most seductive look, eyes lowered, and lips moistened by the tip of her tongue – just then the carriage hits a rock. Blood appears on her lips but is immediately collected by the Duke's hungry kiss.

"The pain enhances the pleasure I hope, my dear. Are you alright? Does it hurt badly?" he inquires solicitously. Lily is grateful for his kiss; it has prevented her from cursing like a gutter wench.

"After *your* kiss, Albert, how could I complain?"

Eyelashes flutter, as does her Parisian fan. She sucks back the irritation caused by her injury and melts into the Duke's broad shoulder. "How much further, my darling?" she asks while dabbing her bloodied tongue with her handkerchief. "I'm feeling weary and, in truth, I'm a little anxious at the thought of meeting Henry and his friends. They may not like me," she says in a small voice.

"You must be jesting, my dear. They will *adore* you, as I do. But remember, please call Henry, Etta – not Henry. Though I don't know why he doesn't call himself Henrietta, ha-ha. Marcus!" The Duke yells, tapping the roof of the carriage with his walking stick. "Could you hurry the horses up a little? Miss Lily is impatient to reach 'Mountain View'!"

"Yes, Sir, very good, Sir, though it's a bumpy road as you have no doubt been experiencing. I'd hate to break a shaft, or Miss Lily's pretty neck, if I may be so bold as to say so, m' lord!" Marcus calls down cheerfully from the driver's seat.

"Just take care and speed up a little, there's a good man." The Duke pats Lily's knee. "Won't be long now, my love, and you will turn all heads in admiration. May I suggest that after our introductions, you have a little beauty nap before dressing for dinner. Please wear that gorgeous satin gown I purchased for you at David Jones & Co. You look stunning in it."

"Yes, Albert, of course," Lily says before yawning widely. She closes her eyes and is soon lost in slumber.

The Duke sits contented. He is enormously pleased with his transformation from pompous peer to worldly lover and caring brother. He can now understand and share Henry's passion for life, despite their different sexual preferences. Also, the rugged untouched beauty of this land, Australia, has day by day worked its spell upon him. He will find it hard to leave, even to finalise his business dealings. And especially hard to return to his toxic wife, and a daughter who is far too like her mother to be promised to any decent man. He frowns at this, but his smile soon returns when they reach the road leading up to "Mountain View".

"We're here, sweet pea. Wakey, wakey," he says with a gentle nudge to his sleeping beauty.

Sarah, Henri-Etta, Pierre, Rosie with two little ones tugging at her skirt, and Melanie, who is trying hard to look inconspicuous, stand on the veranda together, a little apart from Teddy March.

"What's this? The whole tribe is out to greet us! Come, Lily, they all look as if they are not sure who it is. We must put their concerns at bay."

The Duke steps down from the carriage with ease, due to his much thinner frame and the youthfulness that love has imbued him with – thanks to Lily. He offers his hand to Lily and helps her down. The small gathering stands transfixed, their faces displaying a mixture of pleasure, anger and shock. No one speaks.

"Well, what sort of greeting is this?" The Duke asks joyfully, his smile widening. "My friend Miss Lily White and I have come here to celebrate life, and yet you all look like you're at a funeral. Cheer up!" He escorts Lily up the wooden steps. "Come, Lily, allow me to introduce you. This is Etta, my, ah, my sibling – yes, that will do. My sibling." The Duke's smile passes over their faces like a searchlight.

No one moves until Henri-Etta steps, forward, embracing Lily with enthusiasm.

"Please excuse us, Lily. Pierre and I have not long ago arrived from our own travels and have only just found out you were coming to stay. I'm so pleased to meet you." Henri-Etta takes a long look at the Duke. "I say, brother, you look amazing! It seems you and Rosie have been eating from the same feed bin!"

Thank the Lord, Henri-Etta's remark breaks the awkward silence and laughter spreads like a flood.

Teddy March lowers his surprised gaze from the Duke. He remembers the Duke quite well from his years in England before coming to the colonies, but he never would have guessed Henri-Etta was related to his occasional drinking and philandering partner.

Just as the Duke spies a large packed canvas bag on the veranda, a young man driving a buggy approaches the house from the direction of the dusty horse yards. James eases back on the reins and comes to a stop. He looks up at the crowd on the veranda, then toward the Duke and Lily, and asks of no one in particular, "Is Mr March ready?"

The Duke's bushy eyebrows rise as he looks towards Teddy. "I thought I recognised you on my first visit here," he says, slapping the hollow-eyed Teddy March on the back. "Edward March, I remember! One of the greatest practical jokers in the entire country! I say, you even taught an old boy like me a thing or two. I wondered what had ever happened to you, you scoundrel. Kick you out of England, did they? One joke too many, hey what!" Not realising how close to the mark his words are, he gives him another slap for good measure; it makes Teddy's head spin.

"I'm sorry, I can't stay and chat, Sir. I must immediately return to my property in Goulburn. I've been away far too long." The last thing Teddy wants to do is explain his exile from England or his current embarrassing predicament. In his weakened state, it all becomes too much for poor Teddy and he drops to the ground like an autumn leaf.

"Oh, for God's sake!" the Duke shouts as Teddy crashes to the boards. "Come, help me lift the poor man. He looks like he's fought ten rounds with Jem Mace. What on earth has happened to him?"

James leaps from the carriage like a startled gazelle and in four bounds is up the steps. His superb physique does not pass unnoticed by Lily, nor does the attractiveness of Pierre's bulging biceps, as he helps carry Teddy inside to his bed. Lily follows them; she is fascinated. Even the injured man is a fine specimen. She had thought that perhaps this home would be full of rather unremarkable individuals – how wrong she was. The Duke had never explained what to expect, so her expectations were low. Now her interest is piqued, and she is wide awake and eager to hear the story of how and why Teddy March, whom the Duke apparently knows well, lies in his bed, clearly the worse for wear. Not to mention the fact that the other darlings were clearly trying to be rid of him before the Duke's arrival. *Mmm, very interesting.*

Rosie finds smelling salts and shoves them under Teddy's nose. "Wake up, Teddy, please wake up! We need to know you're alright." After a few nervous shakes, Rosie looks over her shoulder. "I think we should leave him be. He seems to be breathing normally, so maybe he'll be alright to go home in the morning." Her customary nod in agreement with her words comes on cue. "I'll just put the kettle on, and we'll all have a nice cuppa. Ernie will be coming soon to fetch me after he's picked up the other four children from school."

They duly troop into the kitchen. "If you don't mind, Rosie, I'd like some brandy in my tea," says the Duke. *Especially with four ankle biters coming.* "This has been quite a shock and I'd like very much to hear what has been going on around here." He turns to Lily. "My dearest, I think you should take the nap we spoke about. Etta will escort you to your room."

"Not on your bleedin' – I mean I would prefer to stay, Albert. It all sounds so interesting." Lily takes a fleeting look around the group. "That is, if no one has any objection?"

"You may as well know the truth," Etta says with a sigh, "if you are going to be my brother's mistress. However, I must warn you, Lily, nothing you are about to hear is to be repeated outside these walls. Do you promise?"

"I promise, Etta. After all, we *all* have skeletons in our closets," Lily nods solemnly, her eyes wide. "Don't we?"

No one can deny her claim; they all have tales to tell, one way or another. Everyone settles around the kitchen table and Etta is about to start when they hear a knock at the door.

"I'll get it," says Etta, rising from her chair, and all eyes follow. They hear Etta say, "Come in, Theobald. Oh, thank you so much! This money *will* come in handy. I'd like to contribute it to Rosie's wedding." Etta, bright eyed and with a handful of gold coins enters the kitchen followed by Theobald. "Look, everyone, Mr Tootle has sold my painting of Satan." Etta excitedly displays the gold coins. "I'd like to introduce you to my brother, the Duke of Harrowfeild, and his lady friend, Lily White. This is Theobald Tootle, a friend of ours and a great artist." Etta draws out a chair for Theobald.

He needs to sit immediately. *The sister of a duke?*

The generous kitchen table seats twelve, and just as well, as it is becoming a tight squeeze, especially when a minute later Ernie enters with four of his children, all of whom carry biscuits and milk. They are sent outside to play, much to the Duke's relief.

Ernie is perhaps the only one who has no secrets to disclose, and besides, he is the law. The stories being told this afternoon would, in normal circumstances, most definitely land people in trouble, if not in jail. It seems unless they form a united front and keep a pact to defend and honour each other, they may all be at risk, particularly Henri-Etta and Pierre. Or they could continue to weave a tangled and dangerous web of lies to disguise their realities. However, Etta has the good sense to realise it is high time for everyone to bring everything out in the open – for better or worse.

Etta turns to Theobald and says quietly and seriously, "Theobald, we are about to confide in each other our innermost secrets as true friends and confidantes. If you wish to stay, you must be sworn to secrecy." Etta looks deep into Theobald's non-winking eye, until he nods.

"I swear I will not breathe a single word of what is said to anyone, dear Etta."

"Good, because I, for one, will feel the weight of the world lifted from my shoulders and my heart will be free at last, that is, if I am able to tell my story to a group of trusted friends, such as you who have graced this gathering today." *A bit over the top, but hard to resist my flair for the dramatic.* Etta takes a big breath and begins. "My time here in Australia came about because Pierre's and my act of true love was looked upon as a carnal sin." She holds Pierre's hand tightly and gives the Duke a pointed look as she braces her shoulders and surveys the faces around the table.

Ernie looks slightly uncomfortable, and Etta notices. "Have you any idea what I'm about to tell you, Ernie?"

"Yes, I do, and it has taken me a long time to consider what Rosie has told me about you, Etta. I'm now at a crossroads. I wish I didn't know. You fooled me good and proper, and I would have preferred to stay ignorant. Now I have to make a difficult decision about what I should do."

Henry's heart crashes through his stomach, and Pierre's face turns a whiter shade of pale. Those who know about Henry look equally horrified, and the ones who don't, namely Theobald, Lily and Melanie, turn their heads to each other with silent questions written on their faces.

"As I'll be among friends, should I wear a frock to the wedding or a suit?" Ernie asks with a cheeky grin.

"Oh! You're a terrible tease, Ernie! I thought you were serious!" Etta laughs with relief and slaps his hand across the table.

"No, I am serious." Ernie coughs nervously. "I've always had a bit of thing about women's clothes," he says, laughing self-consciously.

"You're joking, of course!" protests the Duke.

"Unfortunately, I'm not, m' lord. Though I don't share any of Etta's other, ah, um, desires. I simply like dressing as a woman. But never in public, mind you. Maybe it's because I'm always in uniform. Rosie knows, don't you, love?" Rosie nods and smiles. "I had to give my wife money to keep her mouth shut. But she's gone and now Rosie makes me dresses." He squeezes Rosie's hand.

"Here, take some of this and buy yourself a frock or two with my compliments. Save Rosie the trouble," Etta says with a wink as she places several gold coins on the table in front of the happy pair.

"No thanks, Etta, we're doing okay, aren't we, love?" He turns to kiss Rosie on the cheek.

"Yes, we are, Ernie. Money can't buy happiness."

Melanie finally twigs. "I'd never tell a soul about you, Miss Etta. I promise. I reckon you'll be my best customer when I open my millinery shop. Apart from the fact that I'd like to keep you as my friends, especially if I'm pregnant." She lowers her pretty head and reaches for Sarah's hand.

"Good Lord, who's the father?" demands the Duke, a little stunned by so much scandalous information.

"I can answer that," says Teddy March, standing in the doorway, having dragged himself from his bed into the kitchen.

I bet he can, thinks Lily. She is loving the drama, which, compared to hers, makes her secrets look good.

"Unless you make an oath not to tell another living soul about what is confessed here today, Teddy, you are not welcome. And we shall have no hesitation in knocking you unconscious once again. Is it understood?" Etta says levelly, her neck stretched giraffe-like and her nose in the air to enhance her authority.

Pierre and James sit quietly, calculating. Will this work? Will all that is revealed then be allowed to simply pass into history, without further comment or effect on their tightknit friendships? They hope so, otherwise their lives will descend into turmoil. Everyone must honour the bonds formed from shared confidences.

Rosie, knowing this session will take hours to unfold, acts decisively. "I'll just put the kettle on. Another cuppa won't do us any harm. And I'll make some sandwiches."

"Make mine a brandy, please Rosie, if you don't mind?" asks the Duke, rubbing his forehead.

Rosie is taken aback. *Did he say, 'please Rosie'? Even the Duke's manners have changed for the better.*

They each need to believe their pact will remain intact until they die. The only ones to be anxious about the reception *their* admissions will receive are Lily and Theobald – and perhaps the Duke – but not for long.

"I have something to confess," says the winking Theobald, sitting nervously and wringing his sinewy hands. "I – I was a – a peeping Tom – in my youth." *Oh, goodness, now I'm stuttering as well as winking.* "It is how I came to acquire my winking eye. It was poked hard with a stick. And serves me right! I was lucky it healed, but it left me with this dreadful winking business. I won't ever dare to peek again. It's why I live on my own, in the bush, away from temptation." *Wink, wink.*

"Thank you for telling us, Theobald. I'm sure we all wondered how your dreaded wink came about, although we were too polite to ask," Etta says. *Good on you, Henri-Etta, holier than thou!*

All eyes turn to Lily. However, she isn't entirely sure whether to disclose her past, so she sits on it – *literally.* She can't help but show her amusement at poor Theobald's story. However, the stern looks from the gathering leave her suitably chastened and she shifts uncomfortably in her seat. Giving up her secrets may mean the end of her relationship with Albert. No – it's not worth it.

Etta fixes her with a steely look. Oh, no, here it comes. Go, Henry!

"So, Lily, tell us. Are you as pure as your name suggests? Lily white?" Etta asks with a sarcastic edge to her voice.

"That will do, Henry! Lily isn't here to be interrogated! If you lot wish to wash your dirty linen in public, then it is up to you. And I will give my word – whatever has been said here today will never leave my lips. And so, Henry, Lily's promise is all I will allow you to demand of her. Do you hear me?" The Duke throws Lily a lifesaver, and Lily grabs it with both hands.

"Don't worry, Etta, I most certainly give my word! On my reputation as an honest working woman, I solemnly promise I will *never* divulge to another soul a single word of what has been said here today," Lily says with unmistakable sincerity and an enormous amount of relief.

Well done, Lily! That was a narrow escape.

"Well then," Etta says with a huge sigh, "I shall tell how this saga began." She turns her head to Rosie who is busy making sandwiches. "Rosie, you'll have to pick up on the Teddy and Melanie episode, as I was not here to witness the truth of the matter."

Two hours later, with bellies full of lamb sandwiches and bladders full of tea, the Ten Musketeers make a pledge to keep their secrets hidden among themselves, and to help each other when in need. Although Teddy is a little reluctant at first, he is rather easily convinced, knowing he has too much to lose in refusing to commit to the pact of Henri-Etta and Co.

CHAPTER 44
SARAH

Rosie's wedding fell on a most glorious summer day. White cotton clouds gave pleasant shade just when the bride looked a little flushed. *Perfect!* Rosie appeared before her guests, a vision in a soft pink organza frock with one of Melanie's beautiful hats enhancing her ensemble. Ernie, though tempted to dress alternatively, compromised and chose a dove grey suit and a fetching pink bowtie to match Rosie's dress. Cerise petunias bloomed, cascading over the lips of terracotta pots painted dove grey – Henri-Etta's idea. All in all, the early summer garden had flourished after recent heavy rain. No need for music because the bellbirds chimed their timeless, appealing trill.

My father, the Reverend Timms, stood on a podium shaded by gumtrees where he proceeded to embark on one of his customary long-winded services. An hour passed before I could see that the congregation was cheering raucously and applauding loudly, probably because it was over! No doubt the sound echoed off surrounding mountains – I wished I could have heard it. Straight after, they signed the wedding certificate and, to my father's surprise, he received a written request from yours truly. I guided my father away from the mingling crowd, toward a comfortable chair under a grand peppercorn tree. As a breeze began to play with the leaves, he tugged the collar away from his neck to catch it. I'd filled a glass with sherry, his favourite beverage, and sat it on a side table. I waited nervously as he read my letter. From the corner of my eye I watched, until he reached for the sherry then screwed the letter into a ball as he drank. Slowly, he tipped his head backwards and appeared to be contemplating the branches over his head. He remained in this position, unblinking, until I thought he'd passed out. But no, unhurriedly his head came forward before his eyes sought mine.

Unbidden tears found my cheeks. I should have known this sanctimonious man could not forgive my sins, even though I had been forced to marry a man who had no desire to love to me as I deserved and needed to be loved. I had wanted to love my husband and to have children by him more than anything. These thoughts brought anger enough to dry my tears, and I lunged at him, my fists raised.

"Sarah, Sarah!" I saw his lips form my name. "Please Sarah, look at me." He grabbed my wrists, but the emotion in his eyes could not meet the fire in mine. He hung his head, perhaps remembering the night he'd taken me away from my dead mother.

I'd wanted to give Sarah the best life I could, to see her happy and content. How dare I choose who she should marry? Well, the Duke had arranged it, but I could have protested for the sake of my daughter's happiness. But now, of all days, Sarah wants me to annul her marriage to Pierre – after all, it was never consummated – and then marry her to James, the father of her babies. How could I not do this for her? How could I not give her the happiness she deserves so much? My precious child. However, to marry Etta and Pierre – this is too much to ask! They have fallen in love, she says. What am I to do?

"Please, be still my child." He held me tightly to his chest before releasing me to use sign language. "I love you dearly and I want you to be happy. Just give me time to think about what you have asked. I shall talk with your mother and give you our decision later in the day. Forgive me, Sarah. I know I am the one to blame. Yes, it was I who has brought this predicament upon you, and I'm sorry." His brow furrowed in thought. "Though I beg you tell me: how or when did Pierre change his preference from men to women? Does he truly love Etta? I must say she is a very attractive woman. I presume their love affair began when they travelled alone together."

Had I not already been mute I would have been struck speechless by the fact that my father had not yet realised that Etta was, in fact, Henry! However, I was certain I wasn't going to be the one to break the news to him.

A look of regret shadowed his face, and he shook his head. "I knew it was the wrong descion, leaving them alone. Any wonder a romance blossomed, especially with such a beautiful woman." He realised what he'd insinuated. "I am sorry, Sarah. You are just as beautiful. And look at James, the handsome young man who has fallen in love with you. Why, if I were a woman – well, never mind. I can see why you had babies with James. Pierre never consummated your marriage, did he?"

I shook my head emphatically.

"I see," he nodded. "Give me a little while, Sarah. We must now think of Rosie and Ernie. It's their wedding day and we must not cause a scene."

Father kissed my forehead. I knew then my wishes would be met. I smiled with the warm love I held for this dithering, confused man, who only meant well for me. I squeezed his hand and rested my head on his shoulder, though I must say it was with a guilty conscience. I found it most amusing that he was still unaware that Henry is Etta.

My wish was granted. The annulment was decreed the following week and a double wedding took place under the same maple tree at "Mountain View" two weeks later, though by then the garden, unfortunately, had suffered badly from a hot dry spell. Only the flowers that had been especially hand-watered survived, but that was of no real consequence compared to the happiness we shared that day.

Henri-Etta, as one could only imagine, was in her element. So enchanted was she to be dressing as a bride that Rosie had to keep reminding her, "Less is best, Etta," as she placed even more pearls around her neck and more bows on her frock. Rosie, her matron of honour, gently but firmly removed them. Henri-Etta was indeed the most beautiful, elegant bride that Rosie had ever seen. She cried tears of joy as she and the Duke walked Henri-Etta down the rose petal-strewn aisle to join the dashing Pierre.

I followed, with darling Sascha as an exquisite flower girl by my left side, the kicking baby still encased safely within my tummy, and Melanie, the glowing bridesmaid behind. Mother, in a floating mauve frock and beaming a smile, broke all protocol and escorted me down the aisle on my right. Our happiness reigned supreme.

With a promise to shorten the sermon, Father, through happy tears, gave his blessing, and without further ado, declared the four of us married.

The celebrations called only for the immediate family and friends, including Ernie's six children, who'd been allowed an enormous chocolate cake to keep them silent throughout the ceremony. But now, they were groaning from overloaded tummies and their wretched vomiting could be heard intermittently between the guests chatting and sipping champagne, so I was told.

Our secrets, I knew, were safe. All our dear friends would honour

our pledges. It was the best wedding gift we could be given.

CHAPTER 45
HENRY

I can barely believe I'm married to Pierre and I find no time to worry about the "what ifs". I live each day busy in contented bliss, especially when thinking of my brother Albert and how he has changed for the better. He's even managing without Roberto these days. Roberto returned to England, and good riddance to him. Though I do wonder why when Albert offered Roberto a substantial amount more in wages and one complete day off a week. Oh well, can't please them all. I only hope he keeps his mouth closed about Pierre and me. However, Lily seems to be taking care of Albert's every need. *I'm sure she does.* The Duke has now purchased The Royal Hotel – for a king's ransom – and gifted it to Lily White. *I love her name. Surely, it's made up.* I am so happy we now have extra rooms added to the homestead. It makes everything more comfortable with us all living and working together. We are indeed one big, happy family. Teddy has returned to Goulburn, as a better man he says in his letters of gratitude, but he has not made any commitment to fulfil his obligations to Melanie. Therefore, Pierre and I have made plans for the baby.

I am also excited to think about Mountain Boy racing again soon. Pierre has him fit, sound, and ready to do his best, which I'm sure will be good enough to win the Doncaster at Randwick this fast-approaching Easter Saturday. What to wear, what to wear? It's all I've thought about lately. I have the gorgeous hat, of course, made by Melanie – our incubator. Oh, dear me, I shouldn't say that! Now I've let the cat out of the bag. Melanie is pregnant and has promised Pierre and me that we can adopt her baby. My heart sings with joy at the thought of us raising our child together. Life could not be any better.

Oh dear, something is wrong. I can hear Rosie screaming. What did you say, Rosie? Goodness gracious, Sarah's in labour!

"Come quickly, Etta," Rosie calls again.

"What can I do but boil water?" I ask in a trembling voice. Now I'm trembling all over.

Three arduous hours later, Sarah, after a quick but painful birth, without the sound effects, is nestling a perfect baby boy in her arms. This is the first moment I dare to peek. I hadn't risked it before. I had simply lowered my head when handing Rosie clean towels and given prayers of thanks for not having a womb. Yes, adopting is the far better option for me. Oh, silly me – I don't have any other option! But then, some women are barren and can't have babies anyway, so adoption is their only option, too.

"Thank goodness," Rosie says, eyes raised to Heaven. "Thank the Lord, Sarah, that I arrived when I did. I had a premonition, I did. I said to Ernie, 'Sarah will give birth today and she'll be needing my help'. And I was right. It was a good thing I was here to untangle the umbilical cord from around your baby's neck."

While Rosie wipes the perspiration off her brow with a towel, Sarah nods towards her dresser where her writing pad sits. I follow her prompts and hand it to her then carefully remove the baby from her arms.

Rosie, I cannot thank you enough, she wrote. You have saved my baby's life. I can only honour you by naming him something like Rosie. I know, I will name him Buddy, as in Rosebud. I hope you agree.

Rosie reads the note and bursts into tears of happiness. As for me, I'm not mad about the name; it sounds like a dog I once had.

With self-conscious steps, James comes forward. He stands beside Sarah and gazes lovingly into her eyes before bending over and placing a lingering kiss on her lips. *How lovely.* He straightens and holds out his arms; I hand him his son. It's a tender and moving moment that I shall remember forever. His deep blue eyes glisten with tears of joy and pride. Such a feeling, I'm sure, is the best life can possibly offer. I pray Pierre and I have a similar experience when Melanie gives birth to our baby. *Our baby – it sounds so wonderful!*

CHAPTER 46
PIERRE

The day finally arrives, and we all make it to Randwick Racecourse. Well, except for Sarah, James and pregnant Melanie. Because Buddy is only three months old, the journey would have been too much for such a little babe.

Standing at the Randwick horse stalls, I fail to understand how I can feel so nervous and so confident at the same time. Etta, a quivering bundle of nerves, is standing alongside me. She does look extraordinarily lovely today and, as usual, turns all heads when gliding about the member's enclosure. *Ma belle reine!* I kiss her on the cheek and squeeze her hand. *Mmm, nice gloves. Kidskin?*

I sigh, delighted to see that Mountain Boy's race manners have mellowed since last time he raced. He seems to know what's about to happen. He's calm and self-assured, which is certainly a weight off my mind.

It's time to pick up the saddle. The racecourse is packed tight with racing enthusiasts, fashionable ladies, and the odd pickpocket. I must bump and shove my way through the crowd that ebbs and flows like a wild tide. The bookies, trying to outdo each other, call out the odds. Desperate punters cram closer, their hands waving money about to get the best price. It's a frenzied madhouse, until I finally get a clear passage to the jockeys' room. Hopefully, Timmy will have kept his nerve and not be influenced by the fact that this is a Group One race. As the "experts" have pointed out, he's no top jockey, but I know he's simply the perfect jockey for Mountain Boy. The newspapers are slamming me, too. One paper prints this scathing assessment:

What's this rookie trainer doing? Is he trying to kill this promising horse? Break his heart against the best horses in the land? For the horse's sake, I hope Boyar hasn't made the biggest blunder of his life.

The rest are much the same, except for one. Berny Lipton, with whom I am acquainted, writes:

I admire the ability of young trainer, Pierre Boyar, to have his horse spot-on for tomorrow's Doncaster. He must know what he is doing, to enter this outstanding horse in a Group One-mile race – first up, without a similar distance race under his girth. I'll take the long odds given on Mountain Boy and trust I'll be smiling at the end of the race. Good luck, Mr Boyar!

I choose to focus on Berny's article; it is how I feel. With the miles and miles of training I've done with The Boy, up and down the hills at home, as well as two private early morning gallops at Hawkesbury with a good sparring partner, I feel certain I have The Boy fit and more than ready to do his best.

Speak of the devil, Berny is here to escort me back to the horse stalls.

"Thanks for the vote of confidence, Berny," I tell him while nudging my way through the mob. "I hope you're right, or I'll be tarred and feathered, I reckon." He slaps me on the back.

"Don't worry, Pierre. I've been spying on you at Hawkesbury. I was there the two mornings you galloped Mountain Boy over seven furlongs with Betterthanmost. He's no slouch, and there's not too many horses who can beat him in a track gallop. The Boy left him standing. I feel sorry for the old timer. Here, let me carry the saddle of a winner!"

I must say Berny's confidence lifts mine.

"I've taken twenty-to-one and had the biggest bet of my life. So, we'll both have the jitters before he proves himself," Berny says with a toothy grin.

He stays with me to help saddle The Boy, and escorts Etta to the grandstand while I take The Boy to the mounting yard and get Timmy up. Neither of us says much; we are both too tense. Although I manage to tell him, "If you are in front at the final two hundred meters, look across and give me a smile if you think he's goping to win." Timmy nods his understanding.

I choose to watch the race alone, directly in front of the final two-furlong mark, where I will know if he is going to win. He'll either be tiring, with the field catching him, or he'll still be out in front and going strongly.

My stomach does backflips, until the starter lets them go. After

219

being beaten by speed at the jump, Mountain Boy sits third, three wide. I begin to worry. He's never been headed before. Will he settle or fight the bit to lead? I trust Timmy to feel the horse's intent and go with him, rather than push or pull him into position. Slowly, The race begins, and The Boy eases his way to the front; the rest of the field sits off him. I reckon they think he'll stop in the home straight because the pace is such a cracker. How can any horse keep up this speed for a mile, the race caller asks – and I wonder too? Will he prove himself better than I imagine, or can his will to win outlast his stamina? Coming to the home turn, The Boy is a length in front and going steadily, although the backmarkers who've had an easy time are gaining ground, being ridden hard, hands and heels, and not frightened to go wide on the bend. Mountain Boy rounds the turn perfectly balanced and Timmy just sits, seeming to wait for any challengers. He hasn't moved his position, as the jockeys' whips crack and their screaming threats can be heard above the thundering of hooves. Now is when Timmy lets him really stride, The Boy gains ground. He's three lengths in front at the final two-furlong post where, as Timmy flashes past, he looks across at me with a smile that would crack ice. I throw my hat in the air – it is over! We've won. Nothing looks like getting within cooee!

Breathless and ecstatic, I make my way to the winner's enclosure where I am virtually swamped by Etta, the Duke, Lily, Ernie, Rosie and Theobald, with Teddy March waiting at the side to shake my hand. To try and explain how much this means to me is impossible. My elation in knowing I have a true champion, despite it being perhaps a little early to make such a claim, is the highest of highs. My dream has begun. And with Henri-Etta by my side, my world is perfect.

After the speeches and trophy presentation, all of us –friends and confidantes – settle in the Committee room where we drink a toast to our future together, as Henri-Etta and Co.

"I say, Pierre, I hope you never forget who gave you this opportunity, young man. Though I'm extremely proud and happy for you, I'd like to purchase a small share of Mountain Boy. Say, half?" the Duke asks, a little more humbly than is normal for him.

We all laugh before I say, "I'll think about it, m' Lord."

As our laughter dies down, a strangely familiar voice behind me chills my blood.

"Don't bother, Pierre. The Duke will have no funds left to buy anything. Not when I'm finished with him."

We turn as one to see the Duchess and Gertrude, smiling like Cheshire cats.

"And how are *you*, Henry?" Gertrude sneers, then adds with a spiteful laugh, "My, oh my. I am compelled to admit, Henry, for a *man*, you *do* look lovely in a frock!"

www.ingramcontent.com/pod-product-compliance
Lightning Source LLC
Chambersburg PA
CBHW070018120726
47909CB00003B/985